KRILL

WHEN THE GOOD CHOICES ARE GONE

Also by Susan Hasler

Intelligence

The Flat Bureaucrat

Project HALFSHEEP

KRILL

WHEN THE GOOD CHOICES ARE GONE

Susan Hasler

Bear Page Press
Asheville, North Carolina

Published by Bear Page Press, Asheville.

Bear Page Press and the Bear Page Press logo are trademarks of Zreil Global Marketing, Inc., or its affiliates.

This is a work of fiction. Names, characters, places, and incidents are a product of the author's imagination. Locales and public names are sometimes used for atmospheric purposes. Any resemblance to actual people, living or dead, or to businesses, companies, events, institutions, or locales is completely coincidental.

Book Layout ©2015 BookDesignTemplates.com

Cover design by Susan Hasler.

ISBN 978-0-9840584-0-2

First Edition: July 2021

To Stephen White and Martha Woodroof

"It is difficult to get a man to understand something when his salary depends upon his not understanding it."

Upton Sinclair

Greenland, 2060

Her screams cut deep into the crevices. All the while, no one felt like eating or engaging in any other normal daily activity. Some pressed their heads into the soft folds of lichens to mute the sound. Others wandered off by themselves. A dog howled. Those closest to her held her hand or mopped her forehead. They knew what was going on, even though they had never been through this before. They didn't know whether or not it would turn out all right. It could be wonderful or disastrous. They lost all sense of time and for a while felt that time had stopped altogether, stranding them on this island of suffering.

She didn't hold back on the screaming. She gave it all of her breath and force. The intensity of her expression made her face almost unrecognizable. She frightened them, but they stayed with her until the final grimace. The baby dropped into their hands like an alien suspended in a bubble. The look of panic on their faces elicited one final scream of anguish from the mother. Then they clawed the birth caul from the baby with their fingernails, and it—he—cried.

With this sound, the breath that had been held in their lungs was expelled all at once. The mother's face softened into its usual beauty. When news got round that all was fine, laughter bubbled up from the rocks, and people suddenly remembered that they were hungry or thirsty, or needed to relieve themselves.

Things were different after that. The general fear and discombobulation that had plagued them for months eased. The baby gave them the sense that things would continue, that there was a future that held more than just the struggle to survive. He gave dimension to what had been flat. They felt a burning need to tell him stories and weave him a history to wear. It helped them recover their language and their voices.

CHAPTER ONE

That's Human

By 2030, the window to a recognizable future had been closed for a decade or more. It shut without even the sound of a sash hitting a sill. But humans still clung to the familiar and the moderate. The twenties had been dubbed the "Greenwash Decade," because political leaders made much of their efforts to protect the environment and "the future of our youth." They came up with pithy slogans, slick Earth logos, and ambitious action plans. They avoided any talk of real sacrifice that might make them unpopular. They fought hard for compromises that fell far short of what was necessary.

That May, developers planted a sign advertising "Steeplechase Manors" on a weedy tract of abandoned farmland west of Manassas, Virginia. The "manors" would be 350 narrow, vinyl-clad townhomes. Evidently the people who came up with names for housing developments drew their inspiration from those who had decided that "super colossal," "mammoth," and "super mammoth" were reasonable terms to describe the size of olives. No time for ceremony with the groundbreaking. Spring flooding had delayed construction for two months already. The site manager gave the signal. Fifty yards beyond the sign, an excavator bit into an old, shallow well and brought up a pelvic bone.

The operator cut off the engine, and workers gathered round. "That's human," somebody said. The word "human" echoed around the circle. The site manager said nothing. He was thinking "delay" and "money." He was already teetering on the edge of bankruptcy. He walked away from the group, pulled out a cell phone, and held a whispered conversation. When he returned, he shouted, "Ignore it. Get back to work."

The driver of the excavator protested. "Don't we have to report it? I don't want to chew up somebody's body. It don't seem—"

"I said ignore it," the site manager said. "Ignore it or some of you and maybe all of you get laid off."

When the bucket came up again, it held three human skulls. Impossible to ignore. Work stopped.

The bodies—seven in total—were females ranging in age from nineteen to twenty-eight. They had died over the previous two decades. Forensic teams searched the area and found a single, gold cufflink with the initials MDR.

Matthew Dmitriev Rabdanov was a second-generation Russian immigrant, a widower, a high official in the State Department, and the father of one beloved daughter, Mary, or Masha as he called her. She called him "Marsh," not "Daddy." Marsh was short for Marshmallow, the nickname she gave him for his high, fluffy, white pompadour. His daughter came late in life, and his hair had lost its color early, so she had never known it other than white. When he carried her around as a toddler, she always grabbed a fistful of the soft stuff for security. She didn't have a mother, so she clung hard to her father.

She watched from an upstairs window as a policeman clamped a hand over that proud pompadour and shoved her father's head into the squad car. It was two hours until dawn, but Masha could not see how the sun would ever come up again. As the car drove away, flashing blue lights swam across her face and the watered silk of the curtain. It gave her the sensation of drowning. *He's a spy*, was her first thought when the police cars had pulled up. She realized now that had been wishful thinking.

Masha turned her back to the window. She didn't switch on the lights or dress so that she could drive to the police station. She didn't burst into tears. She stood, swaying and barely breathing, and let her Potemkin village fall. For years she had ignored things she should have found suspicious. One by one they popped into her head, and she said "oh." Mud-caked shoes she found in the trash. Oh. Her father's car driving off in the middle of the night. Oh. A bald spot that had suddenly appeared in the pompadour when she was eleven. When she had asked about it, her father had invented a hilarious and highly involved story about tripping over a State Department rat and falling down the stairs while chewing gum. The gum ended up in his hair, and his secretary had cut it out. The story was ridiculous— Masha had never seen her father chew gum for one thing—but it made her laugh so hard that she didn't ask questions. Now she realized that they would identify and date all of the bones and she might soon know the name of the woman who had pulled out a fistful of her father's hair in a vain attempt to fight back. The thought terrified her. Oh.

"I knew," she said out loud. She knew when the police-woman outlined the crimes he had committed that it was true. Deep in her subconscious, she must have known earlier. That made her an accomplice.

Masha turned her head toward the photograph of her mother on her desk. It was lost in the darkness, but she didn't need light to see the strain in the soft Tatar eyes. Zifa Rabdanova fell into the Potomac at Great Falls when Masha was barely a year old. Stung by a bee while climbing on the rocks, her father had told her. A family picnic, he told her. Zifa had never learned to swim, he told her. Oh. Oh. Oh.

"You figured it out," Masha said to the photo. "You were brave enough to face the truth and you died for it. I was too much of a coward to admit it, and other women died for it."

Also lost in the darkness were the trophies, blue ribbons, and award citations that crowded the room along with other tokens of Masha's abundant talents and bottomless need to earn attention. She had gone off to Stanford at the age of sixteen. In the center of her wall of achievement was her degree in Statistics, bestowed only six months earlier. Everything she did, she did to make Marsh proud. His lavish praise could lift her feet right off the ground.

She had never thought of herself as an addict or thought about the nature of addiction. Her self image was one of a strong young woman. She realized in that moment, however, that this image was too simple to be true. She had lived for Marsh's praise, craved it, turned herself inside out to get it. All the while, her father had nurtured in her an intense streak of competitiveness and drive for achievement. She had excelled in math, field hockey, diving, and dance. Her Russian nanny had taught her to do beautiful needlework. Masha had done up her motto, "Effort, Excellence, and Integrity," in cross-stitch and hung it on her "Wall of Honor." Now she knew it was all distraction and a carefully cultivated addiction. None of this meant anything, but her father had subtly convinced her that this life of achievement was important enough to preserve at all costs. She had never acknowledged the truth because it would have destroyed all of this. But now it was gone anyway.

There are two kinds of life-changing events: those that change your future, and those that change your future and past all at once. If her father had died in a car accident, that would have fallen under the first category. This fell under the second.

Masha felt hot and cold and oddly distant from her own body. A physical sensation of melting in her chest made her gulp for breath. She didn't fight against the process of disintegration. She simply waited to see if anything would be left when it was over.

When the phone rang, Masha knew her father was dead before she said hello. "Of course," she said when the officer told her they had found him slumped and unresponsive when they arrived at the police station. "He would do that," she said, when they related how he died without regaining consciousness and the coroner suspected suicide. Her father would have had a backup plan, a stash of pills that would allow him to escape the consequences. She was the one with no backup plan.

Masha quit her brand new job at the Census Bureau and walled herself off in her room. For months, she saw no one but the ancient, doting nanny-turned-housekeeper, Tanya, who fussed and brought her food she could not swallow. Tanya lowered the blinds against reporters camped in front of her house. Masha slept all day. At night, the television provided the only illumination. She watched all the sensational coverage of the crimes while playing countless games of solitaire. The sound and feel of the cards kept her from screaming.

It turns out that her father didn't always kill the women he preyed on. A number had survived his predilection for rough sex. Masha replayed the videos of women describing her father's laughter, which she could still hear in her head, a sound she had loved, a sound she would call forth with all sorts of crazy antics when she was a child.

"And the moral of this story is," Masha later told a friend, "that people who are into 'play' strangling should avoid custom-made, monogrammed accessories. Seems like a no-brainer, doesn't it?"

It took the better part of a year for Masha to emerge from her depression. She found what was left of her father's deadly stash of Seconal and Nembutal. She kept it in her medicine cabinet next to her toothbrush, but only to remind herself of her father's cowardice and to challenge her own courage. Then she began the long task of rebuilding herself from the ground up, using tougher and coarser materials this time. Her new personal motto was "Fuck the Patriarchy." She worked it up in cross-stitch and put it in the frame that once held "Effort, Excellence, and Integrity." The old sampler went into the box containing all the rest of her awards. She carried it down to the back yard and built a fire in the pit. She burned the sampler first and then took tongs and laid the blue ribbons out like bacon on the grate and watched them curl and blacken.

"Bait," she muttered. "This shit was just bait."

Next came the award certificates and the lanyards that held medals. Masha stuck marshmallows on a skewer, held them over the coals until they turned black and burst into flame. She blew on the molten centers while she tried to figure out what to do with the medals and the gaudy trophies, which were made from a variety of materials, including metal, wood, fake wood, glass, acrylic, and plastic. She wondered how she had never realized before how utterly worthless and hard to destroy these things were. In the end, she buried them in the garden and covered them with a big rock. She took a Sharpie and wrote, "Here lies Masha Rabdanov."

Masha changed her last name to Campbell after spotting an old print of Andy Warhol's *Campbell's Soup Cans*. It was exactly what she wanted, to be one ordinary can on a shelf full of ordinary soup. No more standout performances. No more spotlight. No more notoriety. After a couple of months, she sold the family manse, set Tanya up at a nice retirement home, and moved into a huge, generic condominium complex with pale gray walls and carpeting. She left the walls blank, because she had no idea who she was anymore.

Mary Campbell took a job at the Central Intelligence Agency, where she could hide in a vaulted room behind razor-wire fence, and where reporters and the general public couldn't get at her. She discouraged people from using her first name in a place where everyone went by first names. She was simply "Campbell." She mostly succeeded in burying her past, but informed any man she dated that she had "a shit-load of baggage" that might be dumped on him at any time without warning, explanation, or apology. "So don't get attached," she said. She ended relationships swiftly and without sentimentality at the first sign that her trust had been breached.

During the day, Campbell studied flows of migrants and refugees. At night she pursued a series of master's degrees to fill out her education and reduce the amount of time she spent alone in her condo.

She became a world expert on refugees. As the subject and the globe heated up, she grew blessedly and mind-numbingly busy. She managed her own unit of analysts before she turned thirty.

◘

Campbell finished inking up a draft intelligence assessment. It had been written with abundant pride and purple pretension by a brand new analyst, Brian Foster, fresh out of grad school. He had spent enough time in school that he was Campbell's co-equal in age. She had overheard him questioning her credentials under his breath. Now she was going to have to tell him that his shit did, in fact, stink. She called him up and said, "I've reviewed your paper and I'm ready to go over it with you. Visit the men's room first, because this is going to take a long time and it will be traumatic."

Having been given fair warning, Brian hesitated outside the door.

"I see your toe. You might as well come in," Campbell said. Her unspoken nickname for Brian was "Baby Groucho," due to his heavy eyebrows. Now those brows were furrowed with a distinctly defensive expression. He was going to argue. Well, she had no time for that. She gestured for him to sit down and saw his face blanch at the sight of his work covered in red ink.

"Several of my professors told me I was an excellent writer," Brian began.

"None of them were English professors, were they?" Campbell said.

"They were statistics professors," Brian said. "They make a lot more money than English professors."

"They probably make enough money to hire editors so they don't look like idiots," Campbell said. "You don't make that much money."

Brian's face registered a mix of offense and panic. He blurted out, "Writing the paper is my job and correcting the grammar is your job."

Campbell fixed him with a look intended to corrode the skin on his face. "If you ever again tell me what my job is, I will cut you. If you don't learn how to use an Oxford comma, I will cut you. If you start a paper with the words 'Doubtless there are those who believe,' I will cut you and toss your pieces down the burn chute." She held up his paper. "This is full of drivel, filler, bloviation, cow manure, whatever you want to call it. I can tell that you spend too much time with a thesaurus. But we are going to fix this paper together, if we have to sit here through dinner. We are going to yank out every adjective, adverb, and redundancy. We are going to examine your biases. We are going to figure out what the hell you were trying to say and then put it down clearly and concisely. Then you are going to break up with that thesaurus and take the *Intelligence Style Guide* to bed with you tonight and become intimate with the rules of hyphenation."

Brian would later claim that he lost four pounds sweating out that session with Campbell, but he eventually became a passable writer.

◻

Personnel issues aggravated her, but Campbell thought of numbers as cool in temperature and smooth as polished pebbles. Playing with them calmed and centered her. But as her first decade in the Agency wore to a close, the numbers grew hot, jagged, and sticky as they increasingly came to represent desperate and endangered human beings fleeing drought, flood, unrest, and megastorms. People with nowhere to go.

Campbell's unit had been inputting data for days. Now she stood before a big touchscreen showing a detailed topographic map of Africa. She added a transparent overlay of average rainfall, then another showing various ethnic groups. She added and subtracted transparencies showing population density, disease outbreaks, wars, crop failures, and even locust swarms. She sipped strong black coffee as she visualized and internalized the data. She phoned country experts, military experts, agriculture experts, and her favorite meteorologist. They answered questions and she took notes. It was already ten o'clock at night when Campbell took up a stylus and began to draw colored lines indicating flows of refugees. Where the lines met, there would be violence; where they ended, loss of hope and more death.

No one was more accurate than Campbell and her unit in predicting where people would go. Or in predicting how many, how, and when they would die. One day she overheard Brian crowing over this accuracy and the award the unit had just earned.

She called him into her office and closed the door. It had been a long time since she had given him anything but praise, but now it was time to clip his wings again. "You don't get it," she said. "The idea isn't to be right in your predictions. It's to provide the information necessary to avert or at least ameliorate the expected outcome. When is the last time we averted anything or saved any lives? We're failing every day."

"That's not our fault," Brian said. "If people don't listen to us, it's not our failure."

"It's not our success either, despite the stupid certificates. Or if it is success, it's only the most abstract, meaningless, cold form of success. It's not something we can feel good about when we go home at the end of the day. Not if we're going to retain our humanity." Brian looked so shamefaced that Campbell gently added, "I don't mean to say that you're callous, just young. It takes some people a lifetime to figure out what I've just told you. Some never do. I'm just giving you a heads up. The longer it takes to wise up, the more it hurts." She looked at Brian's slumped shoulders and red face. "Cheer up. I'm going to take you all out to lunch."

□

A month later, Campbell went up to the Operations Center to watch the live satellite images of a sudden lethal crack snaking through the center of the West Antarctic Ice Sheet. A tipping point. It was 2038, and this shouldn't be happening yet. The warm waters flowing beneath the sheet had brought the rupture sooner than predicted. Footage taken by airplanes played on another screen. Both sets of images were oddly beautiful: the one like a moving black and white mosaic, the other a silent blue and white symphony of crashing ice. Campbell didn't have much time to linger. She had to go downstairs and recalculate the speed of ocean rise and its impact on coastal populations. There would be nothing beautiful in that.

As the seas rose, the number of 100-degree-plus days in the nation's capital multiplied. The haves turned up their air conditioners, and the homeless died in the streets. Seeping salt water reached the roots of the cherry trees along the Tidal Basin and killed them. Basements took on water. Anacostia and the Naval Yard turned into a toxic swampland. *Aspergillus* spores floated in the air and colonized in lungs. *Stachybotrys chartarum* blackened walls. *Acremonium, Fusarium,* and *Mucor* raced through ductwork. New strains of mold evolved. Black, green, white, gray, pink, orange, and brown molds. Powdery, hairlike, flower-like, and slimy molds. Fungus among us. Face masks once again became everyday wear, but mycotoxins still played havoc with the health of the local population, especially small children. Dead opossums and For Sale signs began to appear on lawns. The opossums were the victims of a mysterious bacterial disease. The For Sale signs were useless. No one was buying in but the rats, who set up housekeeping in newly emptied ecological niches and began to breed like young couples after World War II. Businesses moved their headquarters to other cities. The question of moving the seat of the United States government out of what people had come to call "Dismal Swamp North" came under serious discussion. A city didn't actually have to be under water to become unlivable. Then, in 2039, a tornado-spawning category 6 hurricane, Edgar, blew in and stalled over the area.

Campbell decided to ride it out at work, and volunteered for emergency duty in the Operations Center. She assumed that the tremendous concrete and steel bulk of the Old Headquarters Building would protect her as it always had. She turned her back on the chaos outside and scanned incoming cables. A young analyst ignored Campbell's order to stay away from the windows and spotted an approaching tornado. She screamed. Campbell jumped up to see a black hole out of deep space bearing down on the building. "Move!" she yelled and herded everyone out into the corridor and then down into an inner stairwell. The electricity went out, leaving only the red glow of emergency lights. They huddled and listened to the freight train roar and the sound of exploding windows.

Meanwhile, under the cover of torrential rain, the swollen Potomac met the incoming storm surge. Water did something unprecedented, something it was not supposed to do. It crossed the GW Parkway and entered the CIA compound without showing a badge. It shorted out the electric fence with a display of snapping blue arcs. It ignored the tire slashers, concrete barriers, and the big humvee sitting just inside the entrance. The muddy swirl rose up the steps of the front entrance and poured into the basement. The George H. W. Bush Center for Intelligence became part of the Potomac.

Campbell and the other employees camped in the dank building for days while the rains continued to descend. The emergency lights faded, leaving the windowless inner corridors dark even in the daytime. All of the steel vault doors were locked, so there was no way to let in any light except for the one door they could open—the Ops center. Disregarding all rules of security, Campbell propped that door open. As others went from floor to floor to forage in fast-emptying vending machines, she felt her way down the stairs and ran into muddy water as she reached the first floor.

"Well fuck a duck," she said. She didn't like the idea of wading into what was probably a toxic soup, but she had a sudden urge to visit the mostly men hanging on the wall. The water was only ankle deep on the first floor, but she had to force the door of the stairwell open. She sloshed down the main corridors that surrounded the inner courtyard, which was now a dirty pool where magnolia branches, paper, and other debris floated. Some windows were intact, some cracked, and many gone altogether. Rain blew in. When she reached the portrait hall, she saw that half the Agency's former heads had fallen face forward into the muddy soup, while the others hung at drunken angles. The blue velvet rope that had protected the distinguished leaders from the rabble now snaked through the waters, diving under canvases and rising up the few stanchions that still stood upright.

Campbell waded slowly down the line of portraits, addressing a select few as she passed. "I bet you felt like hot shit sitting for that painting, didn't you? I see that smirk of superiority. Never mind that you got your job by marrying into a rich and well-connected family. You honestly felt you earned everything you got. Meanwhile, all the people who worked for you thought you were an idiot." She moved farther down the corridor. "Look at you patting that globe like you owned it, while all the time United Fruit owned you. You should have worn a sticker on your forehead just like a banana." Campbell moved on to a portrait floating face down in the water. "Don't even try to hide your head. I know who you are and how you got your fortune." Campbell waded over to the next portrait. "Actually, you were a pretty decent director." She addressed the whole group. "I have something I want to say to many of you. Not all of you. Some of you believed in speaking truth to power. Some of you actually lost your jobs because you refused to prostitute yourself to political expediency. This lecture is for the rest of you, and you know who you are. This is for the skanky corridor walkers, the hired pens, the unprincipled career climbers, the clueless political appointees, and assorted pricks. I know your type. I know what the veneer covers. I know what you got away with, what you covered up, what you left out of those self-serving books with the portentous titles. Some of you were even friends of my dear daddy. He told me your secrets. Such funny stories." Masha addressed the portrait of an uptight-looking man with overly rosy cheeks. "You made a summer intern lean into a burn chute and scream obscenities while you plowed her from behind. Honestly. What was that about? Why are so many powerful men so perverted? Eww." Campbell stopped for breath. "Yet you, all of you, took yourselves so fucking seriously. What you didn't take seriously was climate change, at least not until it was too late. You treated Mother Earth like she was another 'hysterical' female who could be ignored. Well now you can suck the muddy waters of the Potomac."

The Agency wouldn't let civilian rescue teams onto the compound, what with all of the classified information literally floating around. These teams were busy anyway scouring surrounding neighborhoods for survivors. Finally, a military helicopter landed on the rooftop helipad for the first of several trips.

Campbell took her turn last, partly because she wanted to make sure everyone else was out, but mostly because she was terrified of helicopters. She was fine with planes. She got planes. They were aerodynamic. They looked like they belonged in the air. Helicopters were another thing altogether. They appeared heavy and ungainly and always on the verge of dropping straight to the ground. They were held up by fragile-looking blades that could break or decapitate someone at any second. Campbell had a very short list of things she was afraid of, but helicopters sat at the top of it, underlined and in boldface.

When she couldn't avoid it any longer, she took a deep breath and grasped the hand that reached out to help her into the craft. It was a dry, strong, clean hand belonging to a naval officer who had volunteered for rescue duty. As he pulled her up, she panicked and shouted into his ear, "No. I don't want to fly. Can't you send a boat instead?"

He squeezed her hand and said, "No, you'll be fine."

"What good is a fucking navy that can't send a boat?" she shouted.

He laughed as he helped her into her seat. His face was wide open, honest, earnest, intelligent, and bore no trace of the cynicism that grew like fungus in the intelligence world. There was something heartbreakingly unguarded about it. When he began to blush, Campbell realized she was staring too hard. She looked down and grew aware of her own stench. The officer reached into his pocket and pulled out a Baby Ruth bar and offered it to her. She grabbed it, tore the wrapper, and took a big bite. "I love you," she said with her mouth full. This was meant to be facetious, and she doubted he could hear her over the noise of the helicopter blades. Then, after she had finished chewing, she shouted in his ear, "*You* would never lie to me."

CHAPTER TWO

Red Flags

When Sam Bostock thought of what he wanted out of life, the same childhood scene always played in his memory: a campsite on Lake Michigan, a picnic table fitted with a red-and-white plastic checked cover and a Coleman stove, and the prayer before breakfast. His father, Navy chaplain George Bostock, clasped his hands over a paper plate laden with fried fish and began. "Dear Lord, we thank you for leading this excellent bass to our hook this morning—"

"God rest its smelly soul," Iris Bostock cut in.

George continued in a louder voice. "As I was saying, thank you for this fine breakfast, which includes pancakes I made specially for my dear wife, who would turn up her nose at a fish hooked by Jesus Christ himself."

Iris frowned with eyes closed. "I believe Jesus Christ served the fishes for lunch, not breakfast, because he understood that some smells are rebarbative in the early morning, not to mention the fact that they taint all of the surrounding foods, so that blueberry pancakes become blueberry-bass pancakes—an abomination."

19

"Lord knows," George continued in a mock stern voice, "the Japanese eat fish for breakfast every day and are grateful for it."

"I thank you, dear Lord," Iris said, "that I was not born in Japan, where I would have starved."

Sam's stomach growled. "I pray that I may some day eat a warm meal," he said in a plaintive voice.

"Amen," his parents said in unison.

Lots of laughter, lots of teasing, lots of love, and no truly hard feelings. That was how Sam grew up and how he assumed all families lived. He followed in his father's footsteps and joined the Navy, but as a pilot, not a chaplain. He transferred his love of Lake Michigan to the wide sea. To recreate the happy memories of his childhood in a new generation, he began the search for a wife. He anticipated a happy and fulfilling wedded life featuring several lovely children blessed with a legacy of good genetic material and attentive parents—children who would be taken fishing on Lake Michigan every summer. It was a solid plan, he thought. Find a woman you love and treat her like a queen, modeling your behavior on that of your wise father. All you need is love. Right? What could possibly go wrong?

By the time he met Campbell, Bostock had broken off three wildly unsuitable engagements. Actually, the words "broken engagement" were inadequate to describe those ugly explosions of emotion. Tears, bitter words, and even screaming, something he had never experienced in his family. With Gwen Gilbert, his second fiancée, there had even been minor violence: slapping, the hurling of projectiles, and scratches to the face. Whenever he thought of her, he touched the scimitar of a scar her nail had cut across his temple.

Bostock finally figured out that the idea of marriage he carried in his head was so vivid it blinded him to reality until it was almost too late. The women he had chosen were not ones who could step blithely into the role he imagined for them. They were children of unhealthy or downright poisonous relationships. Just treating them well was not enough to expel their demons. They needed a level of understanding he was ill-equipped to provide. So he stepped back from romance for a while to lick his wounds and reassess.

Then he reached out his hand one stormy day, and the most wildly unsuitable woman of all grabbed it—Mary Campbell. Her naked gaze left him uncomfortable, intrigued, and aroused despite his better judgment.

▣

When Bostock awoke in the motel room the day after his rescue mission at the CIA, Campbell was propped on one elbow beside him, once again dissecting him with that look. "Just so you know," she said, "I have a shitload of baggage that may be dumped on you at any time."

Bostock ran a finger over the scar on his temple. "Thank you for the warning. I mean that. I've been blindsided by enough women that I truly do appreciate it."

"Sweetcheeks," Campbell said, "you have no utter idea what it is to be blindsided."

Red flag, Bostock thought. *She has issues.*

Campbell sat up. "Normally about this time, I would be looking for my underwear so I could go home. I wore that underwear so long, however, that I never want to see it again and I'm not sure I have a home to go back to."

"While you were showering last night," Bostock said, "I sent your clothes to the hotel laundry. I specified extra hot water. They'll be ready at 9:30. Meanwhile, we can order breakfast and figure out what to do next."

"Wow," Campbell said as she settled back into the bed. "Are you from the mythical planet of wonderful men?"

"I'm their leader," Bostock said, but he thought, *Another red flag.*

"I'm not sure I believe in wonderful men," Campbell said, "although I did at one time. Feel free to try to convince me, however. Perhaps I should develop some sort of test along the lines of the twelve labors of Hercules."

"Make it multiple choice. I don't want to slay any beasts."

"Not a hunter? Good. Too many military types take obscene pleasure in blasting away the dwindling fauna."

"I don't even fish anymore."

"Also good. Fish stink."

"You remind me of my mother," Bostock said.

Campbell made a face. "You know, it's a red flag when a man says you remind him of his mother."

Bostock nodded. "I suppose I wouldn't like it either if you told me I reminded you of your father."

"No you wouldn't," Campbell said. "My father was a serial killer."

Bostock laughed, then something in her expression made him stop.

"Yes, I am dead serious," she said. "I never tell people that. I don't know why I told you, except that you do have the most open face. Makes me want to overshare."

After a week of intense sex and bizarre conversations, Bostock left for a tour at sea with the feeling of having escaped with his life. At least he hadn't given her an engagement ring.

CHAPTER THREE

New Hope

On Valentine's Day, 2040, something was in the air that was not love. It had a richer, oilier smell, an intoxicating mix of high-end toiletries, dirty money, and lemony cleaning fluid. Greed. It was driving the lobbyists mad.

In a crowded corridor of a rented office building, a chic young woman hauled off and swung her Birkin bag at the head of a man in an Armani suit. He ducked, but the swivel clasp caught him in the scalp, specifically in the tender recipient site for two thousand new hair plugs. He bellowed and took her out at the knees with a blow from his briefcase. She fell, struck a drinking fountain, and broke her nose. Blood spattered over the fine fabrics of nearby trousers. By the time the ambulance and police arrived, the situation had devolved into an awkward scuffle among people who had no idea how to wage physical battle. Women lurched on stilettos. Punches missed their targets. Ligaments tore at the wrist and ankles. Soon everyone was retreating to call their lawyers and get back to a familiar battleground again.

The source of the tension was the question of where to put the new U.S. capital city. It had to be decided quickly because there was an outbreak of Legionnaire's Disease in the ruined old city, and the government was in diaspora, working out of a confusion of rented temporary spaces with inadequate security. The stakes were high. States vied for the revenue and jobs such a city would provide. Political Action Committees waged influence campaigns. Lawmakers lobbed f-bombs on national television. The flow of bribes almost matched the strength of Edgar's storm surge.

The argument that the capital should be in a central location ran up against the view that it should be in an area that would be as livable as possible for as long as possible. The climate toward the center of the continent would be as miserable in summer as the old Washington, DC, which suggested that it should be near the coast but on high ground and not so close as to be wiped out in the next hurricane. A spate of seismic activity on the West Coast turned the focus on New England.

When the dust settled, an empty site was chosen in northern New Hampshire. The capital was planned as an entirely new city, featuring stormproof architecture, a power grid entirely reliant on sun and wind, and pedestrian-, bike-, and electric-scooter-friendly streets that cut wide, graceful curves through gentle hills and along a scenic river. This was to be the shining city that would show the way for the rest of the world. Its roofs and buildings would be white to reflect the sun's rays and pay homage to the birthplace of democracy—Athens. Its solar-power-absorbing streets and sidewalks would glow at night. It would be a city of solutions, a triumph over an ever more challenging climate. Its construction would be a moment of optimism for the century. Its name would be New Hope.

While New Hope was being built, Congress punished the CIA for the latest scandal by hacking it up like a starfish. When the city was ready for its first occupants in 2042, the severed parts of the Agency each moved into their own new headquarters building on the new Wisconsin Avenue, soon to be known as Intel Row. This broad street lined with freshly-planted lindens was the route Bostock biked on his way from his apartment to the new Pentagon, where he was beginning a two-year tour after returning from the Mediterranean. Intel Row was a couple of blocks out of his way. He told himself he chose it for scenic reasons, but the streets and buildings in New Hope were all remarkably alike, having sprung from one central plan.

Bostock had made no effort to contact Campbell since he had left Washington, but he slowed his pace when he passed the Intelligence Analysis Agency. He never saw her, though, among the bureaucrats filing through the scanners in front of the building.

Bostock was serving as executive officer for a Rear Admiral, a rather humiliating ticket punch involving a great deal of paperwork and door opening. One morning, the Admiral came in grumbling about briefings he had to attend on the security implications of migration trends. "Fucking downer if there ever was one," he said.

Bostock was so quick to volunteer to take the briefing the Admiral grew suspicious. "What are you, a masochist?" he asked.

"Yes, sir," Bostock said. All the while, he kept up the inner fiction that he was not really going out of his way to see Campbell again. After all, he wasn't even sure he remembered what she looked like. Slavic cheekbones. A trace of Tatar around the eyes. Frizzy, disheveled hair.

⊞

Campbell glided into the Pentagon conference room looking polished and professional, with hair smoothed into a knot at the nape of her neck. A line of young analysts followed her. She took her place at the head of the table. Bostock could see a hint of anarchic mockery in her eyes as she evaluated the self-important brass. Her eyes slid over him without pause.

Campbell was old enough now that she didn't need to be fierce to command respect. Her attitude toward her charges had grown more maternal. Her analysts, for their part, copied her movements, her speaking style, and her lead in all things with the fidelity of ducklings imprinted on her from birth. It struck Bostock as funny. He had to make an effort to maintain a serious face. The longer she spoke, the more he felt like beaming, but that would have been inappropriate given the grimness of the subject matter. Instead, he began to pepper her with the most difficult questions he could come up with. She handled them easily and coolly, giving no indication that she recognized him. Then he made the mistake of trying to trip up an earnest analyst named Brian. Campbell stepped in to rescue her charge and gave Bostock a blistering look that said, "I know who you are and I know how to deal with you." He didn't do that again.

Bostock collared Brian after the meeting, apologized, and praised him lavishly for his briefing. He did this within earshot of Campbell. She came over afterwards and whispered, "What do you think that will get you?"

He winked at her and pulled a Baby Ruth out of his jacket pocket. "What would it get me if I added this?"

She took the candy bar. "No wonder your face was flushed after the break. How many vending machines did you have to go to to find this?"

"Seven on three floors. What time should I pick you up for dinner?"

"Eight," Campbell said. She scribbled her address on his notepad before running after one of her ducklings who had wandered off in the wrong direction.

▣

When Bostock awoke the next morning, Campbell was once again propped on one elbow, scrutinizing every detail of his face.

"Something's changed," she said. "Have you accepted it?"

"What?"

"The end of humanity. You hadn't accepted it last time."

Bostock rubbed his eyes and glanced at his watch. It was Saturday and it wasn't quite 6:00 a.m. "Could you at least start with 'Good morning'?"

"That would be denial. I'm so over denial."

"I need coffee," Bostock said. "I smell it. I hear it gurgling."

"It should beep shortly," Campbell said. "The machine is set for six."

"On a Saturday? Don't you ever sleep in?"

"I'll catch up on my sleep later. I'm not in sleeping mode right now." She hopped out of bed and took five quick steps to the kitchen. It was an efficiency apartment, half the size of the one Bostock was renting. "How do you take your coffee?" she asked.

"Black."

"That's how I take my attitude," she said, "black and honest. There's a stark beauty to looking death in the face and not blinking. It's more honorable than indulging in silly distractions." She handed Bostock his coffee, took hers to the window, and sipped while staring at the white city pinkening in the sunrise. "Look at this city, built fifty years too late. A beautiful human idea about to run up against the reality of humanity."

"What do you mean?"

"I saw them bulldozing squatters' sheds on the edge of the city. 'Non-code construction,' in the bureaucratic parlance. 'People's homes,' in human terms. They're trying to build a perfect city, but to do that, they can't let too many people in. That's the story of the century. Solutions are too small and too late, and people are too many and too needy."

"What did you see in my face that makes you think I've accepted that?"

"It's what I don't see," Campbell said. "A spark of naive optimism. You've changed your attitude toward your future, haven't you?"

Bostock took a mouthful of coffee and let the bitterness sit on his tongue. He swallowed and said, "I suppose I have. I used to think I would get married and have children, but I'm starting to worry about what kind of future they'll have."

"Just starting to worry?"

Bostock stared into his cup. Campbell had a way of dwelling on the things he liked to push to the back of his mind. "There will be some technological breakthrough," he said.

"Will there?" she asked.

CHAPTER FOUR

Mongold

The extinction of bats, frogs, and the only North American marsupial went little remarked, but the death of Adam Smith caused a world of hurt. Yes, he had already died once, in 1790, but he died again, more resoundingly, as people were pouring into the unfinished streets of New Hope. Regrettably, Mr. Smith took the wealth of nations with him this time.

It was a paradigm shift that could have been predicted had it not been so unthinkable. Who could have imagined that an economic system based on unbounded growth would run up against limits? "We are only limited by our imagination," the saying went. But, as it turned out, the laws of nature, demographics, meteorology, physics, and common sense had not been magically waved away by the invisible hand of the market.

The value of housing crashed in coastal regions, the Deep South, and the Southwest, even before waters advanced or desert encroached. People couldn't sell homes that no one would insure and they couldn't sell the transportable contents of those homes, because everyone was selling, and no one was buying. Money increasingly went to pay the skyrocketing cost of food. Only the rich could afford to insure homes, so torna-

31

dos, hurricanes, and wildfires resulted in a permanent loss of wealth for the people affected. Meanwhile, scalpers bought up vast tracts in the more temperate areas and jacked up prices. The bottom fell out of what was left of the middle class.

During the first decades of the century, anyone who had forecast the end of consumerism would have been greeted with derision. Now a distinctly anti-crap mentality took root. The iconic poster of the so-called Doomer Generation was not some twenty-first century Farrah Fawcett in a slinky red swimsuit. It was ... good god, what was it? You had to look at the macabre image for a while and even then it wasn't easy to decipher what you were looking at. Dead jellyfish on a beach? An orgy? The aftermath of a massacre? No. It was a beach covered with polyurethane fanny packs made to look like realistic naked butt cheeks. A container of them had slipped off a ship during a storm, and they had washed ashore en masse. The caption of the poster was "You Sacrificed My Future for This Crap? Asses."

Stuff turned lethal in gale force winds. Teenagers shared grisly pictures of people impaled by petroleum-based novelty items: a flamingo swizzle stick through an eye, a bumblebee wind spinner embedded in a chest, a plastic Excalibur stuck in the small of a back.

Stuff added fuel to wildfires that released more toxins into the atmosphere and destroyed forests that had been counted on to absorb carbon. Accelerating feedback loops like this meant that tipping points came faster than even the most pessimistic of scientists had predicted.

Panic led to extremism. Eco-socialists clashed with nativists. Teenagers spent more time in the streets demonstrating than in the schools. Survivalists bought more guns to protect their food. A group of environmental terrorists, Mother Earth's Avengers, began to assassinate captains of industry. Oligarchs stopped going out in public. "Drill Baby Drill!" lost out to "Keep it in the Ground!" Plans to exploit the Earth's remaining deposits of fossil fuel were publicly cancelled. Secretly, however, an international struggle to get a piece of the vast petroleum under the melting Arctic continued. Because how can you have all of those riches at your fingertips and not touch them? Especially when you know someone else will get them if you don't? You can't. Yet the carbon already in the sky would take lifetimes to dissipate.

This turbulent and contradictory time bred an unlikely hero, a capitalist survivor extraordinaire, a publicly repentant former extractivist and newly minted anthropocene savior selling not stuff, but a solution.

Alexander Mongold pressed the center of his bowtie. Nothing happened or at least nothing that was discernible to the conscious mind. The subtle flicker of gold lights in the shape of tiny crosses was accessible only to the subconscious. At the same time, Mongold's exquisitely tailored Italian suit came to life in a soft azure glow. Again, a subliminal effect resulting in the frequent remark that Mongold was the sort of guy who "lit up a room." Some of his advisors suggested that he tone down his dress in keeping with the solemnity of today's ceremony, but Mongold would sacrifice none of his signature flamboyance or hidden messages. He hummed "Hail to the Chief" as he leaned close to the mirror and adjusted his bouncy blond beard with a tiny comb. He was about to receive the Presidential Medal of Freedom, and he had every intention of presenting a bright contrast—dare he even say alternative?—to the prosaic Commander in Chief. He touched his cheek and frowned as he detected a patch of eczema attempting to surface through his foundation makeup. "Pakpao," he said, addressing a tiny woman in a smock, "we can't have this."

"Yes, sir. Yes, sir," she said rapidly. She always said it twice, which annoyed Mongold. She threw a drape over the bright suit. "Close eyes, sir." She aimed an airbrush wand toward the offending spot and sprayed on an extra coat of Sun-Kissed Peach. She put down the wand and ripped off the drape. Mongold gave her his signature outsized smile. Not because he was happy with her work but so that she could check his teeth for debris. The extra-broad incisors, with their veneer of dental porcelain mixed with ground diamonds, were close together and frequently trapped the odd bit of lettuce. "All clean, sir. Very bright, sir. Very bright."

Mongold stood and turned to a full-length mirror. He straightened the tails of his coat and adjusted his snowy white cuffs. Even with elevator shoes he was not tall, but his presence was huge. People who met him in person said he fairly pulsed with positivity, good humor, energy, and confidence. They were not wrong. The suit's light did pulse, ever so slightly, in rhythm with his heartbeat, transmitting the subliminal message that this man was so full of life he could bring life and hope to others. Mongold was a circus ringmaster, guru, tech wizard, and a smattering of Jesus H. Christ all rolled into one. He had bargained that the world would welcome a change from grimness and gloom. And the world did.

Mongold was about to receive the Medal of Freedom for his philanthropy as well as his inspired, sustainable, and disaster-proof design for the city of New Hope. Also, he had written the award into the contract he had negotiated with the government. His plan for the New White House, in particular, was genius. The president had asked for a building that would be secure from terrorists and safe in storms but that would also give an impression of openness to the public. Mongold delivered in spectacular fashion. The sparkling New White House was of modest size, but astonishing beauty. It sat on a circular lawn that embraced a perfect, round hill. The streets radiated out from it like spokes in a wheel. The solar-powered structure featured tall, mirrored windows set at angles that reflected the sky and caught the sun like the facets of a diamond. The public was invited to picnic on the hillside surrounding the structure, which had no working exterior doors. The only entrances were two adits at the bottom of the hill—the executive adit, used only by the president, and the service adit, used by everyone else. Inside the hill, elevators took people up into the building. Or so it appeared.

In reality, the fragile-looking building was a concrete shell covered with a skin of space-age materials and electronics. The real residence was below ground, but you would never know it from inside the light-filled space, because the "windows" were screens that projected the exact view one would get from the analogous windows above.

Mongold emerged from the green room and stepped into the elevator that would take him up to the residence. With great satisfaction, he felt it rise to the top of the hill. The sensation was false, a trick of engineering that made a trip of a few feet seem several times longer. The fact that the actual residence was underground was a state secret that even those who worked in the building didn't guess.

"Put the right geniuses in the same pot, add money, stir, and you can accomplish anything," Mongold said, after the president slipped the medal over his head. The cameras caught every carefully calculated nuance of the performance, from the subtly dominant gestures that put Mongold visually in charge of the scene to the charming blush of modesty in response to the president's praise. This "blush" was from a tiny red light on Mongold's cufflink that caught the reflective particles in the makeup on his cheeks when he angled his wrist in just the right way. Viewers were impressed by the ceremony in ways they couldn't quite understand. To an onlooker, this might have appeared to be the apex of a career, but it was merely the setup for Mongold's greatest initiative.

▣

He waited a year to announce it, until June of 2044. During this time, he winked and hinted about something big that would change the world, the future, and the destiny of all mankind. People were looking for a change. That intervening year had been a rough one, featuring killer storms, fires, droughts, and blistering heat. People were anxious, angry, restless, and ready for something—no one knew what.

The venue for the announcement was the New Hope Pavilion, an auditorium designed by Mongold, of course. It featured architectural tricks and distortions of perspective designed to amplify the presence of the speaker and to facilitate subliminal messaging on a grand scale.

When the capacity audience filed in, they saw the sky projected on the domed ceiling. Lazy clouds drifted from west to east. People tripped over each other as all eyes were riveted on the spectacle above. When everyone had finally stumbled to their seats, the sky dimmed, and a spotlight lit on a figure in the center of the stage who had seemingly appeared from nowhere.

Mongold flashed his brilliant smile and gestured to the ceiling. "A stirring image, was it not?"

Nods, exclamations, and a smattering of applause greeted his words.

"Come on," he said. "Are you stirred? Stirred to your loins?"

Applause and cheers. The audience was indeed stirred, if not by the majesty of the sky, then by the pale images of copulating nudes Mongold had tucked into the billowing cumuli. A stickler for detail, he had curated and edited the images himself, spending over two hours at the task in a locked office.

Mongold threw back his head and let out a loud, rude, unbridled laugh that made them join in, even if they didn't know what they were laughing at.

"Laugh," he encouraged them. "Bring it up from your belly and laugh because it's been hard on everyone. You've suffered. You've lost. You've worried about your little ones' future. But now, now, we can laugh like maniacs, because, my people, a new day is dawning. A new day and new hope!" Once again he broke into his irresistible guffaw, and everyone joined in with all of their hearts because there was something unbelievably comforting about seeing a genius laugh like worries did not exist. An optimistic genius! Not like that late wet blanket, Stephen Hawking, with his prediction of human extinction within the century.

The relief was so great that some began to cry, including a lovely, fragile woman in the front row. She wore a portable oxygen machine with clear tubes snaking to her nose. Next to her sat a tiny, wide-eyed toddler who stared up at Mongold with a mixture of fear and awe. When he caught her eye and winked at her, she quickly looked down at the notebook and coloring pencils in her lap.

Mongold came down off the stage and kneeled in front of the pair. "Hello, there. What's your name?" he said to the little girl. She shrank up against her mother.

"Her name is Alison," the mother said softly. "She's shy."

"And your name?" he asked.

"Latisha."

"Latisha. A beautiful name for a beautiful woman. Even in this beautiful, clean city, you have trouble breathing the air, don't you, Latisha?"

She nodded.

"The hotter it gets, the harder it is for you to breathe, isn't it? You hardly go outside anymore?" Mongold put his hand gently on hers, and his eyes filled with tears.

Latisha nodded. "I used to garden. I love flowers."

The screen behind the stage projected the scene for all to see. Alison looked up, saw her own magnified image, and slapped her hands over her face. She would remember this as one of the most terrifying moments of her life. The audience laughed, but gently.

Mongold touched the notebook in Alison's lap. "What a pretty drawing. Can I see it?" He held it up for the cameras. It was a blue sky, a fluffy white cloud, and a rainbow. This was all so perfect for his purposes that one would think that it had been planned ahead of time. This was only partly true. Mongold had ordered up a front row of "pitiful yet attractive" patients from the nearby respiratory health center, but it was luck that one of the patients had brought her camera-cute daughter and that this daughter had drawn an image of the sky. Pure luck, and Mongold was a man who knew how to exploit luck.

"This young lady has drawn a vision of a beautiful, clean sky and air that her mother can breathe. It should be her birthright. It is a glorious vision that the scientists have called impossible. 'A thousand years,' they tell us until carbon levels in the atmosphere abate. Until then the sun will beat down on us, and fields will go to dust, and fish will die in acid seas, and people like Latisha will suffer."

Mongold leaned over and gave Latisha a peck on the cheek. He stood and began to mount the stairs to the stage. On the first step he turned back to the audience and said, "Doom and gloom is what they give us." Another step and he turned again and asked, "What are we supposed to do with that?" A third step and his voice grew angry. "Nobody can thrive on a diet of doom and gloom." He bolted up the remaining stairs, took the center of the stage and whirled on the audience. "What does mankind need to thrive?"

Silence, then a man called out, "Hope."

"Louder," Mongold said.

"Hope!" the man screamed.

"Help him out people!" Mongold said.

"Hope!" the audience screamed.

"Yes! Yes! You have it right because you are smarter than the scientists and the pundits and the doom and gloomers! Do you know what else we need?" Mongold asked the audience.

They did not.

"Solutions!" Mongold yelled. "What did I say?"

"Solutions!" the audience screamed back.

"Did the scientists give us solutions?" he asked.

"No!" the audience screamed.

This was not entirely true, of course. Had the scientists' recommendations been followed in time, the Earth would be far more livable, but it was not prudent for Mongold to point this out since he was one of the people who had ignored those scientists. If he had not ignored them, he would be a millionaire and not a billionaire, and what could a millionaire accomplish? Very little.

"And now what are they doing?" he asked in a voice trembling with outrage. "They are testifying before Congress trying to outlaw solutions. Amazing, marvelous, ingenious geoengineering solutions that would shield us from the cruel heat of the sun."

The audience booed.

"'You can't make it work,' they say." Mongold gave the scientists a high, whiny voice. "'It's dangerous,' they say. 'Unpredictable consequences,' they say. 'It will cause droughts,' they say. Then they wring their hands and pee themselves." Here Mongold went into an elaborate show of wringing his hands. A startled look came over his face, and he quickly covered his crotch. A mini-spotlight turned his face bright red, while another turned his crotch bright yellow. The audience roared.

"So I guess we're all supposed to roll over and die. But I have never accepted that. I have spent more than a decade and countless dollars coming up with a real and miraculous solution to climate change. I have assembled the best minds and given them the best facilities. Just the same way I came up with the design for this city. Do you like, no, do you love this city?" he asked the audience.

They cheered.

"Then you will love the solution to the problem of climate change. A real solution that avoids the pitfalls. We call it Project Panacea."

Mongold didn't mention how long and how many consultants of various types it had taken to come up with this name. The first name they had rejected was Project Pinatubo, after the 1991 volcano. The volcanic ash released by Pinatubo had blanketed the Earth and had caused a fifteen-month, one-degree Fahrenheit drop in average global temperatures. The geoengineering solution would be a sort of artificial Pinatubo that would spray aerosol sulfates into the stratosphere to reflect radiation back into space. So Project Pinatubo seemed an obvious name, but consultants pointed out that Pinatubo had negative connotations due to all of those it left dead and homeless. They didn't want anyone thinking about unintended consequences. The next working title was "Project Parasol." The word "parasol" had only happy associations, the happiest being Mary Poppins and Bert dancing through willow branches. But Mongold himself rejected this name as too frivolous, although the term "Aerosol Parasol" would be used in marketing. For the overall project, he wanted a name with a hint of majesty to it.

"Project Panacea," Mongold said in a slow deep voice, letting the words fall on the audience like manna. He launched into an explanation filled with high-flown language, technical mumbo jumbo, and blank verse intonation. On the screen behind him, wind whipped through the branches of trees silhouetted against the sky. Hidden within the flickering image were clips of John F. Kennedy challenging America to put a man on the moon. At key moments, Mongold dropped a final "r" to give a *soupçon* of Kennedyesque flavor to his speech.

Mongold reached into his interior coat pocket, pulled out his Presidential Medal of Freedom, and slipped it over his head. "You may say I'm being immodest to put this on," he said. "Well, I don't believe in false modesty or false anything else. I want you to believe in me, because I am the real deal. And this is the moment. The moment we can turn things around. I will give you a new sky, a new hope, and sunsets. Panacea will create spectacular sunsets."

CHAPTER FIVE

Nasal Spray for Cats

Bostock allowed himself to fall in love with Campbell, despite the red flags and issues. There was something oddly liberating about not having the weight of future generations— or even a future—to worry about. He just thought about what he wanted to do with his next few hours or few days. The answer to that was often hiking with Campbell in the countryside or biking together through the increasingly chaotic streets of the Capital. People from around the country and around the world flocked to this place, many drawn by glowing advertisements placed by Alexander Mongold himself. Teenagers covered his sterile white walls with graffiti in a profusion of languages. Tiny ethnic restaurants proliferated, filling the air with char and spice. Without the overlay of exhaust fumes, it was a sensory rush biking through the streets.

Bostock asked for no commitments. Campbell would have said a prompt no to any marriage proposal.

She was right when she had said that he had changed his attitude toward the future. No one could deny that things were getting worse fast. And fast got faster every year. He coped by looking down and focusing on the work in front of him. He

couldn't help admiring Campbell for her courage in staring re-
lentlessly ahead, but he couldn't completely accept the inevitability of the horrors she predicted. He had a deep faith in
the energy and innovative spirit of the human race. She didn't,
and it took a heavy toll on her. He was more than happy to provide tenderness and support. He would have happily moved in
with her, but she didn't want that. He stayed with her on week-
ends, but she insisted on having her bed to herself on week
nights.

Bostock provided a sounding board for Campbell during the
Project Panacea debate that raged in the months after Mongold's big announcement. She was virulently against it. He
woke one Saturday morning to find her standing in the middle
of her apartment, muttering and gesticulating. She was still
naked from the night.

"What is it?" Bostock asked.

"Fucking lunacy, that's what it is," she said. "He's acting like
it's a cure, when all it will do is mask the symptoms while the
disease spreads."

Bostock got out of bed and headed for the coffee pot. Campbell was about to go on a naked riff. Naked riffs were now one
of his favorite things in life. He got his coffee and settled back
into bed to watch.

"Do you know how fucking old this idea is? It's been out
there for decades. Do you know why it hasn't been tried before?"

"No," Bostock said.

"Because it's a fucking stupid idea. Like nasal spray for cats."

"Nasal spray for cats?"

"It's how my cousin lost his middle finger," Campbell said.

Bostock smiled. This was going to be a good one.

Campbell continued. "It was his first year of practice after vet school. Someone came up with the brilliant idea of delivering vaccines to cats via nasal spray instead of a shot. Yes, take a cat that's already pissed because it's been stuffed into a carrier, driven across town, and pinned down on a metal table, and then spray something up its nose. Brilliant. Anyone with half a brain could tell you what would happen, but some genius was so enamored with his idea that he ignored the obvious pitfalls. The first time my cousin tried it, the cat chomped down on his finger. The puncture wound got infected, and he ended up losing his middle finger. Just try driving in rush hour traffic without a middle finger."

"So Panacea is like nasal spray for cats?" Bostock asked.

"Exactly. Mother Earth is already in the throes of a killer menopause. She's on a tear. Now we're going to spray something up her nose. Snap her bra strap. Goose her buttock. What could go wrong?"

"They say it will cool things down," Bostock said. He was willing to play devil's advocate to keep the riff going.

"Yeah, well, you can lower a patient's temperature by putting her in an ice water bath, but that's not a cure. You can't just leave her in the bath and not address the symptoms. Eventually, you'll freeze her ass off."

Campbell paused to refill her coffee; then she started in again. "And let's talk about unintended consequences. At least we can try to talk about them. We can take a wild guess because nobody really knows what the fuck will happen. The unknown unknowns have unknown unknowns. Mongold did say that cooling down the Northern Hemisphere might create some 'losers.' Translation: some parts of the world are going to get royally screwed. Probably Sub-Saharan Africa, which always tops the Most-Likely-to-Get-Screwed list. They'll get more drought, but what the hell, they're used to not having clean water. They're not hooked on it like we are. Then there's the Indian subcontinent with their religious strife, overpopulation, and rattling nukes. Just for funsies, let's see what happens when we take away the monsoons and people starve. Of course, they could always get back at us by deploying their own aerosol parasols. Sulphur here, sulphur there, sulphur, sulphur everywhere. Sounds like Hell, doesn't it? It will be. Hell for everyone, good, bad, and indifferent. And it will not lower the level of carbon in the atmosphere by even one part per million. Nope. It's all staying up there. And the acid is staying in the oceans."

"They can turn it off if it doesn't work," Bostock said. He knew what she would say to this, but he wanted to hear how she said it, wanted to see her throw her arms in the air, spin, and rant.

"But they can't!" Campbell said, "because all of that heat will still be up there. If they turn it off and it comes down all at once, we'll broil our giblets off like Thanksgiving turkeys. When will humanity learn the lesson that just because you *can* do something doesn't mean you *should* do it?" She stopped and looked at Bostock. "You're laughing at me, and this isn't funny."

"No it's not, but I really don't think Mongold will get his way for all of the reasons you've just stated. Congress and the president aren't total idiots."

"Really? 'Congress and the president aren't total idiots?' Take that statement to the bank and try to deposit it. I'll wait here."

CHAPTER SIX

Blessed Relief

Mongold's nature was too sunny to tolerate negativity. He had been well briefed on the downsides of solar geoengineering, but he refused to make them real by believing in them. "When you come upon a problem," he was fond of saying, "you tweak it out of existence." He had developed his own proprietary recipe for an aerosol sulfate that would, he was certain, avoid the drawbacks. His manic enthusiasm wouldn't let him believe in anything but possibility. He hadn't earned his billions by hesitating and listening to naysayers. He earned them with bold, unexpected moves made at the right time with panache. He saw himself as a savior of men, someone who would one day be venerated. He wanted to give Latisha cleaner skies. Deep in his heart, he believed he could.

The liability issues did give him pause. Whole countries could potentially sue for any side effects. So Mongold tucked away billions in offshore accounts, front companies, and even gold bars buried on his private island. He had had fun with that one, creating a treasure map that he stowed in a Swiss bank. Finally, he came up with what was perhaps his most brilliant idea of all—a way to monetize one of the negative impacts of Panacea.

He got the idea from technology he had developed for the New White House. One of the effects of aerosolized sulfur in the stratosphere would be to take the blue color from the sky. Mongold figured out a way to sell that blue back to people—Paradise Windows. They could be installed in residences, offices, and automobiles. People spent most of their time indoors now anyway. With Paradise Windows, they could enjoy a near-constant boost in mood and psychological well-being. He could sell a range of products from a cheap basic model, which provided pleasant but pale blue tints, to deluxe, programmable models that created a continuous light show. You could order up tomorrow's sunrise from a menu including "Maui Morn," "Dominica Dawn," and "Phuket, But It's Gorgeous." The daylight hours could mimic the high clear light of the Greek Isles or the softer glow of a Cotswolds afternoon. At night you could enjoy the Aurora Borealis or a fireworks show. The best part was that even the most diligent financial sleuth could not connect the Paradise Window Company to Alexander Mongold.

Paradise Windows were waiting in warehouses now, ready to burst on the scene as soon as the skies began to fade. Panacea had only to be switched on. All Mongold needed to start the ball rolling was the approval of Congress. Not one to leave things to chance, he had contributed heavily to campaigns and employed a swarm of lobbyists. Between the costs of building Panacea and the Paradise Window Company and the hefty price tag for Congresspersons, he had to tap the billions he had stashed away. He even had to dig up the gold bars. Everything was riding on this decision.

Tensions began to rise in New Hope the week before the vote. July was waning, and in just a few days, Congress would adjourn for the August break. It was now or never for the legislation that would greenlight and help fund Panacea. If it failed, or if the opposition delayed a vote, it was over. The Capital Police called in reinforcements to keep the pro-Panacea and anti-Panacea demonstrations apart. Foreign leaders phoned in last-minute appeals to the president.

Mongold peeked between the curtains of the penthouse suite of the best hotel in New Hope. Motley crowds blurred the pure geometry of his city. The uncertainty was eating at him. He couldn't afford to linger over the view. He popped another breath mint and told his assistant to show in the next in the long stream of visitors he had been entertaining all weekend. Congresspersons, all of them. They were giving him a primer on euphemisms for bribe: bakshish, bung, campaign contribution, dropski, payola, palm grease, sweetener ....

"We're losing population and tax revenue," said the senator from Nevada.

"Panacea will cool down your deserts," Mongold said.

"Maybe, but what I'm really talking about is a ..." The senator let his words hang.

"Little brown envelope?" Mongold said.

"No, an *opportunity*. For you. Not something that would fit into a little brown envelope. Nevada needs a pleasure dome."

Mongold shifted in his seat. This sounded expensive. "I thought pleasure domes were all you had out there," he said.

"I'm talking about a massive, climate-controlled pleasure dome filled with casinos, restaurants, theaters, fountains you name it." The senator's eyes glittered as he elucidated his vision. His arms stretched out to encompass it. "Huuuge mother fucker. You could design it."

"And fund it?" Mongold said.

"Like I said, our tax revenues are dwindling."

Mongold forked over money he wasn't even sure he had. By Sunday night, he was retiring to the lavatory between meetings for an inhaler and benzodiazepene break. Despite all of his efforts, the pundits predicted that he would lose by a hair. It would all depend on the messages the most politically insecure of the congresspersons were getting from their districts.

Mongold was not a religious man, but he planted his knees in the thick blue-and-gold-swirled carpeting of the suite, clasped his hands, and bowed his head. It was awkward, but sincere.

"God? Mongold here. It's been a while. I'm praying in regard to Project Panacea. I'm sure you've heard about it. It's humanity's last, best hope, and you have to help me get it deployed. Help me help humanity. You're still pro-humanity, aren't you? Actually, that's a good question. For all I know, you've given up on us and this is your way of clearing the slate. But if you're still willing to give us another chance, it would be such a small thing for you to help me on this. We've already got el Niño acting up, and the jet stream is sluggish. I just need you to make it blistering hot for the next few days, focusing on the districts of undecided senators, if you can do that. Of course you can do that." Mongold paused, trying to remember how to properly end a prayer. "Thanks in advance, Mongold. Amen."

Mongold's arrogance was such that he believed God had answered his personal prayer when temperature records began to shatter across the country before noon on Monday. The homeless and the elderly were hard hit. By Wednesday, the day of the vote, some ten thousand deaths nationwide had been attributed to the heat.

Mongold won approval for Project Panacea by two votes. He celebrated with a vintage Bordeaux aboard his private jet. That night he flew to an undisclosed location where giant hot air balloons, bearing the blue and gold Panacea logo, waited. The size and majesty of the balloons thrilled him. The next day, July 29, 2045, they rose into the blue sky trailing silver hoses. Mongold broke into tears. He, with his own money, hard work, and herculean persistence, was bringing relief to the masses. With the press of a solid gold button, he turned on the hoses, and they began to spray a proprietary mix of sulfates and chemicals into the stratosphere. "Relief!" he cried. "Blessed relief!"

CHAPTER SEVEN

Sleep Mode

Bostock was nearing the end of his extended Pentagon tour. He was considering doing something that would make his colleagues question his sanity—asking for another one-year extension. The paperwork was on his desk, but he hesitated. How could he ask for more of this bureaucratic torture when he yearned to get back out to sea again? But the timing was bad. Campbell had not taken the deployment of Panacea well. She was going quiet, deadly quiet, and he was worried.

Bostock picked up the phone and punched her number at work. Brian picked up.

"She's home sick," he said.

"Sick?" Bostock had never known her to be sick, and there was something in Brian's voice that troubled him.

"She gets sick sometimes, and then she's out for a while. You should check up on her."

Bostock would have gone immediately, but he had to attend yet another meeting. It would include a handful of disputatious souls who promised to turn it into an interminable pissing match. This was why most military officers dreaded their mandatory Pentagon tours. Bostock wondered that his training had taught him how to get out of every sort of dicey, unlikely situation, but had neglected instructions on how to escape from the most distressing and common of snares—the senior-level staff meeting. Perhaps this was the Pentagon's way of turning men into killers. Two hours in, and Bostock would have happily terminated with extreme prejudice the Rear Admiral who kept yammering on about "vertical interoperability of C3 elements," while snuffling back a rivulet of snot. Meanwhile, worries milled about in the back of Bostock's mind muttering something he couldn't quite hear.

It was a few days short of the winter solstice, so it was dark by the time Bostock reached Campbell's apartment building. He looked up to her window on the fifteenth floor and found that it, too, was dark. Perhaps she was sleeping off whatever bug she had contracted. He passed through the lobby where a handful of elderly women hung out to watch the human traffic, talk, and do needlework. They were an incongruous sight settled into the asymmetrical contours of cheap, bright orange modular couches. They smiled and nodded at Bostock, and he smiled back. None spoke English. Campbell could speak Spanish and had learned their stories. It was her way of putting flesh on the dry numbers she dealt with every day. They treated her like a favorite granddaughter. Campbell could have afforded to live in a much nicer building, but she preferred the *abuelas* to the sort of people she grew up with.

Bostock's heart pounded as he rode the elevator to the fifteenth floor. When he knocked on Campbell's door and no one answered, he felt a sickness rising up his throat. He knocked again and then used his key to open the door. He flicked on the light.

It felt like death inside the apartment without the electricity of Campbell's personality. Bostock had never noticed before how bare the walls were or how plain the furnishings. This was something beyond emptiness.

"Go."

Bostock started. She was sitting in the corner of the couch. He hadn't seen her. She seemed shrunken into herself, or into a distance that was spiritual rather than physical. She didn't look at Bostock. The light shone on the sharp Slavic plains of her face, but caught no movement. He wanted to go to her and hold her close, but he felt a barrier, an icy density in the air that surrounded her as if she had wrapped herself in a scrap of the Russian winter.

"Go," she said again. "I need to sleep. I'm in sleep mode now. I just want to sleep. Go. Get out of here."

The vast, barely suppressed anger in her voice astonished him. He left.

◨

Bostock arranged to meet Brian Foster in the underground Pentagon cafeteria. It was as good a place as any for a private conversation. The low ceiling and hard surfaces set the background noises against one another. Chairs scraped, flatware clattered, an occasional raucous laugh rose above the confusion of conversation. Pull chairs close together, maintain a low voice, and you could have all the privacy you needed. Still, Brian glanced around nervously as he answered Bostock's questions. Otherwise, he looked down at his plate, added another layer of salt, and addressed himself to the food. He avoided looking Bostock in the eye.

"It's happened before?" Bostock asked.

"Sure. It lasts for a few weeks." Brian studied a forkful of pasta salad before shoving it into his mouth. He spoke before he finished chewing. "Months, one time. Management puts her on leave and lets it pass because she's Campbell and you can't replace her. We cover for her, too. She's covered for us enough times."

"Has the Agency given her any counseling?"

Brian snorted. "They tried. They sent in a cleared psychiatrist. She spit him out. He came back muttering about taking her out in a pasture and shooting her."

"What should I do? How do I reach her when she's like this?" Bostock asked.

Brian screwed up his woolly brows and shrugged. "Oh, man. Don't ask me. Human relations is not my thing. I'm a numbers guy. And she's my boss. It's like talking about my mother to my father."

Bostock didn't feel the least fatherly emotion toward this awkward man, but he let it pass.

Brian continued. "She almost took my skin off once when I tried to talk to her during one of these episodes. I told you to check on her because I wanted you to see for yourself what she's like. It was easier than trying to explain it to you. We just let her be until she comes out of it. Our senior analyst, Maeve, says she's doing battle. I'm not sure what she means."

That was about all the insight that Brian could offer. Bostock asked him for Maeve's number. Maybe she understood more about human relations than Brian.

▣

Maeve suggested they meet at a *pupuseria* a few blocks from the Intelligence Analysis Agency. It took Bostock a while to find it tucked away at the dead end of an "unofficial" alley. New Hope had a map before it had streets. Everything that appeared on that map was "official," whether it had been completed or not. While work crews labored to lay out the sweeping curves on the approved map, an influx of refugees drew crooked lines connecting the gaps and threw up non-code structures in wee hours of the morning. The city no longer bulldozed the unofficial parts of New Hope for fear of unrest. Immigrants named their ersatz hoods for the countries they had left: Panama, Honduras, Guatemala. Domestic refugees named theirs for cities that had slid off the coastal map: New Orleans, Miami, Charleston. Bostock guessed that this place served largely illegal immigrants from El Salvador. He bought a glass of water and sat down at one of the mismatched tables that crowded the narrow space. He waited for someone who looked like a senior intelligence analyst to come in the door. After about ten minutes, he heard a laugh at his elbow.

"You need to check your assumptions. Otherwise how can you anticipate anything in this unprecedented century?" The voice was female, but it came from a figure Bostock had assumed to be male. Maeve was somewhere in her sixties. She sported a buzz cut, skinny gray-striped pants, and a "blaze-out," the plain gray collarless jacket that had replaced the blazer as standard office wear.

Bostock shook her hand and moved to her table. "You weren't with the unit when they came to the Pentagon."

"I'm rather loosely attached," Maeve said. "Campbell allows me a lot of autonomy. Of course, at the present I'm the acting chief, which I find annoying because I have to deal with the baby analysts' drama as they discover they're not as special as their mothers led them to believe." She leaned back to allow a waiter to lay out paper-wrapped *pupusas* and small bowls of salsa. "I ordered for you," she said to Bostock. "You're welcome."

"Now," Maeve said, "I assume you're here because you're worried about Campbell. "

"Yes." Bostock said. He watched Maeve unwrap her lunch and flatten the paper against the table.

"I'm not going to tell you not to worry. We all worry. She's the strongest woman I know, not counting myself, of course, and this thing she's going through may be stronger than she is." Maeve looked up from her lunch and focused her sharp gray eyes on Bostock's face. He had the feeling he was being sized up, but he didn't look away.

"It may even kill her some day," Maeve said, "but not yet. You're about to ask me what you can do." She slapped her palm down on the table with a noise that made nearby diners start. "Nothing. I can't emphasize that enough. Not one fucking thing. Don't treat her like she's sick. She's not sick; she's engaged in battle, and you will only distract her. It is her battle. You have to retreat and let her deal with it herself. The worst thing you can possibly do to a woman is to try to fight her battles for her. You might as well shoot off her legs. Wait for her to contact you." Maeve let Bostock consider her words as she dredged a pupusa in salsa and tucked in.

"But..." Bostock said. His voice trailed off. "How can I ...?"

Maeve put her food down and wiped the salsa from the corner of her mouth with a napkin. "How can a superbly trained military man such as yourself accept 'do nothing' as an option for any situation? How can you resist going in for the rescue with all guns blazing? How can you make a choice that will drive you utterly crazy, even if it's the right choice for the woman you love?" Maeve said. "Is that your question?"

"Yes," Bostock admitted.

"Suck it up."

A month later, Bostock left for a tour at sea without having seen Campbell again.

CHAPTER EIGHT

Faulty Parasol

Those hoping for cool breezes were sorely disappointed. Panacea made it less hot, but less hot was still pretty damn hot. Mongold had started with a fairly low dose of sulfates, so he upped it, bringing average global temperatures down half a degree Celsius in the first year. No one liked the new, dirty beige color of the skies, but then Paradise Windows came on the market. People went into debt to buy them. Surveys showed that people with Paradise Windows in their homes were less worried about the environment and more positive about the future.

Then the ozone hole over the Antarctic began to reopen, leading to a diplomatic crisis with allies Australia and New Zealand, who countered with tariffs on U.S. imports. Acid rains ticked off our polite northern neighbor, Canada. Ongoing droughts in the Sahel, the Indian Subcontinent, and the Amazon River Basin worsened. The great rainforest, the lungs of the planet, blackened, burned, and failed.

Americans were perfectly capable of putting faraway disasters out of their minds, especially those Americans sitting behind Paradise Windows, but air quality was getting worse in the

United States as well, especially after India deployed its own version of Panacea, designed to counteract the original. Epidemics of emphysema, lung cancer, and pneumonia culled the elderly population. Childhood asthma incarcerated a growing number of youngsters in their own homes. U.S. meteorologists blamed the Indian solar geoengineering project for an unprecedented drought in the Appalachians.

Mongold asked for patience to adjust his system, but air quality deteriorated swiftly in the second year after deployment. Activists gathered crowds on the lawn of the New White House and demanded that Panacea be turned off.

But, as Campbell had pointed out, it wasn't as easy as flipping a switch. Heat had built up above the aerosol parasol, and if it was turned off, that heat would hit the Earth all at once with deadly consequences. Scientists coined a name for it—the Big Broil.

As the realization sank in that the damage could not be undone, angry crowds demanded that Mongold be thrown in jail. A newly created organization, Lawyers for the Earth, began to assemble the largest class action suit in history. Mother Earth's Avengers declared a goal of assassinating him. The slightly less bloodthirsty Defenders of the Planet voted not to attempt assassination themselves, but to offer a hefty reward for anyone else who would do it.

Mongold had never gotten such bad press. On the right wing, he was portrayed as an evil scientist who had sold the world on the hoax of climate change in order to destroy capitalism. The left wing penned articles with titles like "Alexander G. Mongold: Why We Should Have Eaten the Rich While We Still Had the Chance." *Time* magazine dubbed him "The Man Who Killed the Earth."

Mongold stopped reading the papers, stopped going out in public, shaved his signature curly gold beard, and abandoned his flamboyant dress. He no longer bothered to ask why no one talked about his good intentions. He had put all of his energy and much of his money into an effort to save the planet. He was a failure, but he wasn't evil. Yet now Alexander G. Mongold was the new, real-life Lex Luthor.

Pakpao no longer wielded her makeup wand, but she continued to give her boss shampoos, manicures, pedicures, and hot stone massages. The doll-like beauty of the Thai immigrant soothed Mongold's growing paranoia. She was a lost feminine ideal: pleasant, frivolous, subservient, and soft around the edges. Not too bright.

Pakpao placed her tiny foot on the pedal of the hydraulic chair and lowered it to a reclining position. She snapped a drape over Mongold. "I found papayas for mask, sir. Very rare and expensive now, but best for exfoliating. Take skin right off."

"That sounds wonderful, dear," Mongold said. "The tension is playing havoc with my complexion." He closed his eyes as she applied the thick gloop to his face with a brush. She massaged the mask into his face with gentle movements of her tiny, gloved hands. The question "Why is she wearing thick gloves?" almost surfaced to his consciousness, but she began slow, delicious effleurage movements under his cheekbones and the question dissolved.

"I give you hot towel, sir, and we wait twenty minutes." She removed her gloves, lowered the towel gently to his face, and squeezed his shoulder. She slipped his hairbrush with the solid gold handle into the pocket of her smock and left the room, locking the door on her way out. She kicked off her high heels, sprinted to her car barefoot, and left the compound. As the gates closed after her, she stomped her foot down on the accelerator. The guards raised their eyebrows. "She must have a hot date," one of them remarked.

Pakpao glanced in the rearview mirror. "You can't say I didn't warn you, you collapsed bowel. 'Take skin right off,' I said *to your face*."

Mongold attempted a grimace under the rapidly hardening mask. Exfoliation was not supposed to burn this much. A few seconds later he was screaming and stumbling toward the shampoo sink. The majordomo came running and found the door locked. He yelled at Mongold to open it, but his boss was too busy with the shampoo hose, trying to wash off the burning gunk stuck to his face. By the time his staff broke down the door, Mongold was convulsing in a pool of water and the hose was still spraying and dancing across the tiles like something live.

Fortunately, Mongold's onsite entourage included a doctor, Herbert Evans, who had been reading up on poisons, including contact poisons, ever since Mother Earth's Avengers had put the price on his boss's head. He had collected a cabinet full of antidotes and set up a mini intensive care unit next to the bowling alley. He had also been reading up on trauma from explosion, gunshot wounds, and other assorted methods of assassination. A former Eagle Scout, he believed in being prepared. He had been painfully bored for months, but now he was excited, almost happy to see all of his work pay off. After weeks of care, he managed to save his boss's life, but he could do nothing to ameliorate the facial scarring or the terrible psychological effects of the incident.

Before Panacea failed, Mongold had never known anyone who wanted to do him serious harm. Now the whole world wanted to see him dead. As the extent of the environmental damage done became more evident, angry crowds gathered outside whichever of his homes he happened to occupy. He tried to move in secret, but they always seemed to know where he was, and this terrified him. One day he woke up to gunfire, as demonstrators tried to breach his walls before dawn. Two weeks later, he got up in the middle of the night to use the bathroom. He was just about to return to bed when a bomb concealed in his nightstand exploded. When they dug him out of the rubble, he had more scars and less reason.

Mongold's growing paranoia turned against his own staff. He would fire half of them one day; then, feeling exposed with fewer people around, he would rehire them the next because how could he trust unknown people? But how could he trust known people after Pakpao? He ordered the construction of additional fortifications around his compound, but what good would they do if someone inside wanted to kill him? Mongold's behavior grew increasingly erratic. His tantrums increased in frequency and intensity until they fused together into one long, loud paroxysm that lasted from morning to night. The staff resorted to ear plugs against the relentless noise. Then, one morning, it was silent.

"Is he still asleep?" the valet asked the majordomo. "I usually wait until he rings for me, but it's almost noon. Maybe you should check on him."

"You check on him," said the majordomo.

"If he's still sleeping and I wake him, he'll kill me. Maybe we should wait a little longer."

"Maybe he's dead."

It was three o'clock before they finally opened the door to Mongold's bedroom and found it empty.

"Did the Avengers finally get him?" the valet asked.

"Wouldn't there be a corpse?" said the majordomo.

"They might have kidnapped him."

"Oh, come on. If you had the choice of killing him or kidnapping him, would you really choose to put up with that asshole?"

The mystery went unsolved.

CHAPTER NINE

The Obadiah Caves

When Jezebel, wife of Ahab, began to cut down the prophets of the Lord, Obadiah hid a hundred of them in two caves, with fifty men in each.

The Obadiah Caves of the twenty-first century numbered far more than two. They were spread up and down the Appalachians. Not true caves, they were underground shelters that combined the functions of bunker, man cave, armory, abattoir, church, and rathskeller. Filled with military-style weapons, dehydrated food, home-brew, Bibles, chewing tobacco, and carefully hidden stashes of porn, they were home to the Holy Wallbangers, a religious paramilitary group and a fringe of the fringe of the right-wing nationalist movements that rose in response to the waves of incoming refugees. The Wallbangers believed in guns, barriers, and five "Right Things," which were printed in blackletter font and hung in every Obadiah Cave:

Right Things

1. The Ungodly shall not take what is Ours. If we need what is theirs, we shall take it in God's Name.

2. The sins of modern-day Jezebels—the feminazis, Foreigners, homosexuals, transvesites, libtards, and other Perverts—have brought the Vengeance of God upon the Earth in the form of storms, drout, and Peschilence. This is Obvious to All.

3. Like Samson, We will rely on strength and never let Delilah shere our Locks.

4. When the Blessed Donald John Trump returns to Earth, he will lead the Righteous to the Golden Thrown of Heaven.

5. Until this Glorious Day of Rapture, we will Arm ourselves and march as God's Own Army on Earth.

The Wallbangers did not hold regular jobs. They had created a lucrative source of income by offering temporary shelter to wealthy men who needed to go off the radar for a while due to assassination threats, public scandal, or the prospect of jail time. They did not offer this service to women, of course. The caves had housed captains of industry, bankers, mafia heads, and one disgraced Catholic cardinal. All were anonymous to the Wallbangers. It was safer that way. Usually such men stayed a short while in the caves until a more comfortable safe haven in another country could be arranged. Now the caves were housing Alexander Mongold, who had gotten a referral from his former senator.

On his first morning in an Obadiah Cave, Mongold awoke from yet another in a long series of nightmares. He had dreamed that Pakpao had him stretched on a rack, which she operated with a tiny foot pedal. With her soft hands, she pulled out his intestines and wound them on a spool. When he tried to move, he found that he ached all over. He opened his eyes to a confusion of stacked crates and litter. He smelled blood, sweat, sour laundry, and something peppery. His eyes rolled toward a corner where a headless deer carcass hung. He was about to scream; then he remembered where he was. Remembered that he had willingly exchanged his custom-made mattress and satin sheets for this none-too-clean bunk and cramped underground space. He had paid the Wallbangers a fortune and assumed the accommodations would reflect the luxury price tag. He pulled himself up with difficulty and looked around.

Gorillas began to emerge from the visual chaos like figures in a hidden picture puzzle. No, not gorillas, guerrillas. Guerrillas covered in hair like gorillas. Mongold had never seen so much hair. It puffed out from their undershirts and armpits. It flowed down their backs and chests. It stuck out of their ears and noses. Mongold himself had once sported longish hair and a beard, but it was shampooed, conditioned, moussed, sprayed with a proprietary formula that made it bounce and shine. Elsewhere, he manscaped. He had a brief, cruel fantasy about Pakpao being forced to wax these men. But she was free, and he was stuck here with these monsters. The injustice of it almost brought him to tears.

The men paid no attention to Mongold. There were cleaning weapons or reading Bibles in the bunks that lined the wall. One arranged hand-carved wooden figures in a small crèche set up on a crate, while another scraped tin trays into a bucket with a sound that set Mongold's teeth on edge. It was eerie being ignored. He could not remember a time when he was not the center of attention, when people didn't hover and attempt to anticipate his every need. He searched his pockets for the printed set of dietary requirements he always kept on his person. He unfolded the paper and addressed the man with the trays. "Excuse me, but I've forgotten your name."

"We didn't give you no names, and you won't never get no names," he said, "and we call you the Sinner. That's your only name now."

"Are you the cook?" Mongold asked.

"No."

Mongold stood and held out the paper in his hand. "Could you please pass this along to the cook before he makes my breakfast."

Bucket Man spat on the floor but he took the paper. Mongold backed off a few steps. He felt the grit of a dirt floor through his silk socks. He looked down. It was not a dirt floor, but a very dirty steel floor. He supposed it would be useless to ask about dry cleaning.

"Looks like we got us a vay-gun," Bucket Man said as he read the paper. "And if we feed him gluten, his pretty ankles will swell."

A wave of derisive laughter seemed to bounce inside Mongold's aching head.

The man crumpled the paper and threw it at Mongold, who cringed when it hit his chest. More laughter. "Your breakfast is over there." Bucket Man pointed to a tin tray on the floor near the cot. "It's been sitting there an hour, sleeping beauty. I was about to scrape it into the bucket. Eat it or starve."

Mongold was ravenous. He stepped over and picked up the tray. His shaking hand made the fork clatter in its tin compartment. Other than the fork, the tray held only a canned peach half in syrup, a lump of white lumps, and some sort of crispy, greasy rectangle. According to the labels on a pile of empty cans near the slop bucket, the white lumps were called hominy. Mongold could not identify the rectangle.

"What is this?" he asked.

"Venison scrapple."

"What is scrapple?"

"Some people call it pon haus. We call it Spambi. Bambi spam. Get it?"

"What's in it?" Mongold asked.

"Cornmeal, offal, and a whole lot of pepper."

Mongold was not familiar with the term "offal," but he sensed that he had reached the limit of allowable questions. He ate the peach and the tasteless white lumps, but he was still hungry. He examined the Spambi. Maybe it was some sort of rural polenta. He put it in his mouth and gagged. He could not swallow. He needed to spit it out into a napkin, but there was no napkin, and he knew it would do no good to ask for one. He spit the lump back onto the fork and lowered it back to the tray. He tried to be subtle, but the man at the bucket caught the act.

"If you ain't going to eat it, give it here." He came over, grabbed the tray, and scraped it into the bucket. His voice slowed and deepened into tones of Biblical solemnity. "And when they had eaten their fill, he told his disciples, 'Gather up the leftover fragments, that nothing may be lost." He picked up the bucket. "We don't waste nothing here. This goes to feed Gertie."

Mongold didn't know if Gertie was some form of animal or someone's benighted wife. He didn't want to know. He longed to have a tantrum, to scream unreasonable demands, throw things, and fire someone, but all the men here looked mean. No one was the least bit impressed with him. They wouldn't even look at his scarred face. He sat on the bunk and was at a loss as to what to do with himself. Then he noticed the Right Things posted on the wall and read them through. He was on the verge of pointing out the misspellings, but another look at his hirsute companions and he remained quiet. On second thought, he found it amazing that they had spelled so many of the words right. Apparently Right Thing number three, the one about Delilah, explained all the hair. They didn't believe in cutting it.

Maybe he could get better treatment if he befriended these men. Glad-handing was second nature. Mongold said, "We have something in common. Not trusting damn women. It was a Delilah woman that did this to my face."

Nobody offered sympathy or even a verbal response. Mongold tried small talk. He addressed himself to the least-threatening-looking man in the room. "So where are you from?" he asked with a smile.

The man scowled. "I am given breath by Our Lord. I am sworn to protect you but not to be your friend. As it says in Jeremiah, 'Friend deceives friend, and no one speaks the truth. They have taught their tongue to lie. They weary themselves with sinning.' We take in sinners here, but we don't soil ourselves with their friendship. We'll do our level best to try to save you in the name of Jesus Christ, but that's all the love you're gonna get from us. Prayer meeting in fifteen minutes." He pointed to a crate. "Get a Bible out of that box and choose a passage for your testimony."

"Am I on trial?" Mongold asked.

"Here we testify to the goodness of the Lord every day and twice a day on Sundays and Wednesdays."

Mongold picked up a Bible and opened it. The pages were thin and the print small. He had never had an interest in religion, except to study the call and response technique of black ministers from videotapes collected by his staff. Now that was some powerful stuff. It had influenced his own speaking style. None of what they said had ever influenced his life, however. He had no idea how to go about selecting a passage, so he opened the book at random, closed his eyes, and let his finger fall. He read the selected verse. It was a long string of begets. He opened the book to another page and another and another until he finally found a passage that was familiar from one of the tapes he had listened to from Father Joseph Caldwell. Okay, he was ready.

A couple of men began to unfold chairs. "Well, get off your hindquarters and help," one of them said to Mongold. He did. They cleared a small space and set up the chairs. Mongold sat in the back.

The spiritual leader of this cave was the only one whose name Mongold was allowed to hear. He was an elderly, white-haired, scarecrow of a man called Leviticus. He had a jaw like a misplaced shoulder blade and pale eyes that called to Mongold's mind hard-boiled eggs. Crazy hard-boiled eggs, if there were such a thing. Leviticus was full of nervous intensity, and his moods seemed to change by the second. He thundered, cajoled, wheedled, and crooned in a performance that was hypnotic and unsettling. Mongold, an expert influencer himself, knew a charismatic master manipulator when he saw one. Knowing this, he was immune to techniques that held the other men in thrall. He watched Leviticus with cool analytical attention, not awe.

The old preacher seemed to understand this, and it infuriated him. He made his way through the chairs and bent over and thrust his face in Mongold's. He began to rant with a fury that seemed to catch his own disciples off guard. Mongold was fascinated, but not cowed. He had the sudden feeling that the old man's heart was about to explode, a prospect that he found himself looking forward to with intense curiosity.

The coronary explosion was averted, however, when Leviticus screamed, "Close your eyes and bow your head before the Lord God Almighty!"

Mongold closed his eyes, and Leviticus went back to the front of the group.

Mongold was the last to testify. He had listened to each man stand and say how he had "got to thinking on" the meaning of this verse or how that verse had "spoke to me." It was all very personal and, to Mongold, painfully monotonous. These men had no talent for preaching. He was nodding, almost asleep, when the man sitting next to him kicked him, and Leviticus screamed, "Stand, Sinner, and testify."

"Can I open my eyes now?" Mongold asked.

Leviticus didn't answer.

Mongold opened his eyes. He saw Leviticus regarding him with a sneer of contempt, and suddenly he felt the need to show up this two-bit, Spambi-eating charlatan. Mongold drew himself up and launched into a fragment of a sermon taken straight from Joseph Caldwell. Normally, he would have adapted Caldwell's techniques to his own speaking style, but he had had no time for preparation, so, relying on his superb auditory memory, he delivered straight Caldwell. When he got to the call and response section, however, there was no response, just a stony silence. Mongold looked at Leviticus and saw a such a raw, seething hatred that it stopped him in his tracks.

Leviticus squeezed his knotty hands into fists, raised his arms to the heavens, and shouted, "What blasphemy is this, Sinner? How dare you stand before us sounding like a damn—" and here he used a word that shocked Mongold.

Mongold's self-awareness was not so well-tuned that he recognized the more subtle forms of racism that still hid in his own heart, but blatant racism and hatred offended him greatly. His love of manipulating people did not mean he didn't love people of all sorts, with the notable exception of Pakpao and those who had put a price on his head. *What have I gotten myself into?* he thought. *What am I going to be like after I've been here awhile?* Because Mongold had no safe haven overseas. The whole world hated him. There was nowhere else to go.

□

As per the contract they had signed, the Wallbangers moved Mongold every few weeks, hiding him in various conveyances, from four-wheelers to Sunday School minibuses. The caves all looked alike to him. Indeed, they were all the same model of shelter—the Bombtastic—from the same company, Survival Unrivaled, Inc. Every cave had the same bearded and surly men, the same five misspelled Right Things posted on the wall, and the same fiery preacher with hard-boiled egg eyes.

Soon Mongold was as unkempt as the Wallbangers. He had lice in his hair, runaway eczema, and the first symptoms of rickets. His ankles were swollen and purple. He went from being someone other people watched, to being the observer. He watched the Wallbangers because he had nothing else to do, except the chores they assigned him—mindless things like stirring the simmering Spambi. He began to notice things about them he hadn't seen at first. The most obvious was that they were filled with fear. Once he saw it, he also smelled it, heard it, and felt it. The fear was in the furtive movements of their and the sudden moments of stillness when everyone cocked their heads to listen to the speakers that had been installed outside the caves to detect the approach of enemies. Everyone was an enemy, a potential taker. The enemy was always present in whispered conversations and expressions of hatred. Mongold felt the fear of the enemy in the hard metal of all the surfaces, the smell of gun oil, and the meanness of the food.

Watching the fear of the Wallbangers eased Mongold's own raging paranoia. He settled into an unthinking resignation. He no longer remembered why he had been so keen to save his own life. He felt like he had gone crazy, like he was paralyzed and could not move forward or backward. All he could do was watch. Oddly, the more he observed of these men, the less he felt superior to them and the more he felt his own meanness, degradation, and guilt. Yes, guilt. It was something he hadn't felt before, but now it stirred like a sleeping giant.

◨

Not all of the Wallbangers were unkind.

A man-child broke the rules by revealing his name—Galen. "I don't see as how it would hurt," he said. "I heard you been in the caves longer than most. You gotta have somebody to talk to." He was the youngest of the Wallbangers Mongold had met, perhaps not out of his teens. His beard was sparse, his face round, and his physique somehow fleshy, despite the diet. He was limping on a broken ankle and therefore stayed in the cave with Mongold while the others went out hunting. He even gave Mongold a pair of his own sturdy shoes to replace the rich man's smelly and failing Gucci horsebit loafers. Mongold gave him the loafers in exchange.

"What would I want with these stupid things?" Galen said as he stared at the custom-made cream and oxblood shoes.

"The horsebits are solid gold," Mongold said.

Galen shrugged. "Well, I'll put one in my pocket for luck. Maybe we can exchange the other one for food or bullets."

Galen was a talker. He could no more follow the rules of silence with the Sinners than he could stop the incessant jiggling of his foot that continued into the night until he finally fell asleep. "My mama died a couple of years back. She got the cancer, but she beat that with chemo. We sold everything we owned and some things we didn't to pay as much as we could on the hospital bills. A lot of people said we shoulda just prayed over her, but the chemo worked. Then the dingy fever got her when she was still weak."

Mongold guessed dingy fever must be dengue fever.

"She just burnt up," Galen said. "We kept putting cold washrags on her head, but she heated 'em up like we had put 'em on a stove. Then she coughed up big old clots of black blood and she passed in three days." Galen wiped a tear with his palm. "She was good, you know. Kindly. Virtuous. Not like most women. We thought God would protect her because she was good. We thought when he saved her from the cancer, she would be all right." Galen bowed his head and watched his foot jiggle for a while.

"Daddy never got over Mama's death. Then the sky went dirty white, and he come to understand it was a message from God telling man that he's just about fed up with us. It was all the evil in the world that made God take up the best to live with him while he left the rest of us to be all hot and hungry down here. So we left the unpaid hospital bills on the kitchen table and swore ourselves over to the Wallbangers. We decided we would fight the evil 'til we're taken and can join Mama at the foot of the Lord."

Mongold had heard other Wallbangers talk about the dirty white sky as a portent from the Lord. He heard them blame the feminists, foreigners, fornicators, et cetera, for pushing the Lord to do it. The one person they never blamed was Mongold himself. For a reason he could not himself fathom, that bothered him. "I heard it was some man who changed the color of the sky trying to fix the climate," he said.

Galen scoffed. "You hear stupid shit like that, but who can change the color of the sky but God hisself? Man don't change the color of the sky nor make the oceans rise or the windstorms blow. What man does is sin, and his sin makes God punish him with the storms and shit. It's as simple as that."

"But aren't you saying that man is the cause through his sins?"

"He caused God to do it, but he didn't do it himself. That's a big difference there."

Mongold would have to think about that for a while. He changed the subject to something he had been wondering about for some time. "What about women? Have you given up on women altogether?"

"Of course not," Galen said. "We just keep 'em in separate caves, safe and pure and only touched by the most holy and righteous amongst us."

"Do you get to touch them?"

Galen blushed and looked down at his bouncing foot. "Not yet, but some day if I work and study the Bible and follow the path, I will."

Mongold's stomach growled. The food had been sparse lately. "For all the time your friends spend hunting, they haven't brought back much deer."

Galen chuckled. "You think they been hunting for deer all this time?"

"They go out with guns."

"Yeah, but most of the time they ain't hunting deer."

Mongold was almost afraid to ask the next question. "What are they hunting?"

"Mexicans what come up from the south like a plague of locusts. More and more of 'em every day on the Piss Ass Trail."

It took Mongold a few seconds to figure out that the "Piss Ass Trail" must be the local name for what migrants from the south called "*La Pista Áspera*," or "The Rough Track." It was a path taken by refugees who had been dumped on the shores of the Gulf Coast states by traffickers running boats up from Central America. It led north through sections of the Appalachians too remote and rough for the immigration patrols to penetrate.

"Are you talking about killing migrants?" Mongold said.

"Well, what else are we supposed to do with 'em? Give 'em our food and let 'em take our country?"

Mongold felt sick. "Children, too?" He had a soft spot for children, even though he had none of his own as far as he knew. He adored his nieces and nephews and devised elaborate entertainments for them. What were they thinking about his disappearance? He hadn't been able to say goodbye or explain anything. What were they thinking about all of the things the world was saying about him now?

"I didn't much like doing that at first," Galen said, "but it was a kid, not more 'n twelve, what shot and killed my Daddy. After that, I didn't care much. 'Sides, they ain't got no future anyhow. It's a kindness to shoot 'em."

The room swam in front of Mongold's eyes. "How do you get away with murder?" he said in a whisper.

"That part ain't hard at all. There are caves all around here. Plenty of places to chuck 'em where nobody would ever look. Not that anybody would care much that we are taking care of their problems. 'Course if the deer hunting don't get better, we might have to butcher the bodies and start eating Mexican steak." Galen looked at Mongold and laughed. "Your face is white as a sheet. I'm just yanking your chain."

Mongold let out a breath. "You had me fooled. I really thought you were killing people."

"Oh, I wasn't fooling you on that. I was just fooling you about eating them. I'd never eat a damn Mexican."

Mongold avoided conversations with Galen after that by pretending to be sick and sleeping when they were alone together. But Galen just behaved toward Mongold with more kindness, sneaking him treats the Wallbangers usually kept for themselves. When the Wallbangers moved him to the next cave, Mongold was relieved. It was easier to live with murderers who didn't try to kill him with kindness.

CHAPTER TEN

The Great Blame Circle

While Mongold hid in the caves, the United States became so Balkanized that it no longer deserved the title "United." It slid into a state of civil war. This time it was not an official war with a declaration and a discernible beginning and end. It wasn't one group of states against another or one uniformed army against another. It was one ideology against another, one class against another, one resource claimant against another. President Hawkins dubbed it the Great Blame Circle because each faction targeted the people, companies, or institutions it blamed most for the dire state of the world. She called for civility and pleaded for her citizens to seek common ground and solutions to benefit all. It was a stirring speech that did nothing but ensure her defeat in the next election and bring the term "Great Blame Circle" into the lexicon of the Anthropocene. Soon it was shortened to an acronym—GBC.

The GBC was not a declared war, but it sounded like one. It had deep, ground-shaking booms as Mother Earth's Avengers turned to bombing coal plants and pipelines. It had the quick, sharp rat tat tat of automatic weapons fire as white supremacists took over ethnic neighborhoods. It had screams of fear as angry crowds of the homeless broke into wealthy enclaves, looting and killing. It had the flash and boom of artillery as state national guards in the Midwest vied over water, blaming each other for drawing down the Ogallala Aquifer.

◻

Leland Mason was glad to be at sea. He was a man deeply committed to civility, and there was little of that to be found on land. He no longer recognized the country he grew up in. His home, Charleston, was gone. His wife and infant daughter had died in an automobile accident during a chaotic pre-storm evacuation. For years afterward, he focused all of his energies on the Navy career that suited him so well. His superiors called him "solid," and his subordinates "fair and square." He was a man of notable balance and good judgment. Even his squat, broad physique was ideal for life at sea. He could move easily aboard a ship without bumping his head or losing his footing. Then his little sister's husband died the same month that she was diagnosed with emphysema. She was left with an infant and rapidly diminishing lung function.

Latisha Leverett and her daughter, Alison, had been the focus of all of Mason's love and panic ever since. Love because they were his and they were dear. Panic because he could never do enough to protect them. He had moved them to an apartment in New Hope near the Respiratory Center so Latisha could get her treatments and Alison could go to a good school when she was old enough. He visited whenever he could get leave or arrange a Pentagon visit, but he was aware that they needed more.

He always came with gifts. This time it was silk roses and a flowery card for Latisha and two brightly wrapped packages, a large one and a small one, for Alison. He knocked at the door of their apartment.

Alison opened it and squealed with pleasure at the sight of her uncle. She wrapped her arm around his legs and called, "He's here! He's here! He's *finally* here!" into the next room. Then she helped him set the roses and packages down on the table. She touched the roses. "Good. You remembered she can't have real flowers. I want to see real roses one day, but they would make her sick."

"You're getting so grown up," Mason said. "How old are you now?" He asked, even though he knew and never forgot a birthday.

"Seven. I have to be grown up because Mama needs me to be."

Latisha appeared at the door. "You shouldn't have to be grown up," she said to Alison.

Mason was careful not to react to the sight of eyes sunken into hollows and skin grown blotchy and gray. He kept a smile of welcome on his face, but it felt frozen and false.

"I know, but look what Uncle Lee brought!" Alison pointed to the flowers. "Aren't they pretty?"

"You shouldn't be spending your money on silly things," Latisha said to her brother.

Mason went up to give her a hug, being careful not to jostle the portable oxygen machine around her neck. "Do you have to wear this all the time, now? Even inside?"

"Yes."

His eye fell on the large air filter in the corner of the apartment. "Can you go out at all?"

"Just to the clinic." Latisha made her way to the couch and sank into the cushions. "How long can you stay? I need your help. I'm so tired of asking for help, but I have to move out of this apartment. The rent went up again."

Mason went to the table, plucked the card out of the flowers, and presented it to his sister.

"You haven't done something silly, have you?" Latisha opened the card to find a large number written inside. "What is this?"

"It's the amount I just deposited in your bank account. And there will be more. I just got the biggest promotion of my life. I'm going to be the commander of newly commissioned USS Colin L. Powell."

Latisha let out as much of a squeal as her weak lungs would allow. "I'm so proud of my big brother!" She leaned forward for another awkward hug. "Will you be the first black aircraft carrier captain?"

"No, but I'll be the first black commander of the first aircraft carrier named after a black man."

Latisha laughed. "But you're giving us all of your money. You can't keep doing that."

"There's nothing I would rather spend my money on."

Latisha gestured to the window. "Have you seen the squatters' shacks? It seems like they popped up over night. That's where all my friends are now, the other teachers at my old school. They scraped and clawed, but they still ended up out there. I would die there, and God knows what would happen to Alison. How can you keep giving so much?"

"What do I need money for?" Mason said. "I live at sea and eat what the Navy feeds me and wear what the Navy gives me to wear, and thank God I don't have to pick out my own clothes. All I need is enough money to buy the occasional gift for someone special." He saw a way to change the subject. "And I see that someone special has her eyes on a couple of boxes." Indeed, Alison's eyes had been darting back and forth between her uncle and the sparkly packages on the table. "Open the big one first," Mason said.

Alison wasn't one to rip into a package. She stretched out the pleasure by picking up the box, testing its weight, and running her fingers over the smooth ribbon. She sat down on the floor and put the box in front of her. For a moment, she sat still and admired the bright rainbows on the wrapping paper.

"Are you trying to open it with your mind?" Mason said.

"No," Alison said with the impatience of a child whose adults will not understand the simplest things. "I'm trying to look at it hard enough so I'll remember it always." She jumped up and got a pair of scissors out of a drawer. "I'm going to save the paper, so I have to be careful." She turned the box on its side, and clipped the knot that held the ribbon. She pulled it off the package and laid it to the side. Then she slid the blade of the scissors between layers of paper and slit the tape that held them. She folded the paper down to reveal a box with a picture of an aircraft carrier on the front.

"That's not just any aircraft carrier," her uncle said. "That is the very one I will be commanding."

After carefully flattening out the wrapping paper, Alison opened the box and began to examine its contents with reverence. It was an expensive model made of balsa wood, not plastic. She ran her fingertips over the thin, laser-cut sheets of wood. "I *love* punching out the pieces. It's my favorite part, except for putting it together and painting it."

"I hope it's not too complicated for you," Mason said in a teasing voice. "The box says ages 12 and up."

"Nothing is too complicated if you go slow and follow the instructions," Alison said.

Mason knew that she was repeating something her mom had told her. Latisha, uncertain of her own longevity, had taught Alison to read when she was three, to cook and do laundry when she couldn't reach the countertops without a step stool. Alison knew how to do lots of things, and that gave her a deep self-confidence that hid beneath her social shyness.

Alison's careful excavation of the box finally revealed the tiny containers of paint and brushes. She held them up and frowned. "It's different shades of gray."

Mason gave her a mischievous smile. "Now," he said, "it's time to open the little box."

"Is it ...?" Alison didn't finish her sentence. She jumped up and got the small box. She unwrapped it quickly, but still with enough care to preserve the paper. The sight of a paint set lit up her face and called forth whoops of pleasure. She took out the tiny pots one by one and called out their names, pronouncing each one perfectly because she knew her colors. "Turquoise. Magenta. Emerald. Heliotrope. Fuchsia. Oh my god, this is going to be the most beautiful aircraft carrier *ever*." She looked up at her uncle. "When I'm done, I'll send you a picture, and then you can paint the big carrier to match it. You can do that, right? You can order people to do anything you want, can't you? Please! It would be spectacular."

Mason laughed. "I think the Navy would draw the line at a requisition for four million gallons of fuchsia paint."

"Really?" Alison frowned. "But you're so *important*."

"The Navy is still full of people more important than me."

"Let *me* talk to them," Alison said.

His first eight months as Commander of the USS Colin L. Powell were the best of Mason's life, or at least the best since his family had died. His whole career had been a preparation for this, and he stepped into his new role not only with confidence, but with joy. Everything in this life made sense to him: the intricate dance of takeoffs and landings, the complex but eminently solvable equations of budget and supply, even the most sensitive of personnel issues. He had a knack for dealing with people.

The experience was made even better by the fact that his executive officer was his old friend Sam Bostock. They had served their first tour at sea together. Now they sat out on vulture's row at night, sipped iced tea, and discussed a little bit of everything: politics, philosophy, meteorology, Latisha's situation, and Bostock's difficult friend, Mary Campbell.

"It's a bad time to be away," Bostock said. "Her depression scares me. It's like she drifts off to another planet."

Mason had never met Mary Campbell, but from what he had heard, he didn't approve of her. His friend deserved someone less complicated and more stable, someone with the same simple faith in goodness that Bostock had. He had sworn to himself to never say a negative word about Campbell, however, because he feared it would only spark Bostock's defenses and push him closer to her.

Even Bostock's mood improved as they reached the Mediterranean and began the pleasant routine of flying daily reconnaissance missions over the Sudan. The weather was so beastly hot they had to shorten shifts on the flight deck and monitor electrolyte consumption, but, still, the press of the work filled their days in a way that soon pushed out other worries.

Then new orders arrived.

"What the hell?" Mason said. "I never thought this day would come."

"What is it?" Bostock asked.

"We're going home," Mason said. "We're going home to sit off the coast of Virginia and launch air operations against the Daniel Boone National Forest."

Bostock had a peculiar way of squinting when he encountered an absurdity. The expression usually made Mason laugh, but not today. This absurdity was too gross, too hard to swallow.

"That doesn't compute," Bostock said.

"Nut cluster," Mason said. "A bunch of goddam nuts have all come together to create one big cluster of Nazi, white supremacist, and nationalist wing nuts. They've dug themselves into the Appalachians with an arsenal of weapons. At first they were operating on a small scale, killing immigrants. Now they're shooting up courthouses, universities, women's groups, you name it. They're bombing police stations and National Guard posts."

"That's for the National Guard to handle."

"They haven't made any progress because the terrain is rough and these bastards know every inch of it. The president wants it squashed quickly. So they're calling us in because we have the best planes and the best pilots and the best tech. All the effort and love we have put into this ship has come back to bite us. The president wants us to bust bunkers."

"Does he know the difference between a real hardened concrete bunker and the little survival shelters these nuts are living in?" Bostock asked. "Ridiculous overkill."

"I doubt he cares. He got elected by accusing Hawkins of being weak on dissent and letting the country go to hell in a handbasket. He hasn't been in office long, and this thing is threatening to sink him already. He's not a real leader and he knows it. He feels himself losing control. The Guard isn't going to get the time they need to do the job. So I guess he's going to go for 'shock and awe.'"

Bostock closed his eyes. "We brag about being the 'tip of the spear,' but it's different when the spear is in the hands of a crazy, angry man and it's pointed at our own heart."

The company of the ship took the news as badly as Mason and Bostock. They blamed the administration in New Hope and not their own sensible officers, but still the air carried the tang of mutiny. The trip back across the Atlantic was filled with overcast days, glowering faces, and a constant low buzz of disapprobation. The pilots yelled and cursed at the slightest provocation. They hadn't signed on to bomb Kentucky. Then there were the members of the crew who hailed from the region. They were tense and silent, like people in the waiting room of a hospital. Mason spoke privately to each one of them and excused them from taking any part in the operation. Everyone prayed that the situation would resolve itself before they arrived.

As the carrier neared the Virginia coast, news of a deadly synagogue bombing dissolved any hope of the president calling off this operation.

Mason and Bostock watched the coastline come into view from vulture's row.

"Fog for days," Mason said, "and now, when we least want it, we have perfect visibility. No excuses. No delays." He lowered his eyes and saw Bostock's knuckles grow white as he squeezed the railing.

"The end of a hot, dry summer in the Appalachians," he said. "We'll set off a conflagration."

"I think that's what the president wants," Mason said. "Grand, fiery retribution. He thinks he can contain it by having air tankers full of fire retardant on hand."

"It will get out of hand. How can we do this?"

Mason saw something in Bostock's face change. "We can't disobey orders, Sam," he said.

"I'm getting out," Bostock said. "I'll do my duty here, whatever that word means these days, and then I'm putting in my papers and resigning my commission." He unclenched his hands and let go of the railing. Then slapped his fists down on it in frustration, and left.

Mason watched him go with a hollow anticipation of loneliness. There would be no changing Bostock's mind. Mason might walk away himself, if he didn't have his girls to support.

CHAPTER ELEVEN

Inferno

Mongold was thinking about leaving the caves, going back to his billions, and trying again to fix Panacea. For weeks, he had occupied his mind with technical issues. He felt enthusiasm rising up through the dirty sludge of apathy that had closed over him. Maybe he could still save the world and himself. If someone didn't kill him first. He hesitated, remembering the poisonous mask, the sound of gunfire outside his window, the explosion in his bedroom. But that hadn't been the worst of it. Seeing admiration turn to scorn was the worst of it.

As Mongold hesitated, life got harder. Mega death hit the deer population in the form of Chronic Wasting Disease. The forest was reeking with bloating carcasses. He and the Wallbangers now sucked the bones of groundhogs, squirrels, raccoons, and weasels. They consumed snakes, catfish, and suckers. Still, they were hungry much of the time. Drought dried up the wineberry vines and blueberry bushes, ramps, mushrooms, and mayhaw. They bought canned goods when they dared, but since the Wallbangers had joined the right-wing insurgency, supply runs were increasingly risky.

Life was stark, but still Mongold hesitated. Then he was moved one more time. He woke to the sound of a fork scraping a tin tray. He opened his eyes and recognized Bucket Man.

"Don't you look like death warmed over," the man said. "Had a rough time, huh?"

Mongold heard a cackle from the corner. He hadn't noticed the old man staring at him with crazy hard-boiled egg eyes. It was Leviticus, crowing over his degradation.

The unreality of it all came home as Mongold realized he was back where he had started. He collapsed back on the cot and closed his eyes. He had no idea how long he had been in the caves, how far he had travelled, where he had been, or what was taking place in the world. He had been swimming at the bottom of a dirty pool, afraid to surface.

That night, Bucket Man woke Mongold with a bruising punch to the shoulder. "Get on your feet. Move."

"Move where?" Mongold said. All around men were pulling on boots. Over the sound of scuffling and scraping, he heard the roar of a waterfall over the speakers.

"Forest fire!" someone yelled, "move or die. Don't take nothing. No time." The entryway trap door was open, and two men were climbing up the ladder. The smell of smoke filled Mongold with panic that released a hot trickle of urine. It seems he still feared death after all. He felt under his bunk for his shoes with shaking hands. "Wouldn't it be safer to stay in here?" he asked.

"They're blowing caves," someone said. Then he was up the ladder.

Mongold didn't know what he meant by "blowing caves," but he remembered now that the storage space under the metal floor was filled with ammo, grenades, and explosives. That was what his money had bought rather than the luxuries he had naively expected. He scrambled up the ladder with one shoe tied, the other loose.

It still sounded like water to him at first, beating down, splashing, roaring. Then he climbed out into hell. The fire was coming down from the hilltop.

"Downhill, follow me," someone shouted.

Two men got on either side of Leviticus and half-lifted, half-dragged him along, while the old man turned his face to the sky like a wolf and howled a prayer for deliverance.

Mongold lost one shoe. Rocks tore at his feet, brambles grabbed at his clothes. A branch bit into his cheek, just missing his eye, but he ran headlong down the steep slope, falling, rolling, getting up, running again as nearby trees exploded into flame. Beneath his feet, the sere leaves curled and grasped for sparks. The wind picked up and the roar of the fire hollowed out his skull. He had a dreamlike sensation of paralysis, of being suspended in the split second before doom. He expected to be swept up into the air, another burning ember in the maelstrom. But he was moving and he kept the men ahead in sight. Smoke burned in his throat, lungs, and eyes.

The men in front reached the old camouflaged army truck they had parked just off a dirt track. Mongold heard the roar of the engine. "Don't leave me!" he screamed. He reached the truck, and the men pulled him into the back. "Thank you for waiting."

"We wasn't waiting for you. You can burn as far as I'm concerned. We're waiting for Leviticus and the men with him. Did you see them?"

"Just outside the cave. Not after that."

"We can't wait much longer," someone said. "The burning is going to block the road."

"We have to wait."

A man moved to jump down from the truck. "I'm going to go up the hill and look."

Hands pulled him back. "No."

The next words were drowned in the sound of an explosion that made the ground buck under their feet. Suddenly the fire was all around them and pouring from the sky.

The truck took off, canting from side to side as it encountered gullies and branches. It stopped when a burning tree fell into their path. The men got out with a chainsaw, cables, and hooks and cleared the path, all the while praying out loud. Even Mongold, with his bleeding hands and feet, helped drag the tree off the road. The next tree was too big. They abandoned the truck and ran down the stony dirt road. Behind them, the truck caught fire, and the gas tank exploded. Mongold had never felt so much pain in his feet, legs, lungs; he was ready to give up and let the fire take him when they reached the Cumberland river. Muddy and much shrunken in its banks, but it was still deep enough that they could wade in to their necks, pick up their feet, and float downstream.

Mongold floated on his back, watching a canyon of fire rise on either side and in the middle, a sky that held no stars, only a boiling pyrocumulus cloud glowing with bloody light. He watched a fire devil spin up from a ridge and twist a hundred feet into the sky. It roared and writhed like evil itself, self-consuming evil made manifest.

Even if there had been no smoke, the stars would be almost invisible through the sulphur dioxide particles. He was the man who had taken away the stars, and the blue sky, and hope. The whole world hated him. He should die. He should stop making the small movements that kept him afloat and sink under the waters and drown. But every time he tried to do so, some stubborn life force made him spit out the filthy water, kick, and gulp the foul air, because existence, even degraded, was existence.

⊞

After the fires subsided to a smolder, a helo flew over the scene of devastation looking for survivors. The rescue team spotted the first body lodged in charred branches on the shore of the Cumberland. A second was caught on rocks farther downstream. The third and fourth had washed up on shore. The fifth, the one that would be identified as Mongold, was half in, half out of the water, face up, arms outstretched, as if still staring at the sky. A representative from the Mongold Foundation, summoned by an early morning phone call, arrived at a temporary morgue set up in a highschool gymnasium. He held a whispered conversation with the coroner and then handed over a thick manila envelope labeled "dental records" and filled with one-hundred-dollar bills. In return, he got a death certificate for Alexander G. Mongold, born April 12, 2000, died September 5, 2049.

CHAPTER TWELVE

Misplaced

The eastern United States had never seen anything like the Boone Fire. Even though the president had fire crews and planes at the ready, it quickly got out of control. "It's like the Balrog," one firefighter said, referring to Tolkien's fiery demon. "You can't bring it down." The fire charred hundreds of thousand of acres, destroyed countless homes, and wiped dozens of small towns off the map. The full death toll could never be accurately calculated.

The president moved quickly to contain the damage to himself. He ordered that Commander Mason be court-martialed. "I asked for surgical strikes, and that idiot laid waste to the Appalachians."

Bostock was furious. He delayed resigning his commission so he could call in his chits in the Navy and get support for Mason's cause. He found a lot of it. Mason was not only well-respected, but well-loved. Moreover, the president had issued a string of nonsensical orders that had undermined military morale. The Chief of Naval Operations was already chafing at the scapegoating of Mason.

Meanwhile, Mason sat in the brig awaiting trial. He was there when the chaplain brought him news of his little sister's death.

"I should have been there!" Mason howled. "Where is Alison? I need to be there for her."

The chaplain promised to find out. "Call Sam Bostock," Mason said. "Tell him to go get her."

It should have been easy. Bostock was already in New Hope, working his Pentagon contacts. He went to the hospital where Latisha had died. "We couldn't locate any relatives," the nurse said, "so we called Social Services." The Social Service Office was crowded, dirty, and chaotic. A harried and distracted woman gave Bostock the address of a foster home, but when he got there, he found a girl named Alice Lester. He went back to the office. They checked their records again and sent him to another office.

"How can you lose a child?" Bostock yelled at a consumptive-looking man in sweaty shirtsleeves.

"We lose them all the time," the man said, not without sympathy. "We have a fraction of the staff we need. Don't you know that the name of this city is a bad joke?"

At the third Social Services Office, Bostock found the staff gathered around a television screen.

"Excuse me," he said loudly, "can someone help me?"

"Hush," a woman said, pointing to the screen. "They got rid of him."

"Who?" Bostock asked.

"The president. They invoked the 25th. Hauled him out in a straightjacket."

Bostock got on the phone and found that Mason had already been released and was on his way.

◘

Kristin's parents had held their daughter between them as they jumped off an overpass into rush hour traffic. She survived but lost her leg. Jade's mother washed down the contents of her medicine cabinet with a fifth of rum and then put a plastic bag over her head. Joshua's father put a pistol in his mouth and fired. These were Alison's best friends during the chaotic year between the day that her mother died and the day her uncle finally found her. It was a time of skinny-armed hugs, tears, cockroaches, dirt, and stifling hot apartments.

Children of suicides, alcoholics, and drug abusers overwhelmed the foster care system, turning it into more of a trap door than a safety net. There were too many kids to keep track of. Traffickers got hold of some of them. Children slipped into hidden pockets of horror never to be seen again. When the government started skipping some monthly payments, thousands were simply dumped on the streets.

The spike in suicide and addiction was called the Panacea Effect. Project Panacea was not only failing; it was setting off a spiral of climate anomalies that would, not too far in the future, make human survival impossible. Slow boil or Big Broil. Damned if you do. Damned if you don't. It was only a matter of time. Each day was bad, and yet much better than the day that would follow. The news was finally hitting home, even to those who had done their best to ignore it.

Alison understood this with the matter-of-factness of a clever eight-year-old. She sat at the table with Kristin, Jade, and Joshua trying to scrape every last bit of breakfast off her plate.

It was awful stuff. Their foster "mother," Sophie, worked at a car charge station and convenience store. Every night she brought home whatever food was left over from the day: hotdogs that had been spinning on the roller for hours, gelatinous nacho cheese scraped up out of the warmer, rock-hard bagels that they gnawed on like puppies. The kids suffered such bad diarrhea from this diet that their butt holes were always sore. They were constantly dehydrated. Still, they ate it.

When her plate was clean, Alison put down her fork, and in her quiet, solemn way made an announcement. "We all should kill ourselves. Everybody is doing it."

Kristin considered this. Like many children in the system, she was so malnourished and undersized that it was hard to tell her real age. Forty-year-old eyes in the body of a five-year-old. Chronic anemia and intestinal parasites had left her too listless to give anyone much trouble. "Is there a way to do it that won't hurt too much?" she said.

"I don't care if it hurts," Alison said. "The important thing is that you get it done and don't end up a vegetable."

"What's a vegetable?" Jade asked.

"Well..." Alison tried to think of an example Jade would be familiar with. "You know when Sophie brings home those left-over sandwiches? You know the green stuff? That's lettuce and that's a vegetable."

"I don't get how we could turn into green slime," Joshua said.

"You don't really turn into lettuce if you don't kill yourself all the way. You just can't move or talk or think, so you're like a vegetable." Alison spent a lot of time explaining the simplest things to the others. They had attended school rarely or not at all. They hadn't had a mother who read to them every night. So even though Alison was the youngest, they all looked up to her as if she were more adult than Sophie.

Joshua added his opinion. "It would be nice if we could just fall asleep and not wake up. Just die in the middle of a good dream and stay there forever."

"I just have to research it so we can do it right," Alison said. "I'll go to the library and look it up."

The People's Library was only three shabby city blocks away. It occupied the site of a bowling alley gone bankrupt. Its founder, Carrie Portman, was one of those happy people who give without ever asking the question "Suppose there won't be enough left for me?" Giving was a coping mechanism, almost a form of sustenance. It fed her soul at a time when others searched vainly for meaning. It protected her from both fear and despair.

Carrie had installed metal shelves between the lanes of the old bowling alley. She kept the wood floors clean and polished so the kids could slide around in their sock feet. She gave all of the rental shoes to a church to distribute, and now every homeless man and woman in a ten-block radius wore bowling shoes. She filled her library with warped and mildewed books rescued from Atlantic City and other coastal towns. A gun concealed under her vest kept the bad elements out.

Alison loved every inch of the library, even the smell of mold. She went up to the counter where Carrie was using a hairdryer on a damp copy of Little Women.

Carrie turned off the dryer and smiled. "Well, if it isn't my favorite patron. What can I do for you today, Alison?"

"I need a good book on how to commit suicide without a lot of blood and pain."

"Oh, God," Carrie said. She closed the book and came around the counter. "Come sit with me, honey, and tell me why you would want such an awful thing."

They sat on the chairs at the end of the lanes under a sign that now flashed featured books instead of scores. Carrie put her arm around Alison, squeezed her shoulder, and felt the sharpness of the bone. "Do you have any relatives?" Carrie asked.

"Uncle Lee. I thought he would come for me, but I think he forgot me."

"Tell me about him."

"He's Mama's big brother, although he's kind of like my dad, too, because I can't remember my real dad. Uncle Lee paid for our apartment and brought me presents, but he hasn't come for me."

"That sounds like someone who loves you, not someone who would forget you. Do you remember his full name?"

Alison was offended by the question. "Of course I remember. I'm very smart. His name is Leland Michael Mason, and he is the commander of the USS Colin L. Powell."

"Oh. I think I know why he couldn't come get you. I can find him. Librarians can find anything."

Carrie took possession of Alison, fed her, and put her in a hot tub of soapy water. While Alison soaked, Carrie searched online and made phone calls. It was not too difficult to locate Commander Leland Mason. He was famous from the Boone Fire scandal. Besides, the government might lose thousands of children in its care, but it kept careful track of the commanders of its aircraft carriers.

After he got Carrie's phone call, Mason was at the library within the hour. He broke down and wept when he saw Alison.

"Where have you been?"She looked at him with a cool eye.

You're breaking my heart," Leland said. "I didn't mean to abandon you, honey. I've been looking for you. I couldn't come get you right away when your mom died. When I got home, nobody could tell me where you were. I called every government official on the East Coast bad names. I begged them, and yelled at them, and hung up on them. Nobody could give me any answers. I took emergency leave. I've been looking for you all this time. I would have never given up."

Alison tilted her head as she looked into his face. "I suppose that's okay then. I suppose I'll forgive you." She didn't cry with relief at her rescue or return Leland's hugs with any particular enthusiasm. Eventually, her uncle would win back her love and trust, but not yet.

CHAPTER THIRTEEN

Sinking

Bostock paused in front of Campbell's new apartment building and studied the graffiti that covered the walls. He saw words in a dozen languages, words of blame, hatred, anger, and frustration. The paint was thick. Almost every night rival factions covered over each other's slogans. He took a step back, and a bullet casing squibbed out from under his heel and rolled into the sorry strip of weeds by the road. Spatters of blood decorated the sidewalk nearby. This didn't look like a safe place to live, but it was apparently safer than Campbell's old neighborhood.

After weeks of appeals, she had finally agreed to see him. He came bearing rare offerings of flowers and a Baby Ruth bar. Riding the elevator, he wondered who would open the door: the woman with challenge and humor in her eyes or the one with the vacant expression?

Neither. Campbell had come out of the worst of her depression, but he could still see the shadow of it in her eyes and movements. She put her arms around him and accepted him back into her life, but something in her expression reminded him of a soldier returning from a long and bloody war. Looking over her shoulder, he spotted yesterday's blouse draped over the back of a chair, a dirty glass on the counter, and cobwebs knitting her bike to the wall.

"I will come out of it," she told him the next morning. "I'm coming out of it. I just need a little more time."

She no longer treated him to mantic naked riffs. She didn't want to go biking through the streets like they used to do. "Not safe anymore," she said.

Bostock devoted himself to the problem of how to raise her spirits. He monitored her behavior closely to try to determine whether she was getting better or worse, rising or sinking. He couldn't tell. Maybe she was just treading water.

"Let's go to Franconia Notch." Bostock was conscious that his voice sounded too chirpy. It annoyed him and probably annoyed her, too. It was hard to tell. "We could do the bike path or the sky tram or both."

"It won't be the same," she said.

He squeezed her knee. "Please. It would do us both good to get out of the city and into the trees. "

"Fine," she said in a flat voice. He got the feeling she was humoring him.

◘

They rented a car and loaded up their bikes. It took several hours to get out of the city. The squatter neighborhoods had continued their desperate sprawl into the countryside. As Bostock drove, Campbell scanned live drone imagery to navigate around barricaded streets, trash fires, and prowling gangs.

When they escaped the city, the first thing Bostock noticed was the change in color, not an autumn change, for it was June. Familiar greens were gone. Maples, beech, and birch had retreated into the north, leaving gray snags behind. A takeover of the forest by pines had been routed by pine beetles, leaving broad patches of a dull, rusty red. The spruce were also under attack from their own species of beetle. Wooly adelgids had taken out the hemlocks, leaving a carpet of tiny brown needles. The forest was a tinderbox. Indeed, they topped a hill and encountered acres of charred land. Bostock almost turned back, but he bit his lip and drove through in the hope that they would find a less degraded landscape higher in the hills.

Bostock saw a patch of deep green in the distance and sped up. When he reached it and realized what it was, he pulled to the side of the road. He felt dizzy. How could so much have changed so quickly? He got out of the car and stared up at the mats of kudzu that had scaled the trunks of dead hardwoods. The exotic invader not only choked out native species; it released carbon that had been sequestered in the soil. Bostock was looking at an ecological catastrophe. He pushed his way into the vines. The sweet, stifling smell of kudzu, the crepuscular quality of the light, and the absence of bird song shook him. The gentians and pipsissewa that once decorated the forest floor were gone. Bostock turned to look at Campbell, who had followed him into the woods. He saw tears flowing freely down her face.

"It's like crawling over the rotted corpse of a loved one," she said. "Nature has no more solace to give."

"I'm sorry I brought you here," Bostock said. "Let's go home." As they walked into the light, he looked down and saw that their shoes were covered in ticks.

A few months later they shared a meatless, flavorless spaghetti dinner. Campbell didn't cook, so Bostock had bought the food at a grocery store. It was lukewarm, due to an unscheduled brownout as they were reheating it. The particles of sulfur in the stratosphere rendered the solar power grid less reliable. They ate in front of the one big window. It was the builder-grade version of a Paradise Window. Mongold had signed a huge contract with the biggest construction firms in the capital, so these windows were a standard feature in apartment buildings. Unfortunately, the cheap ones began to cloud up after a few months. Now the glass was lending a rather sickly green haze to a dark and crowded city. The only light was at its center, where the New White House shone with an inappropriate sparkle, like a Christmas ornament atop a heap of trash.

When they had finished and cleared the table, Campbell grabbed both of his hands and said, "I have to tell you something."

It had been a long time since he had seen that deep and penetrating look in her eyes, and he felt a surge of hope followed by fear. Something was wrong. *Fatal disease* was the next thing that crossed Bostock's mind as he sat down with her on the couch. She had been sad and subdued all evening, even sadder than usual. *She's dying.* So many people were dying.

"I'm pregnant," she said. "I found out on my fortieth birthday."

Bostock felt hope and the death of hope almost simultaneously.

Campbell continued in a voice that was sad, a little apologetic, but determined. "In a different century, I would have had your baby. Believe it or not, I would have focused my maternal instincts on adorable little rug rats instead of on a bunch of irascible analysts. But not this century. I can't do it."

Bostock squeezed her hands. "I know. I understand." He did, but that knowledge didn't stem the grief.

After the abortion, it was quite clear that Campbell was sinking, rather than rising. Bostock lived with a growing panic, and every day it was harder to keep it tamped down. One morning, the tension in his body erupted in a spastic movement that sent a bowl flying out of his hands. It smashed to the floor, and Campbell turned to look at him.

"It's like watching you die," he said. "What can I do? How can I help? I want to pull you out of this, but you have to at least reach out your hand." He stretched his own hand toward her.

"I can't."

"Try. Please. For me."

"There is one thing you can do that would make it better."

"I'll do anything."

"Go." She said the word just the way she had said it before their last separation.

Bostock drew his hand back.

"I can't snap myself out of this," Campbell said. "I see what it's doing to you, and that only increases the pain and the paralysis. You have to go."

"For how long this time?"

Campbell gave him one of those long, penetrating looks, the kind of look that usually preceded closeness. Now he had the sudden sensation that she was retreating into the distance even though she was perfectly still. He felt the answer before he heard it.

"Forever."

CHAPTER FOURTEEN

Unreal and Real

Bostock took a job with Summit Industries, based in Boulder, Colorado. He thought things might be better in the western mountains. A new decade, 2050, and a fresh start in a place he had never been to before with no memories of Campbell. The pictures in his mind—as well as those on the Summit Industries website—showed glistening snow-capped peaks under a blue sky. Sure, he knew that the pictures must be heavily touched up, but he thought maybe nature might still have some solace to give out west. He arrived in the city on a red-eye flight and the next day opened his hotel curtains to brown peaks swimming in an off-color sky. The sign in the shower explained that the water would come on in two quick bursts with time for soaping up in between. Not much different than a Navy shower. The air was so dry, however, that he got a nosebleed before he had finished buttoning his crisp new white shirt. He got blood all over it. He took it off, stuffed tissues up his nose, and rummaged in his suitcase for another shirt, still in its packaging. He speared himself twice fumbling with pins. He put it on and took a look in the mirror. Tissues up his nose and fold creases across his chest. He didn't have the time to iron them out. He would have to keep his suit jacket buttoned.

As Bostock drove the rental car up to the elaborate gated entrance of Summit Industries, he pulled the tissues out of his nose and stuck them in the drink holder. *Do not bleed*, he instructed his nose. He gave his name to the guard who directed him to park in space 52 on Executive Level One of the underground parking garage. "An orientation specialist will be there to greet you."

A young woman sporting a high blond ponytail, palomino print leggings, and bedazzled cowboy boots waved him into his parking spot. She held a green binder firmly clamped under one arm.

"Welcome, Sam! Good morning! My name is Kyra, and I'll be your orientation partner."

Bostock got out of his car and shook Kyra's hand as she eyed his suit.

"Oh my. Are you on your way to a funeral?" she asked.

"Excuse me?"

"The suit. We don't see many of those around here. Summit style is business casual with a Western flair." She did a little kick that showed off her boots. "Don't worry; you'll figure it out. We have our own company clothing store. It is phenomenal." Kyra pronounced it FEE-nom-i-nal and rolled her eyes heavenward when she said it.

She showed him the cover of the binder, which was printed with his name in gold letters. "This is your *personalized* binder. It has everything you'll need." She began to page through the material. "Here we have a map of the building and the complex, an explanation of our employee rating system, a summary of your benefits, a copy of your contract, the company honor code, some samples of our most frequently used forms, vouchers for our executive dry cleaning service, a list of the personal trainers available at the gym—I recommend Jarrod, he is phenomenal—and menus for our various cafeterias. We also have a company store where you don't need ration coupons. No need for a wallet, of course. We'll microchip you this afternoon." She closed the binder and handed it to him. "We call it the Family Bible. Don't lose it. Now, I'm going to take you to the Atrium Bistro for complimentary coffee; then we'll go upstairs to meet Brad. Okay?"

Bostock followed Kyra. Both her gait and the exaggerated movements of her head as she talked seemed calculated to make the ponytail swing. She peppered her speech with exclamation points and microbursts of giggling. By the time they reached the ground floor of the building, Bostock wanted to swat her with his thick binder.

Kyra waved her hand to open a pair of automatic glass doors that led into a soaring atrium. Bostock recognized it from the pictures on the company website. One wall was an enormous Paradise Window that offered a stunning view of snow-capped mountains and clear blue sky. This was the image that had attracted him here.

A coffee bar in the middle of the room was set in front of an elaborate planting of Aspen trees and columbine. Bostock could only imagine the effort it took the company gardeners to keep this slice of fake nature in perpetual bloom. In most of the world, coffee was now a rarity, but here it flowed like water. They got their frothy lattes and sat down at a table by the window. Given new government limitations on cattle raising, this so-called casual clothing must have cost a fortune.

"The view is phenomenal, isn't it?" Kyra said.

"It's not real," Bostock said. "Doesn't that bother you?"

Confusion showed in Kyra's eyes, but her lips continued to smile. "It's enhanced real. It's more real than real. Who needs ordinary real? I've got Paradise Windows in my home and in my car. I park underneath my apartment building and in the parking garage here. I *never* see plain real, and my life is better for it. So is my productivity. The company did a study. The windows practically pay for themselves."

"But won't we all have to face the reality sooner or later?" Bostock asked.

"I don't see why. The windows have a lifetime guarantee."

"Life doesn't even have a lifetime guarantee anymore."

"Whoa. You cannot be that negative here." A pout of concern crossed Kyra's face, distorting the smile. "We are all responsible for company morale." She reached for the binder and flipped to a page that said, in red 48-point font: We Are All Responsible for Company Morale." She tapped a glittery fingernail on the words. "This is a happy company. We have the Summit spirit. You're not one of those climate change cultists, are you?"

Bostock was temporarily struck dumb. He finally stammered, "You don't believe in climate change?"

"I don't have to and neither do you. This is America. This is Summit. If you work hard and believe in the system, your climate doesn't have to change. We're building our own housing, right on the grounds here. There will be climate-controlled walkways. Pretty soon you won't even have to go into the trashy parts of the city."

Kyra's voice was so full of naive conviction that Bostock mentally dubbed her "Tinkerbell" and thereafter had trouble remembering her real name.

Kyra's smile broke out anew. "Do you like rock climbing?"

"I've never done it, but I hope to try it soon."

"Let me show you something absolutely phenomenal." Kyra led him around the plantings to an artificial rock climbing wall that stretched to the ceiling. A handful of employees were doing a morning climb.

Bostock was impressed. "Wow. This looks like a great place to train until I can try out a real mountain."

Kyra made a face. "Oh, you don't want to go out there." She flipped her hand at the window. "Since the opossums died off, the ticks have gone crazy. An hour and you'll be covered with them." She shivered. "I've seen pictures of ticks so thick on hiking boots that you couldn't tell what color they were supposed to be. You'll end up with Lyme Disease and God knows what sort of cooties. You couldn't pay me to go out there." Kyra looked at her watch. "It's time for you to meet Brad. Let's head upstairs." She led Bostock to a cylindrical glass elevator that took them to the top floor of the building. As they rose, the view out the window shivered slightly. It was a quirk of the glass.

"Are you running for office?" Brad said as he shook Bostock's hand.

"Excuse me, sir?" Bostock said.

"I'm not 'sir'; I'm Brad. We're all on a first-name basis here because we are one big Summit family. Dress is Western casual." Brad himself was wearing a plaid shirt, jeans, and boots. "Let me introduce you to some of the people you'll be working closely with." He led Bostock into a room labeled "Brainstorming Pit." Inside were leather chairs, barn wood tables, and Navaho rugs. A dozen or so people lounged about sipping coffee and listening to a man lecturing in front of a digital whiteboard.

"If I may interrupt for a minute. Let me introduce you to Sam Bostock, former Executive Officer of the USS Colin L. Powell. He should bring some fantastic insider knowledge and contacts to Summit. He'll be great just as soon as we can teach him how to dress." The lame joke brought lame laughter.

Brad named each of the people in the room so rapidly that Bostock had no hope of remembering them.

He heard a few "Hey Sams," but no one stood up.

"Fair warning," Brad said. "These folks will judge you on the quality of your boots. Boots are something of an obsession around here."

"Do a lot of wading in manure?" Bostock asked.

Brad guffawed. "Not in these babies. Whip 'em out, folks."

A series of thumps sounded as boots landed on the low coffee tables. Bostock got an eyeful of tooled leather, snakeskin, and alligator. The women's boots were embellished with embroidery, silver, and beadwork.

"Am I required to purchase boots immediately, or can I shop around?" Bostock asked.

"The only place to buy them is the Summit Outlet. We have our own herd of cattle for meat and leather. But it's an important decision," Brad said, "like choosing a spouse. So take your time and collect a few fat paychecks first. "

Bostock considered his line of broken engagements and vowed to never buy a pair of boots.

□

Bostock did purchase a stack of plaid shirts and a few pairs of jeans. Plaid had the advantage of not showing blood. The nosebleeds became chronic, and he soon developed a dry cough. Bostock's body, which had spent previous decades at sea level, reacted badly to the high altitude.

The job was all writing proposals for government contract work. Requests for Proposal in the inbox. Proposals in the outbox, written in such a way as to achieve maximum payment for minimum work. Of course the inbox and outbox weren't really there. His desk was completely bare in the real world. No pens, papers, or even a computer. The computer was a microchip that had been embedded into his brain the day after the fairly benign procedure to microchip his wrist. It took a week of recovery time and some training to learn how to master the art of commanding an intracranial computer, to learn to access the virtual workspace, and to connect to other users in the system. He learned to use it, but he would never get used to it.

Once Bostock finally mastered use of the "crani," the tedium of the work weighted his eyelids. By early afternoon the effort to stay awake was painful. When he left Summit at the end of the day, the guard at the gate waved a wand over his head that cut the crani off, just in case he hadn't done it himself before he left his desk. It was a security measure to protect proprietary information.

At night, sleep eluded Bostock. He had no friends. The people in this place talked about their possessions, made jokes about exterminating migrants, and engaged in a never-ending game of one-upmanship.

Everything about the place offended Bostock, from the cowboy motifs to the technicolor windows, and the all-intrusive new technology. Summit was a theme park that simultaneously celebrated a sanitized past, an illusory present, and a future that would never come. Bostock had never hated people or a place or a job so much. Unfortunately, he had signed a contract to stay for a year.

Bostock wanted to tell Campbell about all of the idiocies and hear her turn them into a naked riff that would make him laugh until his stomach ached. But he didn't even know if the Campbell who did naked riffs still existed.

Bostock was beginning to understand why people drank. He had tried it a couple of times in his teens and found the sensation of being out of control frightening. Now he found the dull evening hours in the extended-stay hotel frightening. He had elected to stay in the cheap hotel because he didn't want a Paradise Window, but that gave him a long drive through the poorer sections of Boulder and the sort of misery once reserved for the third world. The sights were one more reason he couldn't sleep at night.

The only thing Bostock enjoyed was watching the fierce beauty of storms breaking over the mountains. It gave him the sensation of being at the center of the final conflict, a place he felt he should be. He set out to turn his amateur interest in meteorology into a more disciplined study. This sparked an interest in storm chasing and a yen to see a tornado. The Colorado mountains were not the best place for it. By next year's peak tornado season, however, he would have enough vacation days saved up for a trip to Tornado Alley, which had shifted southeast. It covered a broad area, but Bostock chose south central Alabama because its flat terrain would make for the best viewing.

Planning this trip gave him a destination for daydreaming during the tedious workday. He guessed that he was the only

person in Boulder Colorado fantasizing about the Alabama flat-
lands. His trip was planned for April, when it should be only in
the upper eighties. He was thinking about storm-chasing supplies as he returned to the hotel from a long day of costing helicopter seats. He was in the process of hurrying past the aggres-
sively friendly receptionist when she called out, "Mr. Bostock.
Valentine's Day and it looks like you have a letter and it's not
even in a fancy envelope." She put emphasis on the word 'letter.' Snail mail was a rare thing. She leaned over the counter and
waved it at him. "If it's a Dear John letter, you can always come
to me for sympathy."

He grabbed the envelope with mumbled thanks, not slowing
down enough to be mired in small talk. In his suite, he threw it
on the bed, opened the mini fridge, and took a long swig of water. He didn't pick up the letter until he was stripped to his
shorts and lounging against the raft of hotel pillows.

His eyes went first to the sender's name, Andrew Gilbert,
and then to his town, Defiance, Ohio. He was tired, and it took
a minute for the associations to gel in his mind. His former fiancée, Gwen Gilbert, was from Defiance, Ohio. Her father's
name was Andrew. He would be an old man now, just the sort
to use snail mail. The only reason he could think of that Andrew Gilbert would be writing to him would be to inform him
of Gwen's death. He tapped the scar on his temple and put the
letter aside to read later. He felt bad that he barely remembered
her face. Then he felt bad about putting the letter aside, so he
picked it up again and opened it.

Dear ?

I don't even know what to call you. Mr. Bostock seems too formal, and I don't have your permission to call you Father. I am your son. I am sixteen years old. My mother is Gwendoline Gilbert. She told me that you were dead, that you were a Navy pilot, and crashed into the Mediterranean. I recently came to live with my grand-parents and found out that this was NOT true. Maybe you don't want to have anything to do with me, but I hope you will answer this letter. I almost sent an email, but then I thought it would be too easy for you to delete. I'm sorry if I'm being presumptuous.

Sincerely,

Drew Gilbert

In a moment of skewed perception, Bostock thought it was the letter shaking and not his hands. He put it down and tried to remember Gwen's face. Only the wide, clear blue eyes stared back from the past. When he met her, he couldn't imagine how anything but an angel could hide behind those eyes. He was so young and naive back then. By the time he discovered her temper and vindictive streak, he had already given her a ring. He panicked and drove all night to his parents' place in Pennsylvania and poured his heart out to his father. "You have to end it promptly and kindly," George Bostock said. "To do anything else would bring pain to everyone involved."

Bostock had followed that advice and walked straight into a buzz saw. He had never seen anyone so angry or out of control.

One wrenching evening, though, and it was over. Did she know then that she was pregnant? Did she find out after he had left for his first tour overseas? He had told her how much he wanted children. Was this her way of punishing him?

He had a son. He sat down to his computer. "Dear Drew," he wrote, "I would consider it the greatest honor of my life if you would call me Father or Dad or whatever feels right to you."

Bostock used an old-style laptop on his own time. He leaned forward and peered into its screen at his son, who returned the gaze with equal intensity. Due to a trick of genetics, the small muscles between their brows operated in the same quirky, asymmetrical way. The shallow and ephemeral furrows in Drew's forehead matched the ones etched deep into Bostock's face. They saw this simultaneously and sat back. Nervous laughter came from both sides.

"We get this from my father," Bostock said. "His name was George. He was a good man, the best man I ever—." It hit him that these ripples from the past would likely not extend into the future, and his voice faltered for a second. "The best man I ever knew," he finally said.

They did not have the same eyes. Bostock's were hazel, while Drew had his mother's righteous blue orbs. Gwen's eyes had deceived Bostock so thoroughly that he felt a twinge of panic at seeing them again. Drew had his mother's curly dark hair as well. This combined with Bostock's good bone structure to produce exceptional beauty, beauty that could translate into shallowness and meanness if over-indulged. Sam touched the scar Gwen had left. What kind of upbringing had she given Drew?

A rough one that did not involve indulgence of any sort. The story came out in bits and pieces over a number of evenings of father-son computer chats. Drew wouldn't criticize his mother directly, but careful questioning from Bostock elicited a few disturbing facts.

"So, Gary was your stepfather?"

"One of them, the only one I liked. He was with us for four years when I was in grade school. He had a business, a farm supply store. I loved that place. It smelled like grain. It had tools, seed corn, bird feeders, and all sorts of cool stuff. He said he would add "And Son" to the sign when I grew up, but then he went bankrupt and Mom left him. He tried to get custody of me and almost did."

Bostock caught the wistfulness in Drew's voice and wondered how bad Gwen must have been to almost lose her son to a man in bankruptcy court.

"How many stepfathers have you had?" Bostock asked.

Drew looked at the ceiling as he silently counted. "I think seven or so. She didn't marry all of them, though, so I don't know if they were really stepfathers. Not that it makes much difference."

"Have you lived in Ohio all your life?"

"Oh, no. We've been all over. We were even rich once for almost two years. We lived in Maine with a lawyer."

"Did you like being rich?" Bostock asked.

Drew had to think about this for a minute. "I should have liked it because everything was nice and clean, but it was, like, too nice and clean. I got yelled at a lot for being too messy or loud or having bad table manners or for not being grateful enough. Rob, that was his name, was always listing the stuff he had bought me. I didn't have any friends at school because I didn't fit in. I was kind of relieved when he kicked us out, but I missed the food."

A cloud passed over Drew's face and he asked, "Do you drink?" Then he quickly backtracked. "That's none of my business. I'm sorry."

"It is your business," Bostock said, "and I don't drink. Never have."

Drew's obvious relief was as telling as anything he had said.

In their third conversation, Bostock discovered that Gwen was doing jail time for defrauding her employer. That's why Drew was living with his grandparents.

"It's boring here," Drew said, "but I've seen worse things than boring."

□

Bostock could no longer abide the boot-obsessed dung heads at Summit Industries. When his first year ended, he did not renew his contract. He had the microchips removed and took a series of puddle-jumper prop plane flights to Ohio. It was hard to get direct flights these days, with the rationing of jet travel. Besides, he had lost touch with what was happening to the country during his tours at sea. He had to admit now that it was deliberate avoidance. He owed it to Drew to take a hard look at the world he had left him.

Taking off from Denver, he saw the pine beetle damage and the scars of fires fueled by the dead trees. It was an uncomfortable reminder of the role he had played in the Boone Fire, as well as that sad day with Campbell at Franconia Notch Park. Leaving the mountains and flying over the flat expanse of Nebraska, he encountered an eclipse of geometry. The center-pivot irrigation circles that had been the most conspicuous feature of the landscape from the air were now faint ghosts where they were visible at all. A decade-long drought had drained the Ogallala Aquifer, while windstorms had lifted the topsoil into the air. The plane pulled above the dust clouds. Where the view cleared, Bostock could see that nascent dunes had erased large sections of abandoned rural roads. Where were all of the people who had drawn these circles, squares, and lines? Thanks to Campbell, he knew far more about migration in other countries than he did about the United States.

From Des Moines, Bostock flew to Grand Rapids over Lake Michigan. It was out of his way, but he wanted to see the lake where he and his father had caught so many bass. He smelled it before he saw it. A recent fish kill gave the surface of the water off the Waukegan shore the look of silvered pebbles. Despite record rainfalls, the shore was stretching farther into the lake, stranding piers in sand. The Great Lakes Compact had been broken, allowing water to be diverted out of the basin. The fish kill was left behind after a few minutes, but they encountered the eastern shore of the lake far too soon. After a minute of confusion, Bostock realized that they were flying over thick mats of some sort of water plant and not solid ground. The weed had taken hold along the southern tip of the lake and was moving northward.

On the final leg of the trip over Ohio, geometry reasserted itself in the form of the long, thin rectangles of the industrial polder farms. The Netherlands was losing its battle against the rising sea, but its hydrologic engineers were in high demand around the world. All along the Ohio Valley, they built dikes to hold back frequent floods, while the pumping stations brought relief from periodic droughts. Family farms were virtually extinct. It required big capital to make land produce these days.

Where could his son get a foothold in this landscape? What kind of ambitions could he have?

He's so thin, Bostock thought when he saw Drew waiting at the gate at the Defiance Memorial Airport. He had been thin himself in his teens, but this was different. He could see the shadow of malnutrition in the delicacy of bone structure. When he hugged his son, he could feel a frailness that put a lump in his throat.

⊞

Bostock rented a car, and they drove to Drew's grandparents' house through miles of razor-wire fencing broken by guard towers. "All I see are fields. Why the fences?" Bostock asked.

"You can't leave food unguarded," Drew said. "Have you always lived in cities?"

"No, but I've never lived in a place where farms had prison fences."

"How did they keep people from stealing?" Drew asked. "You can't just leave food out in an open field."

"People did," Bostock said.

"And why didn't people steal it?"

The answer, of course, was that they weren't hungry enough to steal it back then. Bostock preferred to change the subject, however, rather than give that answer. "How are your grandparents doing?" he asked. He vaguely remembered two accountants who read little beyond their church bulletin, yet held unyielding opinions on everything.

"Umm, they're old and angry most of the time."

"Angry at you?"

"Angry at everything. They keep saying that their investments should have left them better off, but they're not starving. Although they keep complaining that I'm eating them out of house and home."

"Are they making you feel unwelcome?"

"The only one who ever made me feel welcome was Gary," Drew said. "And you," he added with a blush.

The house was dark, sour-smelling, and crammed with collections: commemorative plates, dolls in elaborate national costumes, and decorative signs with trite messages. Bostock was amazed that it was all exactly as he remembered it. The things had been collected by Drew's great grandmother. Nothing had been moved. A photograph on the mantel confirmed it. It was a picture of the great grandmother sitting on a chair next to the fireplace with her daughter at her feet. Item for item, he could match the tchotchkes on the mantel to the things in the photo. Everything was in exactly the same place, just as it had been seventeen years earlier, when he had done just what he was doing now. It was an eerie double echo that made his head spin. He picked up a porcelain cherub and was surprised it left no footprint in dust. There was no dust. How much time did the old woman spend dusting?

"Be careful with that!" Drew's grandmother snapped. She entered from the kitchen, carrying a tray of some yellowish drink.

Bostock remembered that she had scolded him before with almost the same words. He knew before she did it that she would put the tray down, pull a grimy cheesecloth from her pocket and wipe off the cherub before repositioning it in the exact spot it had always occupied. He knew she would say, "That is a collectible. It gets more valuable every year. My mother told me that these are like money in the bank, except that we get to enjoy their beauty every day."

The collectibles were completely worthless, of course. Even museum curators were beginning to wonder why they were preserving Rembrandts when soon there would be no eyes to see them.

"I'm sorry," Bostock said. He was sorry they cared for things more than they seemed to care for their grandson.

The drink was foul, made with some sort of artificial lemon powder. Nevertheless, the elder Gilberts acted as if they were offering something rare and delicious at great personal sacrifice to themselves. Bostock could see that Drew was embarrassed at their behavior.

After dinner, Bostock pulled Drew aside. "Pack your things; we're leaving tomorrow."

"For how long?"

"How long would you like?"

"Forever," Drew said.

"Forever it is."

◨

They left the next morning before dawn. For a couple of miles, Drew stared straight ahead with a severe brow.

"Is everything okay?" Bostock asked.

Drew made a sound that might have been positive or negative. Then his mouth began to quirk.

"What is it?" Bostock asked.

Drew cleared his throat into his hand. He seemed to be trying to get hold of himself. "I ... um ..."

"Come on, what is it?"

Drew leaned his head back and let out a whoop of laughter. He beat his hands against the dashboard.

Bostock caught the contagion and began to laugh so hard he had to pull over to the side of the road. A car passed, and its stern occupants gave them a glare of suspicion and disapproval. The car slowed almost to a stop, the people spoke among themselves, and then they continued on their way.

"They were trying to decide whether to call the police on us," Drew said.

"That's exactly what they were doing," Bostock said. "I guess we'd better move, but first you have to tell me what we've been laughing at."

Drew looked sheepish. "I moved stuff."

"What?"

"All the collectibles. I moved each one. Just a little bit. I switched some around. Turned some backwards. I was up all night. I did the mantel and the hutches and breakfronts and windowsills and side tables and the ones above the kitchen cabinets."

"That was childish," Bostock said. "That poor, elderly woman will be doddering around for the next month trying to put things straight."

Drew hung his head.

"It was childish, diabolical, and more than a little bit brilliant," Bostock said. He began to laugh again, imagining the sour old woman huffing and fussing over utterly unimportant things while he drove away with the real treasure.

⊞

Bostock still wanted to see a tornado, and Drew was more than game. They had collected maps, a scanner, weather radio, good camera, and a cooler full of drinks and sandwiches, and headed south to Alabama. Now they sat in the parking lot of an abandoned Bojangles and waited for a supercell storm to intersect the warm front that stretched across the center of the state. A dozen chasers had gathered in the lot in assorted vehicles from dedicated storm-chasing vans, to regular cars, to one ancient DayGlo green monster truck. Bostock spotted two other father-son pairs. He felt a deep contentment at sharing this experience not only with his son, but with the other fathers and sons, with a whole tradition of fathers and sons. For the first time in his life, he felt like he was coming into his own. The small interior space of the car took on a singular aura. It felt holy to Bostock. As they scanned the wall clouds for the appearance of a funnel, he explained to Drew the dynamics behind tornado formation.

"The difference between a regular thunderstorm and a supercell is a rotating updraft. It's called a mesocyclone," Bostock said. He used his hands to demonstrate how warm, moist air from the ground could flip a horizontal rotation into a vertical one. "What happens next," Bostock said, "is that ...." He looked up at Drew. His child's face was so full of adoration that it stopped him in mid-sentence. So many kids these days blamed and hated their elders for destroying their future, yet Drew, who had more to complain about than most, loved him without reservation. The knowledge took his breath away. On the way to Ohio, he had prepared himself to face teenage sarcasm, rebellion, and blame. He hadn't been expecting unconditional love. It destroyed him.

All he had ever done was let Drew down and live a selfish life. Bostock had regarded climate change as something that had been done to him, something too large for him to contemplate. Now the dishonesty of the passive voice came home to him. He had loved piloting fuel-guzzling jets and standing on the deck of an aircraft carrier breathing the fumes. All the time he had felt like a good and honorable man who was serving his country. He was living a life that would have made his Navy chaplain father proud. But all this time Bostock had done absolutely nothing to ensure his son's survival. His existence had hinged on carbon consumption. He thought back on something Campbell had told him: "there are things that change your past and future all at once. Then you have to rebuild on thin air." Now he understood. He needed to talk to her about all of this. She would understand better than anyone.

"Go on," Drew said. "What happens next?"

Bostock wanted to throw his arms around his son but didn't want to risk spoiling a moment of closeness.

"Are you crying?" Drew asked. "What's wrong?"

"Nothing," Bostock said. "Allergies." In a shaky voice, he returned to his explanation: "When the updraft flips the rotation, that's when we see the funnel descend ...." He trailed off. It occurred to Bostock then that Drew should already know most of what he was telling him. He himself had learned much of it in a sophomore science class. "I hope I'm not boring you with things you learned in school."

"Oh, I haven't learned much of anything in school," Drew said. "School is a joke and everyone knows it. It's a place to go, but it's like the teachers barely try anymore. One day one of the history teachers says in this stern voice, 'Those who don't know their history are destined to repeat it.' The kids shouted him down because, well, we won't get a chance to repeat it anyway." Drew laughed.

This time, Bostock couldn't laugh with him.

"There!" Drew cried. "Look! There it is!"

A section of cloud swirled; then a tube appeared below it like something sentient, an elephant's trunk or the tentacle of a squid. It hesitated for the space of a breath, and then it darkened and dropped, drilling down to the ground and swelling with startling speed.

Drew whooped.

All around them engines started, and the chasers moved out onto a two-lane road that would take them first in the direction of the storm and then parallel to its path. Bostock had already marked three escape routes, roads that intersected this one and would allow them to turn east at a right angle to the path should something go wrong.

Bostock was in the middle of the line of cars moving at just above the speed limit. He was uncomfortable with the speed and the darkening sky. He eased his foot up on the gas, but the car behind him, full of college kids, sat on his tail and he sped up again. "Maybe we should turn off at the next road," he said.

Drew was filming the widening tunnel. "Nooo," he cried. "I may never get to see something like this again. Please, just a little farther."

They passed the first turnoff. Bostock drove with the boiling tornado in the corner of his eye. As it hit a farm, the debris of shattered buildings flew up at its base.

Drew was in such a state of excitement it was all he could do to hold the camera still. The boy started begging two miles before they reached the second turnoff. "Please, please, please stay on this road. I'm getting fantastic shots. Oh, look, upward lightning! It's like fire trees. I've never seen that before!"

When they reached the road, one car turned off and the rest of the caravan continued. Bostock reluctantly followed them.

A mile later, a sudden sheet of rain slapped the windshield with a noise that made Bostock's tense back muscles spasm. The line of cars slowed for a mile and then resumed speed when the rain stopped as suddenly as it had started. The tornado was changing direction. A couple of cars did U-turns and headed back where they had come from. Bostock was waiting for his chance to do the same when a volley of hail hit them like artillery. The lead van slid off the road. Behind it, the other cars fishtailed. Bostock swerved to the side, but the car behind caught his bumper, and they spun out of control.

Bostock had a generous share of physical courage that kept his hands and mind steady when piloting a jet through the most perilous situations, but now he was terrified he would see his son die. When the car came to rest against a fence, he had to swallow back a mouthful of vomit and grip the wheel to keep his hands from shaking. He couldn't let Drew know his mind was still spinning out of control.

Drew didn't appear to be scared at all. He was laughing. "What a rush!"

No one was willing to risk the golf ball-sized hail to get out to survey the damage. A couple of vehicles were already back on the road and moving. Wheels spun as others stuck in soft ground. The monster truck started pushing the mired cars back out onto hard surface. A couple of bumpers were bent and hanging, but all the cars were still drivable. They headed back with the intent of taking the road they had just passed. When they got there, they were surprised to see cars coming toward them.

"There's another one!" Drew pointed to a second funnel a few miles behind the merging cars. They had no choice but to continue on this road and try to stay ahead of both tornados.

The hail ended abruptly and melted, but the wind started gusting, making it difficult to stay on the road. Drew twisted around and continued to film. Bostock had no choice but to drive and silently beg whatever higher power he could summon to let him keep his son. He lost all concept of time.

The worst came close, but did not happen. The tornados dissipated and the sky lightened. Bostock did a U-turn and drove back toward their hotel hoping that it was still standing.

"This has been the best day of my life," Drew said.

Bostock didn't have a voice to answer him.

"Are those cows?" Drew pointed to light-colored objects scattered across a field ahead. When they got closer, the shapes resolved into cuboids. The tornado had deposited stoves, refrigerators, washers, and dryers more than a mile from the destroyed houses from which it had taken them. As Drew stared, his body grew still, drained of animating excitement. "Where are all the people who owned those things?" he said.

CHAPTER FIFTEEN

Northern Foothold

The analysts were roiling, and Mary Campbell seethed at the center of the disturbance. Outrage had cleared away the last of her depression. The absurdity of the executive decision that had seemingly sprung up out of nowhere. *The sheer ...*

Campbell sat back in her chair and took a deep breath, searching for a word. *Pissedness.* It wasn't actually a word, but it had the right sound. "The pissedness of it all," she said out loud. Then she pounded the word into the keyboard along with a few other choice phrases. It was well after close of business or COB in office parlance. But intelligence agencies never actually closed for business, and the vault was full of people who had stayed after hours to vent their spleen on the office discussion board. Cogent, clever, and convincing arguments crawled across the page. Anyone who read them could not fail to be persuaded of their wisdom.

But this was not a situation where "wisdom" was relevant.

"It's a done deal," Leila Anderson said the next day when Campbell placed a petition on her desk signed by some ninety-five percent of analysts in the agency.

Leila was the head of the Intelligence Analysis Agency. She was a competent administrator who had risen out of the analytical ranks, but she was not a "people person." She preferred to communicate electronically, but Campbell had demanded a hearing in person. Campbell had had occasion to visit this office before, under previous directors. Those meetings were held in the seating area in the corner, where comfortable chairs surrounded a coffee table. Leila, however, preferred to keep the expanse of her desk between her and her visitor. She carefully avoided looking directly at Campbell, even as she tried to explain that opposition was useless at this point. "The decision has been made."

Campbell looked down at the polished surface of the desk, which reflected the unlikely blue of the Paradise Windows that stretched across the east wall of the office. *Fucking fake blue.* She lunged forward and slapped her palm down on the wood with a noise that forced Leila to meet her eye. "Don't try to hide behind the passive voice. Who made this decision?"

Leila's broad, bland face reddened. "It was above my pay grade."

"Don't give me that. You're head of the agency."

"Yes, but I'm hardly the most powerful person in New Hope."

"Who even came up with the idea?" Campbell asked. "The president? This president doesn't seem that creative or that crazy."

"I heard it came out of private industry."

Campbell slapped her forehead. "Bingo. Someone found a way to make a buck."

"Look," Leila said. "I wasn't given a choice so I can't give you one. Considering the current security situation in the capital, it might all be for the best. We'll be safer."

What Leila called the "current security situation in the capital" was elsewhere referred to as a "Code Red State of Emergency." A terrorist bomb had gutted the Department of the Interior. A half dozen extremist groups claimed responsibility. The FBI was scrambling to sort through the long list of entities that wanted to bring down the government. Meanwhile, a series of storms had flooded low-lying districts along the river. Out of this confusion sprang new buzz phrases: dispersed command, executive redundancy, and northern foothold. These phrases drifted through the capital for weeks before it became clear what they meant.

Dispersed Command. Parts of the government were going to sea. Six elderly Nimitz-class aircraft carriers were already in the process of being refurbished to house critical civilian government functions. A legislative branch carrier, for example, would hold roughly half of Congress along with their assorted staff. If "something happened" to the capitol building in New Hope, the seagoing version of Congress could continue to make decisions without interruption, thereby providing executive redundancy.

"Northern foothold," related to the recent acquisition of Greenland. Caught in a power struggle between Russia and the United States, Denmark finally agreed to sell Greenland to Washington. "Agreed" might not be quite the right word, as Copenhagen had little choice in the matter. Niceties like respecting the sovereignty of foreign nations weren't observed as much now as they had been in the past. At any rate, the United States had a vast new territory in the north. Moscow, however, didn't recognize the sale. So the six refurbished government aircraft carriers, along with accompanying destroyers and one active-duty military carrier, would be stationed in Baffin Bay for most of the year, moving only to avoid the dead of winter and major storm systems. This would give the United States a "northern foothold" to secure its claim. Meanwhile, a large new U.S. military base was already under construction near Nuuk.

So that was the done deal. Six civilian government aircraft carriers would be going to sea over the next year. The first would be the one housing the Intelligence Analysis Agency.

◫

"The utter pissedness of it," Campbell said. She was lunching with Maeve in the agency's cafeteria. "They give us six weeks notice. Six weeks. You know they didn't just start refurbishing the carrier. It's probably been underway for a year or more."

"They didn't want to give opposition time to build," Maeve said. "I've never seen this place so mad. Do you smell the bile?"

"Is that what that smell is?" Campbell wrinkled her nose. "Does bile smell better or worse than dead fish? I prefer to look at the sea from a distance. I don't want it under my feet."

"Not everyone will go to sea," Maeve said in the calm, slow voice she always used when she had to talk Campbell down off a ledge. "There will be an appeals process."

"Yeah, but the only ones who will be able to successfully appeal are those who would have to leave behind small children. If you're single or if you're part of an agency couple, you won't have a choice. No, we're fucked. So fucked."

CHAPTER SIXTEEN

DeepWater

The first time Mason put on the DeepWater uniform, in June of 2051, he felt like a fool, a fake, and a clown. He stared at himself in the mirror of a motel in the recently built port city of Newfolk—pronounced NewFuk—west of the submerged city of Norfolk. Newfolk was one of the new "pick up and go" port cities. Almost all structures were built on slides ready to be moved when waters advanced or hurricanes threatened. Non-military structures, including this motel, were cheap and generic. Military structures were costly and generic. The gaudiness of the DW uniform was jarring against this neutral background. Mason wasn't even sure what to call the color of the thing. It was one of those shades wedged between blue and green on the color wheel. "What is this color?" he asked Alison.

She was sitting cross-legged on one of the beds reading a book. She looked up and frowned. "I would say it's a bright aquamarine. It's like the color they paint the bottom of swimming pools."

That answer did not give Mason confidence.

"What did you win all of those medals for?" Alison asked.

"Nothing. They're fake. Fake medals, meaningless braid. Ridiculous froufrou." Mason pronounced the word "froufrou" like it was two different four-letter F words stuck together. "I'm going to have to negotiate something less embarrassing before I meet the ship's company."

"Aren't you meeting them today?"

"No. Today the CEO of DeepWater is taking me on my first tour of the carrier since they refurbished it. I'll meet my crew tomorrow, and it will be another month before the intelligence people come aboard."

"When do we go onboard?"

"Tomorrow."

When DeepWater had offered him the position, Mason was working a desk job in the Pentagon. He hated every second of it, but he couldn't go back to sea again and leave Alison alone. She was still subdued and wary. She suffered stomach problems and had yet to regain lost weight. She hated leaving their apartment and could barely be persuaded to go to school.

Then he got a call from DeepWater, the biggest of the giant government contractors that vied with the government itself for influence. They had won the contract to refurbish and run the civilian government carriers. They offered him a position as captain of the first carrier to launch, the one that would house the Intelligence Analysis Agency. It seemed like a perfect solution. He was eligible to retire from the Navy and to negotiate a place on the carrier for Alison. Not only that, but the ship was the one he had served on early in his career. He had a fond feeling for her.

Mason didn't like leaving Alison alone in the hotel room, but she argued that she had been on her own for the previous year in places that were much worse. She preferred to read rather than follow some muckety-mucks around listening to blather. So he had relented. She was touchy on the subject of supervision.

Doubts about the new job surfaced soon as a DeepWater stretch limo the same color as Mason's uniform arrived to pick him up at his motel. As someone who had spent his life aboard carriers where everyone made do with a minimum of space and material possessions, he found excess offensive. Sitting in the back of the limo in his clown suit with a breakfast of fruit kabobs spread out in front of him and a screen playing a Deep-Water promotional video on a loop, Mason felt over twenty years' worth of professional pride and identity begin to shrivel. He picked up one of the kabobs. It was made up of pineapple, kiwi, and strawberry slices drizzled with white chocolate, sprinkled with edible gold glitter dust, and impaled on a DW logo skewer. He put it back down again.

Waiting for him at the dock was Tim Burg himself, the CEO of DeepWater. He advanced on Mason with hand extended and an aggressive big-toothed smile. Burg was a silver-haired, hyper-muscled former special forces commander who was hearty, glib, and frighteningly friendly, like a large dog who threatens to jump on you, knock you down, and lick the epidermis from your face.

"What do you think?" Burg said. He gestured toward the carrier.

The first thing Mason noticed was that the number on the island had been painted over with the strange word "Ayn." He was about to ask about that when he noticed the addition of a bubble-like structure above the primary flight deck and below the radar arrays. It looked to be about fifteen feet in diameter "What is that thing over the Pri-Fly?"

"What?" Burg said.

Mason pointed. "That thing." He squinted. "There's someone in it walking around in circles." Indeed, through the curved glass, a dim, distorted figure was visible. "Who is that?"

"Oh, we'll save that discussion for later."

It would be a number of days before Mason could even get the name "Bextrand" out of a DeepWater representative.

Mason had known that this was now an aircraft carrier that would no longer carry aircraft, but he hadn't anticipated how jarring the change would be to his psyche.

"AstroTurf?" he cried when he saw the new, lime green surface of the flight deck.

"DWTurf®," said Burg. "It is our own seaworthy surface designed to be far more salt-, UV-, and slip-resistant than the old AstroTurf."

"Good God Almighty," Mason said.

"God Almighty himself could not have designed a more durable and foot-friendly surface for the new generation of seagoing bureaucrats."

"Jesus Christ," Mason said.

"Nor him either," Burg said with a laugh. The CEO began to jump up and down. "Go ahead; try bouncing on it."

"No, thank you," Mason said with strained courtesy.

"Oh, come on."

"No, thank you," Mason repeated more slowly.

"Suit yourself. Let me show you something fun." He led Mason to one of the jet blast deflectors. The steel barriers had been covered in DWTurf® and marked up like gigantic dartboards. Burg lifted the lid of a storage box bolted to the deck and took out a large rubber ball printed with the company logo. "It was going to cost a fortune to remove these things, so instead we invented our own game called DWBall®." He stood on a line marked on the deck, dropped the ball, and kicked it toward the jet blast deflector. It hit far from the center. "Damn, only five points for that one. You want to try?"

"No, thank you," said Mason.

"What you knew as the flight deck has been reconfigured for recreational and fitness purposes, as well as al fresco dining. We call it the Lanai Level now."

No we fucking don't, Mason thought, but he said nothing out loud.

Mason remained polite, but the expression on his face hardened as he viewed the dining veranda, the track, tennis, badminton and shuffle ball courts, the softball field, the putt putt golf course, and an herb parterre garden that had taken the place of space once dedicated to flight operations.

"It's all play above, but all work below," Burg said. He led Mason down into what used to be the hangar deck. The cavernous space had been turned into a multi-level warren of tiny cubicles between metal catwalks.

"It looks like a prison block," Mason said.

"It's Bauhaus inspired," Burg said.

Other areas formerly devoted to aircraft and weaponry had also been converted to cubicles or used to expand living quarters. Only one flight elevator remained operational for the use of the helicopters that would provide supplies and transport personnel on and off the ship while it was at sea.

"The berths for your crew are largely the same as they were for naval personnel, but we've made extensive modifications for our intelligence professionals, adding more partitions, more privacy, and more toilet and shower facilities. We've taken into account the older and less fit demographic, so no three-deep racks. GS-11 and below will have eight-person berths like this." Burg led Mason into a room with four racks on each side. Each rack featured a bedspread and curtains in a DW logo print the same color as Mason's new uniform.

"What is that color called?" Mason asked.

"DW Capri Weekend," Burg said.

"Ah," Mason said. He still didn't know what color it was. As Burg led him to the four-person GS-12 through -14 berths, he said, "We need to talk about my uniform."

◨

By the time the new generation of seagoing bureaucrats arrived, Mason had negotiated a new, somewhat plainer uniform in a more muted version of DW Capri Weekend called DW Capri Weekday. He still felt like a fool, but that was the least of his problems.

Boarding day was not going well. Burg had meant it to be a patriotic celebration and had scheduled it for the 4th of July for this purpose. Mason and his crew had the Ayn ready by 0800, but DeepWater's Personnel Security Division had yet to allow the new generation of seagoing bureaucrats aboard. The hamburger and hotdog lunch had already sat too long on warming tables and had to be discarded. While Alison hung out in the ship's library, Mason went down on the docks where the temperature was 110 degrees. He circulated among the sweaty, disgruntled, and loudly complaining bureaucrats. He introduced himself and promised to help facilitate the screening process.

He went looking for the head of security operations. Mason questioned a number of officious young people in DW shorts and T-shirts, and someone finally pointed out a slight, high-cheeked woman sporting a slick chignon and large, mirrored sunglasses. He strode over to where she stood with a clipboard in front of one of the half-dozen trailers they had set up for the check-in. This one was labeled "STD and Other Communicable Disease Screening."

"What's taking so long?" he asked. "These people already have Top Secret clearances."

"Not good enough," she said without looking up from her clipboard. "We have additional requirements."

"DeepWater has more stringent security requirements than the Intelligence Analysis Agency?"

"Special case," she said.

"What makes it special?"

The young woman took a pen from behind her ear, pointed it at the bubble-like structure above the Pri-Fly, and then scratched a note on the clipboard. "We don't question Bextrand," she said, "and that's all I have to say to you." She turned and went into the trailer.

Mason went back to shaking hands and apologizing to the people who stood in the long lines in front of each trailer. It did not take long to ascertain that they were a different breed entirely from the men and women who had served under his command in the Navy.

He had sent out a memo on appropriate footwear and clothing and the number and type of personal items that would be allowed on board. He was now introduced to a paradox that would plague him in all the years to come. These people were highly intelligent and widely read. They consumed cables, reports, books, and magazines. They read political philosophy, history, novels, poetry, and tomes on the most esoteric of subjects. They were capable of delivering an articulate briefing on a wide range of topics at the drop of a hat. They did not, however, read instructions, and they were not capable of following them even if they did read them. Moreover, quite a few of them suffered from a serious deficit of good old common sense. On their feet he saw high heels, flip flops, and other elaborate safety hazards he could not name. Tiny women wheeled heifer-sized duffels across the tarmac. He saw a cello case, a few body pillows, and even a large Boston fern.

If they had been military personnel, Mason would have dealt with the situation by having the excess and contraband items confiscated and put in a dumpster. However, this group was already on the verge of revolt. The word "ridiculous," pronounced with spitting emphasis on the second syllable, was everywhere. Mason decided he would not stop them from bringing their stuff on board. He would let them try to fit it into their tiny quarters and live with it for a few days. He suspected they would soon be ready to give it up.

Late in the afternoon, people finally began to trickle on board as they completed the screening process. Mason returned to the ship and greeted each one. He heard the word "ridiculous" over and over again until he finally resorted to repeating it. "Yes, ridiculous." This was strangely effective at calming people down.

After dinner, after he had delivered the opening remarks at the orientation session the crew had prepared, Mason slipped up to the flight deck for some precious moments alone. He was physically, psychologically, and morally exhausted. He felt a surge of irritation as he spotted a woman standing near the jogging track staring up at the bubble, which was illuminated at this hour with a pale green glow. He didn't remember seeing her earlier in the day. She had an athletic body and an intense expression. The last thing he wanted to do was interact with another analyst, but he put on the friendliest expression he could manage and approached her.

"Do you need help finding your rack?" he asked.

She glared and issued an icy "I beg your pardon?"

Mason quickly explained. "Rack is what we call a bunk on an aircraft carrier."

She appeared to consider this for a moment and said, "No, we're not calling it that anymore. It's a bunk. That term is good enough for the Girl Scouts, and it's good enough for us."

Mason was nonplussed. He wished that civilians wore some mark of rank because this woman carried herself like someone who was in charge of something big. Crap, this must be Leila Anderson, the head of the agency. He had been looking for her all day and somehow missed her. "Is there anything else I can help you with ma'am," he said.

She turned and gave him a long look. He didn't like people who wouldn't look you in the eye, but this woman looked too hard, as if she were analyzing the contents of his skull.

Finally, she pointed to the bubble, where a figure, elongated and distorted by the glass, could be seen pacing in a circle. "Who and what is that?"

"Bextrand," Mason said.

"That's not a real name. What is his function?"

"I have no idea. All I could get out of DeepWater was the name and that he is some sort of philosopher."

"Since when do we have government philosophers?"

"I don't think he's government," Mason said.

"I'll find out who he really is," she said.

After an awkward pause, Mason said, "I'm forgetting my manners. Let me introduce myself. I'm Captain Mason." He held out his hand.

She gave it a firm shake and said, "I'm Campbell."

"Mary Campbell?" Mason asked. "You're Bostock's ...." He hesitated over the noun. "Friend?" he said at last.

"Yes and you're also his friend. I've heard a lot about you. It's nice to finally meet."

"Yes. This is a surprise. He didn't tell me that you would be onboard. Of course, he's been away."

"Well, we broke up awhile ago," Campbell said.

It was an unsettling conversation, and Mason wanted out of it. He started to stammer something, but Campbell cut him off.

"I'm going downstairs now. It's been nice talking to you."

"Good night," Mason said. "If you need anything, let me know."

She was already walking away, but she turned and pointed to the island. "The name of this thing is the Ayn? Seriously? Is that irony or stupidity or what?"

"Ridiculous name," Mason said.

Before she turned away, Campbell added, "And I meant it when I said we are not using the term 'rack.'"

"Yes, ma'am," Mason said.

CHAPTER SEVENTEEN

The Cutest Thing
Onboard

When Uncle Leland first brought Alison aboard the Ayn, it was love at first sight. The Lanai Level was one big playground, while the labyrinth of narrow passages, hatches, and odd nooks below was fodder for the imagination. She turned the spaces into dungeons, a dragon's lair, and Khazad-dûm. The library made her happy. When she discovered book acquisition forms, she was ecstatic. In coming years, she would send in hundreds of these and get marvelous books in return. Real books with pages to turn, not electronic ones. Books that had never been wet. And because these forms were authorized by Captain Mason himself, no one in the bureaucracy ever questioned why intelligence analysts would request so many books about dogs and drawing.

Her first month on the ship was wonderful. The crew was nice, although they treated her like a child. Then all of the analysts came aboard, and suddenly it was overwhelming. People were everywhere, interrupting her games, destroying the somber tension of Khazad-dûm, and frightening away the dragons and imprisoned princesses.

They all loved her, but that was the problem. Some had lost their own families in war or natural disaster. Others only got to see them on shore leave. Most analysts, being pessimists at heart, had chosen not to have children because of the dismal outlook for the human race. The sight of this adorable, frail-looking, little girl with hair done up in two black puff balls triggered their repressed parental instincts. She was almost eleven years old, but looked eight. Everyone wanted to touch her, mother her, keep her safe, give her little presents like a hand-made doll or a stick of gum. At first it terrified her; then it offended her. After years of having to act older than her years, suddenly she was reduced to near-toddler status. Due to their general unfamiliarity with children, many of the analysts grossly underestimated her maturity and capabilities. She spent extra time with the big dictionary in the library and learned to answer their condescending questions with sophisticated vocabulary words and concepts.

"Do you have a favorite teddy bear?"

"No, I'm too mature to anthropomorphize fake fur."

"Oh my god, that is adorable. Jim, did you hear what she just said? You are going to be an analyst when you grow up."

"No," Alison said firmly, "I am not."

During her first year on board, Alison spent much of her time in hiding. She soon learned every recess, alcove, and cubby hole on the ship. Then couples began to discover those same hiding places. "Oh, gross!" she said when she discovered two economists *in flagrante delicto*. She took the problem to her uncle that night.

"People are doing sexual things all over the ship. I found what I thought were popped balloons, but they're apparently called condoms. It is inappropriate, unsanitary, and I don't like it," she said.

"Who?" Mason asked.

"I don't tattle," Alison said.

"How did you know what they were doing?"

"I researched it. I know how to use a library."

The next day Mason sent Alison to the library with instructions to stay put for the morning and read children's books. Then he called the ship's company to the flight deck for a lecture. He thumped the sound system. It screeched. The crew shifted nervously on their feet. They had seen Mason angry before. The analysts were relaxed. They still thought of the captain as a sort of benevolent cruise ship director.

"I'll make my remarks short," Mason said. "My sweet, unspoiled niece caught two of you dirty bastards doing, and I quote, 'disgusting sexual things." As a result, I had to give her a talk I was hoping to avoid for several more years. I am pissed.

"I have set aside two rooms. If you need time alone with whoever to do whatever, go to the events coordinator and sign up for one of them. The sign-up will be confidential. I have given Alison a camera with instructions to take a picture of anyone she catches violating this rule. I have consulted with your analytical publications graphics staff, and they assure me that any photo I bring them can be blown up to poster size and framed for display in the mess. Further, if Alison finds any more used condoms, I will line up every man on this ship and make him take the 'Cinderella' test. In other words, he'll have to try it on to see if it fits. Dismissed." Mason gave the mic another thump for good measure.

Alison had all of her hiding places to herself again.

▣

On a ship full of intelligence officers, it was no problem providing a good education for Alison. Her teachers for each subject were world experts. She even found a cello instructor and someone who could teach her watercolor painting, although supplies were hard to get and there were few good subjects.

In a world with more choices, Alison would have chosen to be an artist when she grew up. In her dreams, she sat alone on a mountaintop and ran a brush full of azure across a white canvas. She was a creator of blue skies and blue seas and flowers of every form and color. She awoke from such dreams with a sense of peace that dissolved in the noisy clatter of breakfast.

The Ayn was not a world with choices. The world was not a world with choices. Alison didn't expect to grow up and she was quite matter-of-fact about it, even in the face of Uncle Lee's awkward assurances to the contrary.

Alison soon discovered that Mary Campbell was the only person willing to discuss the future, or lack thereof, without sugarcoating.

▣

Alison and Campbell sat at a table on deck, under the awning of one of the dining areas, nibbling bland wafers and sipping watered-down juice. It had been over a year since they first came aboard. They set their eyes on one of the destroyers that always accompanied the Ayn. It was the only spot to anchor the eyes on in the broad expanse of water. The whole scene had a sepia tint, like an old photograph. Drifting smoke from Canadian wildfires hung in the air. Everyone wore small filters that stuck over their nostrils. Alison kept wrinkling her nose against the annoying feel of the adhesive.

"I mean we're all going to die. Why lie about it? Why pretend?" she asked Campbell.

"They think you're not strong enough for the truth," Campbell said. "But you're tougher than the lot of them."

"Damn right," Alison said. "You would have to be stupid not to see what's happening."

"Well, stupidity is our most abundant resource."

Alison chuckled. "The Ayn is full of stupid smart people."

"It is," Campbell said. "It's such a dreary day. Have you done any new paintings?

"I quit painting."

"Why?"

Alison chose her words carefully. She had been thinking about this a lot. "Paintings are just stuff. There's too much stuff already."

"But your paintings aren't just stuff. They show how you feel. They let you share your feelings with other people."

"It's a dead end," Alison said. "Everyone will be gone soon. There won't be anyone to look at them. They'll just end up floating in the dead ocean like everything else. Just debris. I don't want to make any more debris just to stay busy."

Campbell let out a long sigh. "That makes me sad. I love your paintings. But fair enough, if you don't want to paint, I understand. But that leaves you with a lot of time. How would you like to be my training partner?"

"What type of training?"

"Running, jumping, throwing. Basic track and field. It keeps me sane. It's the thing to do when there's nothing else to do. Go out and race the fears until you run them down. Are you game?"

"Yeah. I'm game."

CHAPTER EIGHTEEN

A Visit

It didn't take long for Mason to change his mind concerning Mary Campbell. She had recovered from her depression so completely that he could not imagine her as anything less than positive and energetic. He found a lot of things about her to admire. She took her subject seriously, but not herself. She inspired incredible loyalty among not only her subordinates, but other colleagues as well. She treated Alison like a colleague, and Alison loved her for it. Campbell was more of a leader than the agency head, Leila Anderson, who would rather hide in her office and attend to paperwork than interact with people. Campbell could be outrageously funny and irreverent while maintaining a perfectly straight face. It took Mason a while to realize that she was yanking his chain with her single-minded campaign to undermine the use of naval terminology aboard the Ayn. Not only did she make sure that no one used the term "rack" for bunk; she called the jet blast deflectors the "Pop-Tarts," the island the "clock tower," and the head the "tail." "Really," she said to him with an expression of the most sincere curiosity, "Why would you call it the head? It has nothing to do with the head." It was only when he saw people giggling behind their hands that he realized the joke was on him.

Campbell always led with skepticism. For that as well as other reasons, Mason began to consider the possibility that her split with Bostock was not a good thing. Outside the realm of his work, Bostock could be too naive, too quick to trust in basic human goodness, and thus too easily hurt or disillusioned. Campbell offered a rather good counterbalance to these qualities. Perhaps she could protect him as well as she shielded her analysts.

Bostock's communications had been perfunctory when he was in Colorado. It was easy to read depression between the lines. Then, after he found Drew, they went on for pages as he shared a welter of conflicting feelings. In all this time, he hadn't asked about Campbell, although he surely must be wondering whether she was on the Ayn. Now that Bostock was back in the capital, he finally asked about her, wording the question carefully. The pains he had taken to make it sound casual told Mason that he cared a great deal. Then Bostock dropped a hint, saying that someday he wanted to show Drew an aircraft carrier.

Of course Mason would invite Bostock and his son to the Ayn, but he had misgivings. It would probably be a good thing for them to get back together, but as far as he knew, Campbell didn't know about Drew, and she should be informed before they arrived. Which meant that he would have to be the one to tell her. He had long experience at breaking disturbing news to people. Death notifications were a part of his job. He had never had to tell someone that her old lover would be visiting and bringing along a sixteen-year-old son she had never heard about.

Mason issued the invitation with a casual mention that yes, Campbell was aboard. He did not expect Bostock to reply immediately. *He won't want to look eager,* he thought. *He'll wait for a few days to pass. Four. I'll guess four.*

Four days later, Mason got a short but positive response.

⊞

Campbell had a habit of staring down the gaudy post-Panacea sunsets. She would stand on deck and glare at the show of fire and brimstone as if confronting the devil himself. Mason found her there so intent on her task that she didn't notice his approach.

Mason waited a minute and then cleared his throat. Campbell started and for a second burned him with a ferocious glare. Her expression quickly softened when she saw who it was.

"Hello, Captain," she said.

There was an awkward pause as Mason tried to figure out how to bring up the subject. Finally, he just said, "Hello, Campbell."

Another awkward pause. He thought of saying, "So, what are you doing?" but that was blindingly obvious.

A faint smile twitched at the corner of Campbell's mouth. "Hello, Captain," she said again.

Mason opened his mouth, closed it, opened it again, and said nothing.

"Great fish imitation," Campbell said. "Do you do birds?"

"Bostock's coming for a visit." Mason blurted out. "Just thought you would want to know."

"Thank you," Campbell said.

Mason couldn't read her expression. He blundered on. "He's bringing his son."

"His what?" Campbell asked.

"His son. Surprised me, too. And Sam. It was a complete surprise to him. He had no idea he had a son until he got a letter from the boy. A teenager. The mother was one of Sam's fiancées. She never told him. So we are all surprised. I'm sure you're surprised. I, um, should get to bed. Have a good evening." He turned and fled.

After dark, Mason went out to vulture's row to savor his modest nightly bourbon on the rocks. The absence of the Navy's prohibition on alcohol was one of the advantages of the civilian status of the Ayn. He was beginning to appreciate other advantages as well. The big one, of course, was that he had just safely tucked Alison into bed and kissed her goodnight. For the first time in his life he had family and career simultaneously, and it was wonderful. He took another sip. Before long he could share his evening time with Bostock. He was looking forward to hashing out with him all the complex fallout of leaving the Navy behind.

He wished he had had the courage to stick around to get a better read on Campbell's reaction. Suppose she rejected Bostock? What would it do to him if he arrived and found Campbell indifferent? Mason pressed his hand to his forehead. He felt like he was driving out of his lane and about to crash into an oncoming semi. When he let his hand fall from his face, he saw her out on the track.

Campbell was running, not jogging, but racing herself around the track in the darkness. Mason was impressed with her speed and endurance as she completed lap after lap. She must be in her early forties, yet she ran like someone two decades younger. How long could she keep this up? He watched until at last she slowed, stopped, and bent over to catch her breath. Mason checked his watch. It was after midnight. No, Campbell wasn't indifferent.

⊞

Campbell awoke the next day to the near-audible whine of sore muscles. She had overdone it with her late-night run, yet all of that physical activity had not damped the slow burn of anticipation she felt on hearing that Bostock would be landing on the Ayn in days.

She sat up and lowered her aching feet to the floor. "Holy goddamn, shit-slinging, nut-cracking, mother-fucking son of a bitch," she muttered as she coaxed her body into a standing position.

"And good morning to you, too, Sunshine," said Meg, her roommate, who was already dressed in a crisp blouse and sweatpants. Because all briefings were now done via video, most analysts went about looking professional from the waist up and comfortable from the waist down. Meg leaned in to the small mirror above the sink and applied lipstick in a few quick strokes. She pursed her lips, rubbed them together, and ended with the smacking sound that signaled the end of her toilette. "You were cursing and moaning in your sleep, so I decided it would be a good day for me to be up and out early. There's a bottle of ibuprofen in my top drawer if you need it. See you later."

"If you run into Brian at breakfast, tell him I'll be late this morning. I may not make it in at all."

"Will do." Meg shuffled out, still wearing her slippers, badger slippers of all things. The badger was her spirit animal, and an appropriate choice it was. Meg wasn't easy to like.

Meg and Campbell shared quarters because no one else would have them. Campbell's moods were too erratic, and Meg was too gossipy and intrusive. They had somehow worked things out between themselves, however, and lived in as much harmony as was possible in the small space.

When Meg had left, Campbell took a handful of ibuprofen, eased herself back into bed, and pulled the cover over her head.

She had dumped Bostock after watching him grow increasingly unnerved by her depression. She told herself she dumped him for his own good, but it was more because of the anger, a sudden, hot, bitter anger against him. She had no clue to its source. She recognized the irrationality of it and yet could not stir a muscle to change the situation. Some blind, contrary troll buried deep in her brain kept its three-toed foot on the brake.

Her anger over the going to sea had dispelled the depression. Then, to her great surprise, she had immediately taken to the stripped-down, relatively egalitarian existence aboard the Ayn. For one thing, there were no Paradise Windows, or Denial Glass as she called it. She didn't realize how much she had detested things until she was free of them. Mongold had filled New Hope with the windows. From the cheap, fogged-up window in her apartment, to the better quality version in her office, to the technicolor monstrosities that dominated the offices of the high officials that she briefed, they were always there. Transparent lies. Their absence restored a measure of honesty to her relationship to the natural world.

At the same time, the Ayn carried her away from the sound of bullets in the night, breaking glass, and the roar of mass demonstrations that were now a daily feature of life in the capital. She no longer saw awful sights on her way to work: no child panhandlers, homeless elderly, or motionless addicts, who might or might not be dead. This removed a measure of honesty from her relationship to the human race, but it was easier now to concentrate on her work, which was grim enough.

Campbell groaned again and reached into the drawer under her bunk for the jar of smoked almonds she kept there. The magnesium in the nuts might help with painful buildup of lactic acid in her muscles. Might. Probably not. A cool bath with Epsom salts would be better, but there was no such thing as a bathtub on the Ayn. Then Campbell remembered the big, galvanized tubs they used to hold ice and drinks. A soak would be heaven but would require considerable effort to pull off. Then, again, she should probably get up and engage in gentle exercise.

"Fuck it," she said, and sank back into the pain.

She missed Bostock like she missed the blue sky. He was deep, clean, beautiful, and calming to her soul. He wouldn't be visiting the Ayn if he didn't want to see her. Otherwise, he would have arranged to meet up with Mason on his next shore leave. She had treated Bostock abominably, but he wasn't the type to hold grudges, even when he was hurt. He was so much better than she was. Embarrassingly so.

And now he had a son. A son that would bring joy and pain. What a world Drew Bostock would inherit.

Sam needs to talk to me, she thought.

She had broken up with him because she knew that over the long term, depression would win out and Bostock would be too good to abandon her. *What long term?* she thought. *Is there a long term? Talk about something that isn't guaranteed. Fuck the long term.* She needed to talk to him, too.

◼

Campbell's unit rolled their chairs into the narrow space between cubicles for a whispered and impromptu meeting. These
were not the young up-and-comers she had managed in the
early days of her career. The Intelligence Analysis Agency had
little in the way of new blood these days. It was a time of stasis
that would soon become shrinkage. These were old hands who
inured themselves to the lack of room for advancement, the
cramped space, and the unchanging company. They were more
family now than colleagues—dysfunctional family, but family
nonetheless.

Campbell wasn't there, and that was the topic of the meeting. This absence was highly unusual. Normally, Campbell
worked seven days a week, unless she was depressed. She had
already taken off one day this week for sore muscles and now
she was off again?

Bella had trouble keeping her voice to a whisper. She was a
large and enthusiastic woman covered with tattoos in Latin,
French, and English—some rude and others cerebral. Her hair
was blue and her ears pierced with silver rings. She loved her
own opinions too much not to share them with anyone within
earshot. "I think she's gone mental this time," she said loudly.
"Not depressed, but raving mental. I heard her humming one of
those old music box songs." Here Bella demonstrated by humming her own off-key version of the tune.

"Lara's Theme," Maeve said. "I haven't heard that one in
ages. I can't think of anything less like Campbell."

"See? She's gone mental," Bella said.

"Keep your voice down," said a third woman. "You shouldn't say that about her, even in a whisper. Maybe we should call in the psychiatrist."

Bella snorted. "He's useless and stingy with the drugs to boot. She wouldn't go in any case. Maybe we should get Brian to ask her what's up. Speaking of Brian, where is the little twit? Funny, I didn't even notice his absence."

"I hear him coming up the stairs," Maeve said. "I would know that clomp anywhere."

The modernistic catwalk and cubicle system that filled the hangar—now dubbed "the Block"—magnified the sound of Brian's footsteps so that everyone in the room heard him coming. He was almost running.

"What's gotten into you?" Bella asked. "The last time I saw you exercise you were trying to get away from a seagull."

Brian plopped down in a chair to catch his breath. His face was purple. "You will never guess what I just saw."

Bella reached out and grabbed Brian's arm, squeezing as hard as she could.

"Ow! What are you doing?"

"I hate guessing games. Spit it out before I start ripping off limbs."

"Okay, " Brian said. Bella released his arm, and he rubbed the red spot as he spoke. "I saw Campbell pacing the deck wearing a dress. With flowers. And thin straps."

"What the fuck?" Bella said. "I didn't know she owned a dress."

"It wasn't exactly tight, but it was a close fit. She looked hot," Brian added.

"Dearheart," Maeve said, "Remember when you were a baby analyst and we taught you to always keep your audience in mind when you write? Well, that goes for speaking, too. Look around; what do you see?"

"Um, analysts," Brian said.

"And what is the gender profile of those analysts?"

"Um, eighty percent female."

"And the age profile?"

Brian started to open his mouth. He hesitated and said, "I'm not going to touch that question."

"Good boy," Maeve said approvingly. "You considered your audience and elected not to say something stupid. Now go forth and never refer to your female boss's body as 'hot' again, and most especially do not do that in the presence of professional women, because we are sick of that shit and will stretch you out on a desk and neuter you like a tomcat."

⊞

Campbell had seen Brian gawking at her. She knew damn well that the whole ship would be talking about her dress, but she didn't care. It was liberating to do something so totally frivolous and out of character. She'd only worn the dress once before, to a rare night at the theatre with Bostock. "Somewhere a hill," she sang softly, "blossoms in green and gold. And there are dreams...." She reverted to humming. She didn't actually like the tune, but it was stuck in her head.

She heard the sound of the helo and watched it approach from the south. The helo banked and she saw Bostock at the window. Campbell waved and smiled in a way she hadn't smiled at him since before her last depression. Bostock took something out of his pocket and held it up to the window. Campbell burst out laughing. She knew what it was—a Baby Ruth bar.

◫

Alison crossed her arms over her chest and narrowed her eyes in a move calculated to let her feelings be known.

"You'll be there, won't you?" Mason said. "I want you to meet Sam Bostock. He's one of my oldest friends. He helped look for you when you were missing."

"And he failed," Alison said. "I hate meeting people. They fuss over me and talk about me like I wasn't standing right there. Like I was a three-year-old idiot."

"Bostock is not the fussing type. Please, it would mean a lot to me. He's bringing his son Drew to meet us. You should be there, too."

Alison heaved a sigh. She would never actually refuse such a request from her dear uncle, but she needed to set her limits and register her objections, just in case he planned to make a habit of this sort of thing.

"I was hoping you might even take Drew on a tour of the ship," Mason said. "And why don't you wear your purple dress?"

This was too much. Alison was about to protest when Mason said, "Campbell is wearing a pretty dress."

"What? I never saw her wear a dress."

"She is. She's a good friend of Bostock's, too, and I know she would appreciate it if you were there when he arrives."

"Fine, I'll go, I'll even wear the dress, but I'm not giving tours."

Alison and Mason met Campbell at the helipad and waited while the helo set down. Campbell, indeed, looked very pretty.

Alison told her so, and Campbell answered with a quick "You, too," but she was watching the helo as she said it.

That left Alison feeling put out, because she looked adorable—quite adorable—in this dress, and if she had taken the trouble to put it on, someone ought to notice. She squinted at the man who appeared in the door of the helo. This must be Bostock. He was nice and friendly looking, but she guessed that he would take up all of Campbell's time as well as much of her uncle's for the duration of his visit. She prepared to be cool upon introduction.

Then the handsomest boy she had ever seen appeared in the door. He was like a fairytale prince with curly black hair and dreamy eyes. He was shy, too, just like she was. She could tell by the way he kept his head slightly lowered. She lowered her head, too, and was glad for the sunglasses she was wearing. She could stare without seeming to. When Bostock and Campbell kissed, the young prince blushed, and Alison fell hopelessly in love.

"I am so glad to meet you, Drew," Campbell said after she had let go of Bostock. She grasped the son's hand and gave him a warm smile, and then a hug.

"I'm happy to meet you, too," Drew said. "My dad told me a lot about you. And you, too, Captain Mason."

Drew held out his hand, but Mason gave him a big hug and a few hearty pats on the back instead. "You are so welcome aboard the Ayn, son," he said.

Alison wondered briefly if a hug was the way to go since everyone was doing it, but she rejected the thought. She could not be that forward. Instead, she offered her hand and a shy smile. She thought she would faint when she looked into his eyes.

"I was hoping that Alison would take Drew on a tour of the ship, but she is regrettably busy," Mason said.

"Where did you get that idea?" Alison said. "Come on," she said to Drew, grabbing his hand again. "I'll show you the library."

▣

During their visit aboard the Ayn, Drew explored every inch of the ship with Alison, while Bostock spent most of his time alone with Campbell. Mason had arranged for them to have a "married's" room together, while he gave Drew a spot in one of the crew's berths, where the boy could get a flavor for what it was really like to live and work aboard a carrier.

Alison came to get Drew at dawn and kept hold of his hand for the rest of the day. It was all he could do to break free long enough to go to the bathroom. He was occasionally irritated, but mostly amused. For her age, she knew a lot of things and had read more than some people do in a lifetime. She gave stern instructions on what he needed to read, and it was not easy stuff. She took him on a tour of the captain's galley and introduced him to Uncle Luther, an enormous man with an equally enormous grin.

"I call him Uncle Luther," Alison said, "even though he's not my real uncle. I've found that you can adopt an unlimited number of uncles and aunts. You have to listen to him talk."

Luther wiped his hands off and offered one to Drew. "I'm from New Orleans and I got the Cajun and the jazz and the 'gator in my voice."

"Hear how he says 'New Orleans?'" Alison said. "Don't you love it? I've tried and I can't say it like that."

"You need more 'gator," Luther said. With quick, precise motions, he laid out bread for sandwiches. "Mayonnaise or mustard?" he asked Drew.

"Mustard," Drew said. "Where is New Orleans?" He had missed a lot of school.

"Under the acid sea and dead as the shrimp," Luther said. "Lake Pontchartrain and the Gulf of Mexico met right over my old restaurant."

"Luther is the world's greatest chef," Alison said.

"You should have tasted my food back when it was real food. Last time the supply helo came, I got boxes of something called 'protein patties.' It takes a lot of Worcestershire and hot sauce to make that shit taste like food."

"Luther was always feeding me special stuff when I first came aboard," Alison said. "If I didn't come to a meal, he would find me and make me eat."

"You were half starved," Luther said, "and you still walking around on a set of toothpicks. I feed you up, and Campbell takes you out on the track and makes you run until you're skinnier than ever." He turned and looked Drew up and down. "And you could use some feeding up, too. You been through hard times?"

"Yes," Drew admitted.

"Oh," Alison said with sympathy in her eyes. "Me, too. You have to tell me about it."

Luther made them each chew a vitamin gummy; then he sent them off with sandwiches.

❦

"I'm overwhelmed," Bostock said, "and terrified. I put a child—my own son—in danger and I didn't even know it. I put him in danger by putting him on this Earth. Now I discover that every decision I ever made in life was wrong, wrong for Drew. All this time I just thought I was making decisions for myself. How incredibly stupid."

"How incredibly human," Campbell said. "You need to forgive yourself as readily as you forgave me." She placed the tip of her finger in the dimple of Bostock's chin and asked, "What is it like to forgive so easily? What is it like to watch your anger circle the drain and disappear before it can do any real harm?"

"What is it like for you when the anger takes hold?" he said.

Campbell squeezed her eyes shut. "Possession. Paralysis. Distance. Like I'm floating away on a raft caught in a strong current."

"Why do you push me away when I try to help? Do you think I'll be caught, too?"

"Yes, but it's more than that. It's not me making the decisions when I'm like that. I just hang back watching in horror."

Bostock saw her jaw clench. He pressed his lips to it until he felt the muscle relax.

▣

"So how old do you think we'll get to be before the world ends?" Alison asked Drew. "Are you going to bother going to college?"

"My dad wants me to, but I'm really behind in school. I hate it. I'm dyslexic and it's just too hard. Besides, college would cost him a fortune, and there's just rich kids there. He might need that money to survive. I would rather go to work and earn my own keep."

"Do you know what you want to do?"

"Yes," Drew said. "I didn't before, but then Dad took me on a tour of New Hope. Have you ever seen the White House?"

"Yes. Lots," Alison said. "I grew up in New Hope."

"It's the most beautiful building I've ever seen. It's in the center of everything. I loved watching the guards. I got there early in the morning just to see them raising the flag. They never look aimless, even when they're just standing still. They always know what their responsibility is and they always know what to do. Everybody else looks kind of lost. I want to be in the Secret Service."

"What does your dad think about that?" Alison asked.

"He doesn't like it."

▣

"Do you know what Drew wants to do?" Bostock asked Campbell. "He wants to guard the White House. It's the sort of stupid choice I've made all my life—protecting an ideal when you don't even know what it really means."

"Did you try to talk him out of it?"

"A little bit. I didn't want to press too hard for fear of having the opposite effect. I want him to go to college, but he doesn't see the point. How can I argue with that? There's no future to prepare for. We should have been the last generation."

Campbell gave a wry laugh. "I can't stop thinking about all of those crazy doomsday prophets picking dates, assembling disciples, and then watching the day pass with nothing happening. Imagine being disappointed that the world didn't end. Is our human fascination with Armageddon so strong that we had to bring it about ourselves?"

"Are you about to do a naked riff?" Bostock asked. A naked riff would make his visit perfect.

"Yes, as a matter of fact," she said. She jumped up, struck a pose, and began to speak with the intonation of a charismatic preacher. "My name is Father Ludicrous B. Revelation, and I want you to save the date! The end is nigh! On midnight, March third, 1975, the world will end and the Faithful shall be lifted into the sky on the wings of angels!" Campbell raised her arms to the heavens and closed her eyes. Then she peered at a pretend congregation and wagged her finger. "I would remind the ladies not to wear skirts on that day, lest the gentlemen below them look up, think sinful thoughts, fall from the sky like rocks, and perish in the flame. Hallelujah!

"How do I know the exact date? I studied the Bible. I studied the ancient calendars. I studied the Farmer's Almanac. I added, multiplied, and divided by the number of the beast in both human and hellhound years. For a long while I was confounded, and then an angel of the Lord came to me as I sat at my desk and said, 'Behold, the answer is written and it is within your very grasp.' Again, I was confounded, but then I looked and saw that within my grasp was a bottle of RC Cola. And it was glowing with the light of the Lord. RC stands for Royal Crown. The crown is pictured on the bottle. Then it came to me that this crown symbolized the Kingdom of Heaven. It came to me that RC also stands for *Return of Christ*. I examined that bottle, and there, stamped on the neck, was a date, the expiration date for the sinful human race. The Lord himself put this particular bottle in my hand so I could share the date with you."

Bostock collapsed back on the bed, laughing. "What would my father think of me falling in love with such a blasphemer?"

"So what do you think the end will be like?" Drew said. He and Alison were walking the track, munching on a bag of precious peanuts that had come in with the last supply helicopter.

"Less food and more heat until we starve or roast or someone kills us for our food or to make us food," Alison said, "but I'm going to commit suicide before it gets too bad. I decided that years ago. People say it will be 'kill or be killed,' at the end, that you won't be able to survive unless you fight other people. I'm not going to do that."

"How are you going to kill yourself?"

"I stole one of the red pills from the infirmary. They're cyanide or something like that. There's enough of them for everybody on board in case, as Luther says, 'things go south.' Like maybe we get captured by the Russians or Panacea gets turned off and we're all about to broil. I want to decide for myself when and not have to wait for somebody to hand me one. So I stole one. Uncle Leland gave me a pretty diary with a lock. I hollowed out a hole in the pages and I hid the pill in there."

"They lock up the drugs in an infirmary. How did you get them?"

"I stole the key, got the pill, and returned it before anyone noticed. I'm really good at stealing stuff. All you have to do is establish a reputation for being a good kid. Ask anyone on the Ayn about Alison, and they'll say, 'She's a good kid.' And I am, ninety-eight percent of the time. But when I need to be bad, I can get away with it."

"And no one knows that you're a sneaky little monster?" Drew said.

"Campbell knows, but she won't tell because she has used my services. She asked me to steal something for her, and I did."

"What?"

"I can't tell you," Alison said solemnly. "We did a pinky swear."

"What's a pinky swear?" Drew asked.

Alison rolled her eyes. "Honestly, where did you get your education? A pinky swear is like a blood oath, but without the blood. It's just as binding."

"For a twelve-year-old, you're kind of scary," Drew said.

"And this," Alison said, "is my shit-eating grin." She bared her teeth.

◨

It was three days before Mason got his evening on vulture's row with Bostock. Mason sipped bourbon, while Bostock had an iced tea.

"Think about it," Mason said. He had just offered his friend a position as his executive officer. The current EO was not taking well to the transformation of the Ayn and wanted out.

Bostock slowly stirred his "tea." It was not real tea, but an off-tasting substitute. A blight had reduced camellia sinensis to a luxury too expensive for even a captain's table. Like mold and bacteria, quotation marks flourished in the Post-Hope World.

Bostock wasn't thinking about tea or quotation marks. He was imagining life with Campbell in one of the tiny cabins reserved for couples. The look on his face was not one of bliss.

"You're going to say no," Mason said.

"I want to say yes, but I'm more of a realist than I used to be. Tell me, how long have you been at sea?"

"Nearly two years."

"And how many of your couples have split in that time?"

Mason frowned. "Twenty."

"Out of how many?"

"Twenty-seven."

"That would be somewhat above the national average for land-based unions, I think. Don't get me wrong, I want to be with her; I just don't think we would stand a chance under these circumstances."

"You used to be such a romantic," Mason said.

"Yeah." Bostock rubbed a finger over the scar on his temple. "How did that work out for me?"

"Point taken, but if you stay in the capital, you'll get to see her maybe once or twice a year. Will that be enough?"

"No it won't, but when Drew starts school in the fall, I need to be there for him. I have a job prospect, though, that may prove the perfect solution. I have an interview tomorrow afternoon."

"You're leaving already?" Mason said.

"No, my interview is with your philosopher up there." Bostock pointed skyward.

"Bextrand?" Mason sat back in surprise. "Nobody meets with him. You're going to see him in the flesh? I've only ever talked to him on the phone."

"It's because of that." Bostock pointed to Mason's bourbon. "One of the requirements of the job is that the applicant be a teetotaler. Apparently, he won't even grant an audience to anyone who has ever used any sort of mind-altering substance. For 'security reasons.' You wouldn't believe all the tests I had to take to even qualify for an interview."

"I suppose your background as a chaplain's son came in handy."

"It did, indeed."

"What would you be doing?"

"I gather it's like taking your first job in the intelligence world. You don't know quite what you'll be doing until you get in and start doing it, I know part of it would involve serving as a liaison between Bextrand, the Office of Advanced Plans, and his people at MIT."

"He has people at MIT?" Mason said. "I didn't know that, and I've never heard of the Office of Advanced Plans."

"OAP is located in the basement of the Pentagon. It's close hold. All most people know is its name. Its focus is long-shot solutions, crazy sci-fi stuff. I was looking to work with people who haven't given up. Now that I have Drew, I have to do something more meaningful than just make a decent living for myself. The strange thing is that they found me before I found them. They were looking for someone with project management skills and an absolutely clean background. Someone recommended me. I was probably the only person he could think of who doesn't drink. I interviewed with a guy in a Pentagon SCIF and found out that it would require frequent travel between New Hope, MIT, and an aircraft carrier called the Ayn."

"Well," Mason said. "You're way ahead of me. I suppose you'll go up and meet with Bextrand and then refuse to share any details because of some non-disclosure agreement you've signed?"

"You suppose correctly."

"You won't even say a word to your best friend who has been tormented by curiosity?"

"Correct. My word is my bond."

"You're such a Boy Scout."

"Actually, I was an Eagle Scout."

"Fuck you."

Bostock laughed and drained his "tea."

◩

The inhabitants of the Ayn were sure that Bextrand was a name made up by marketers. Perhaps a nod to Bertrand Russell with a twist of sci-fi. It was one of the many elaborate affectations adopted by the philosopher to bolster his status as legend, his ego, his whatever-the-hell-else that needed bolstering. Like the colored smoke and amplified voice employed by the Wizard of Oz, they were special effects.

What was a philosopher doing on the Ayn? Was he a government philosopher? Was philosopher a government position? Did the government hire contract philosophers from the private sector? Who knew. Such relationships were all very murky these days. Maybe it was just another affectation. The name Bextrand did not appear on any government forms or wiring diagrams, but no one on board the Ayn doubted that he had more power than Captain Mason or Leila Anderson. Bextrand was the chief customer for reports out of Campbell's unit. He sent them back dog-eared, crumpled, and covered with barely-legible questions scribbled with a purple pen.

As he took the elevator to the Pri-Fly, Bostock thought about the nickname the company of the Ayn had given to Bextrand—the cuckoo in the Doomsday Clock.

On the Pri-Fly, Bostock found a slab-faced man in a DeepWater uniform guarding a tube near the center of the room. The name on his pocket was "Duff." Duff examined Bostock's ID, checking the face against the photograph with undisguised hostility. Finally, he punched a code into a keypad, positioning his body so as to hide numbers. A door in the tube slid open.

"At the top of the ladder, press the blue button and announce yourself," Duff said.

Bostock stepped inside. His shoulders scraped the sides of the tube as he climbed the ladder. At the top, he pressed the button, leaned into a microphone, and said, "Bostock here."

"You may enter," Bextrand said. He spoke in an artificially slow, measured tone. The lid of the tube slid open. Bostock climbed up into a space filled with the eerie, sulphur-stained light of the afternoon sky. It was too warm. The air conditioning struggled to overcome the constant glare of the sun.

Bextrand paced the perimeter of the room, head bent forward, hands clasped behind his back, legs moving with a regular jerking motion like the second hand of a quartz watch. He was wearing a purple hooded robe, despite the heat of the room, and large mirrored sunglasses that gave him an oddly insectile demeanor. An unkempt beard covered the rest of his face. Bostock could smell the acrid sweat the philosopher left in his wake. Philosopher sweat had a different smell than athlete sweat. A meaty tang of simmering gray matter, like boiling giblets. Did Bextrand really wear this robe all the time or did he pace around in his shorts when he was alone? Bostock imagined the man looked like a plucked chicken or perhaps a larva without his robes. He shook the image from his head. Meanwhile, Bextrand continued to pace.

Bostock used the time to consider to the oddness of the room and what it said about the oddness of the man. It was a sort of flattened bubble with bulging sides. Measuring fifteen feet in diameter, it was sparely furnished. Bextrand slept on a slab of foam inset into the floor. Retractors on the side of the bed contained seatbelt-like straps. Bostock guessed they were there to hold Bextrand steady in case of a storm.

A stainless steel toilet sprouted near the center of the space. Bostock could see spots of urine on the floor around it. Bolts secured a small table and chair. Blinds embedded between the double glass walls of the bubble controlled the level of light. The room was never completely dark, even on a moonless night. Filaments in the glass emitted a pale green glow, giving the effect of a space ship perched atop the island. The lights prompted another nickname for Bextrand down below—the Green Lantern.

Bostock felt like the victim of an elaborate joke. Bextrand didn't shake his hand or even look at him. Bostock would not have been able to tell anyone what the man looked like even if he hadn't signed a non-disclosure agreement. It was like no human interaction Bostock had ever experienced.

Bextrand began to fire questions as he continued to pace the tight circle of his bubble. "Do you believe in the inevitability of human extinction in this century?"

"I'm not ready to give up on the human race."

"How strict is your definition of human race?" Bextrand asked.

This question gave Bostock pause. "What do you mean?"

"Suppose the human race could be tweaked to allow it to survive extreme conditions?"

"Tweaked how?"

"That is to be determined. We are pursuing a number of paths from gene modification to cyborg variations. Would ethical considerations prohibit you from pursuing such options for survival?"

Before he knew about Drew, Bostock would have balked. He would have needed time to weigh the morality and consider unintended consequences. But now he had a son standing on the precipice along with the rest of humanity. No good seemed greater than giving Drew a chance. He didn't have the luxury of hesitation. "I would choose survival," Bostock said.

"Good," Bextrand said. "You're hired. You will be my courier. I do have computer connectivity to OAP and MIT, but I don't trust my voice to electronic channels and I won't use them again unless the situation is dire. So you are my go-between. It is a position of utmost sensitivity, and I expect one hundred percent compliance with all of my security protocols."

"Yes, sir," Bostock said.

◫

"Are you even going to tell me what he looks like?" Campbell asked after Bostock returned from the meeting. They were sitting at a table on the deck celebrating his new job with two cupcakes created by Luther. "I assume the glass distorts him and he's not actually nine feet tall?"

"No, he's not, but I don't know what he looks like."

"What the fuck?"

"Don't ask any more questions, Masha. I signed an agreement."

"You wouldn't even tell me in exchange for sexual favors?"

Bostock glanced around and lowered his voice. "Are you saying you'll withhold sexual favors if I don't tell you anything?"

"No, that would be punishing me, too. I need something that only punishes you."

"Well, that's a relief. I think."

"Actually, I already know how I'll punish you." Campbell took a big bite of the cupcake.

"How?"

"Campbell pointed to her mouth to indicate that she was still chewing.

"This is part of the punishment, isn't it?"

Campbell nodded and continued chewing. Finally, she swallowed and said, "I'll stop playing games with you. To be serious, you should think twice before getting involved with Bextrand. As much as I would love to see you make regular visits to the Ayn, I don't trust our cuckoo."

"Why not? You don't know anything about him."

"I know he's wealthy, powerful, and weird as shit. And my guess is that he's becoming stranger by the hour shut up in that bubble. You know, he's the biggest consumer of my unit's reports. Sends them back with a long list of annotations and questions every time."

"Is that a bad thing?"

"It might be, depending on his motives. I know you won't help me, but I am going to find out who Bextrand really is."

CHAPTER NINETEEN

Hail Mary

A vanilla word, plan. Just the sort of word that you have to watch out for in the intelligence world. If you run across something called "Office of Plans," it's time to start asking probing questions. If the thing is called "Office of Advanced Plans," then you need to get someone from MIT or Stanford to ask those questions for you.

Bostock had spent enough time in New Hope to know that. It was the office's nickname, "Hail Mary," that attracted him despite his misgivings. The desperation pass made when the game is all but lost. He had a son now, and he could no longer afford to resign himself to the end or let doubts stop him. If there were people looking for solutions, then he had to align himself with them.

If Hollywood had created its own version of a highly secret "Office of Advanced Plans," it would have been a cavernous space lit by bluish lights from beneath a translucent floor. The place would be staffed by serious-looking, hyper-attractive people dressed in white. It would have sleek machinery with flashing lights, and arrays of screens and buttons. One button would be large and bright red. According to Chekovian law, that button would have to be pressed by the end of the movie. Then things would blow up in spectacular fashion.

Bostock had worked for the government long enough not to expect any such thing. He knew that secrecy on the working level meant that visitors were few and workspaces were utilitarian and not in the least showy. And they were dirty. Cleaning ladies didn't linger long and didn't dust for fear of seeing something they shouldn't and losing their jobs. A cheese cloth run over any surface would pick up years' worth of black grime. Secrecy meant that there were few visitors so people dressed rather shabbily. There would be ties hanging on hooks in case of the need to give an unscheduled briefing.

Even by Bostock's realistic standards, the OAP was a dump. The office's requests for more people had been granted, while its requests for more space were ignored. As a result, population density in the vault was approaching the human equivalent to a behavioral sink—the point at which rats quit reproducing and begin to display pathological behaviors. Microwave fish, and pretty soon the place would devolve to bestiality or perhaps cannibalism.

Most of the people weren't visible when an OAP escort led Bostock through the vaulted space located in the basement of the Technical Intelligence Agency—another of the detached limbs of the former CIA. They were hidden away behind the partitions of tiny cubicles. The original concept of an open office environment had been vetoed by this introverted group. They collaborated electronically, even if they worked only inches from one another. Bostock could hear voices, coughing, chairs scraping, and other sounds of human habitation. By smell, he could tell that they had enjoyed a pizza lunch, coffee had scorched in the pot, and someone had taken off his shoes. He only saw one person. A scowling, troll-like man stuck his head out from behind a partition and barked, "He cleared?"

"Yes, Ben," the escort said, "to the max."

Hamish Kobayashi wasn't the man Bostock had originally interviewed with. He was the new chief of OAP, only a week or so into the job. Some personnel issue had arisen with the old chief, and no one would give Bostock the straight story on what had happened.

Hamish rose and came to the door with hand outstretched. His amiable face showed more of the Japanese side of his family than the Scottish, but he wore a kilt and sporran. He had a Dutch boy haircut and the body of a caber-tossing highlander. When he spoke, he had a light Scottish accent.

Hamish's tiny office was cluttered with colorful plastic DNA strands and hairy, phallic silicone shapes that Bostock guessed were models of bacteria. It barely had room for an extra chair. When he sat down, his knees were up against Hamish's desk.

"Sorry for the state of things here," Hamish said. "I hope you're not having second thoughts after looking at our office. I know you just came from private industry."

"Yes," Bostock said, "but I didn't fit in."

Hamish laughed. "Well, I've never fit in anywhere—my name is Hamish Kobayashi for crap sake—but my attempt at private industry was particularly uncomfortable. They kept trying to get me to wear trousers, but I can't stand the things. I came back here so my balls could breathe and I could do something more useful than figuring out how to give a rich couple a cute genius baby. Plus, the peer pressure to buy a spot for my brain in a cryogenic chamber was unbelievable."

"People are still doing cryogenics when the human race is under threat of extinction?" Bostock asked.

"Oh, it's more popular than ever. I don't understand it either. Maybe they believe some survivors will thaw them out some day. But think about it. If you found the heads of the people who put us into this mess, would you really take the trouble to revive them? I would chuck 'em straight into a turkey fryer."

Bostock had to agree with that sentiment. He found himself liking Hamish.

"But to get back to business," Hamish said, "we've been trying to fill this job for months, and every single candidate washed out in security checks. I couldn't have passed myself. Too fond of the Glenlivet. We'll have to call you Saint Sam."

"I appreciate the sentiment," Bostock said, "but please don't. I would rather not be known as the office Pollyanna."

Hamish laughed. "I must admit that left to my own devices, I would never hire a rule follower. I need people wired to break the rules. They're the ones who push things forward. But you don't seem the type to take yourself too seriously, and that's my main problem with rule followers. Your job will require different skills. I think we'll get along."

Hamish grew serious. "After all the time and effort it took to get you here, I don't want to scare you away, but I also don't want to be anything less than honest about our work. We are rule breakers, but that doesn't mean we aren't concerned with ethics. We struggle with them every day. We don't sleep well and unintended consequences haunt our dreams. I know you've heard OAP called 'Hail Mary,' but do you know our other nickname?"

"No," Bostock said.

"OOPS. We earned it with a few fatal errors. Not that we've killed anyone yet, but a building did have to be evacuated. However, it is likely that we will kill someone—or worse—in the future during testing. We don't have time for caution."

"And that will eventually lead to something positive?" Bostock asked.

"It will." Hamish slapped his palm down on his desk for emphasis and sent a cheap government pen flying into the corner. "It hasn't yet, but it will."

"Everyone I've spoken to has been vague about what you're trying to do."

"No less than find a path for survival of the human race," Hamish said. "And by that I don't mean that we are trying to ameliorate environmental conditions. That's not our particular mission, and that window closed long ago. I mean we are trying to find ways to make the human race more resistant to the heat and pollution we can't get rid of, all while making it less of a burden on the surrounding environment. All the odds are against us, of course. That's why we push so hard against the bounds of ethics. We don't have a lot of time."

"Can you be more specific?"

"Not yet. We're still in Phase One. What used to be called blue skying, back when the sky was blue. All options are on the table. No one is allowed to say something is impossible. The actual experimentation isn't done here, of course. We don't have the facilities, and we certainly don't have the necessary sterile environment. We're battling rodents, to tell you the truth. No, we set requirements, lay out research paths, and try to anticipate problems. We act as a sort of dating service for brainpower, searching out the expertise and putting people together. The Advanced Planning Center at MIT does the hands-on work.

By the end of this year we will have narrowed options down to a few of the most promising. Bextrand will make the final decision on where we focus our energy. That's where you come in. You present our ideas to Bextrand and bring his thoughts back to us. Thus far all of the communications have been written and painstakingly slow due to all of the precautions he demands. He won't even talk to us over the phone." Hamish shook his head. "I can't get a feel for him. I don't know whether I'm dealing with a benevolent force or an evil genius or a mad man. I can look in your face and see that you're an open book. I can see you evaluating me. I want you to evaluate Bextrand just as closely."

"Well, I'll try, but from what I've seen thus far, he is rather inscrutable. I can't get a look at his eyes. He wears sunglasses."

"Really?" Hamish said. "I have to say that gives me pause."

"Me too," Bostock said. "Although he struck me as sad rather than evil."

"Who isn't sad these days?" Hamish said. "May I ask what brought you to this office?"

"I found out I have a son. He's sixteen."

Hamish nodded with sympathy. "We have a support group here for parents."

"These times," Bostock said. "I think I would like to join that group."

CHAPTER TWENTY

Scabies

Bostock took great pains to score his son a spot in one of the best high schools in the city, New Hope Academy, but Drew dreaded passing through its fancy Paradise Glass doors. He guessed that it would be as bad as the rich kids' school he had attended in Maine. He was wrong. It was worse. It catered to the children of high government officials, diplomats, and lobbyists. They were smug kids who bragged about the important things their parents did and even smugger kids who bragged because what their parents did was too secret for them to even tell. Drew could have attached himself to this second group, because his father did secret work, but he wasn't a joiner and he could have never fit in.

On the first day of school, Drew watched the others spill into the building and coalesce into whispering cliques. Cute girls side-eyed him, giggled, gestured, and spoke louder to get his attention. Their hair was shiny, their skin clear, and their clothes rich in color and texture. They were not all frivolous and vain, but Drew didn't give any of them a chance. They were of this place and he had never been of any place. He didn't know the in-jokes, the in-spots, or shared history. He didn't care to learn it, either. He was aware of the chip on his shoulder, but he was quite attached to it, thank you, and planned to leave it securely in place. He kept to himself, because he didn't have acceptable answers to the questions they would surely ask. He wasn't going to talk about his past in front of these kids.

In his first-period history class, Drew chose a seat near the middle, avoiding the conspicuousness of the front, where the best students sat, and the unpleasantness of the back, where the obnoxious boys congregated. This turned out to be a mistake. It gave the obnoxious boys a view of the rash on the back of his neck.

Bostock had taken his son to the doctor, who said the rash was a result of compromised immunity from past malnutrition and that it would soon go away.

"Look at his neck," someone said. "Is he one of the Scabies?" "Scabies" was the name these kids gave to the squatters on the outskirts of the city, after the disease that ran rampant through their streets.

Drew felt his face and neck grow hot, and he knew that his rash had reddened and become even more noticeable. He heard girls whispering, heard the word "Scabies" echoing from one corner of the room to another. Then he heard a comment that surprised him: "This place was great until they showed up. If the Scabies would just hurry up and die off, the merit class would have a better chance." It was a sentiment that he would hear over and over again in coming months. On this morning, however, it was new. He had never heard the term "merit class" before, but he was about to hear it a lot.

Drew had been homeless more than once. He had suffered lice and hookworm and other shameful diseases of poverty. He had made it through all of that. He had gone to poor schools where everyone blamed the rich who took almost everything. It had never occurred to him that rich kids were blaming poor kids, that people with more than their fair share would blame others because they couldn't take it all. The kids in this school hated the Scabies for bringing disease, using up resources, and spoiling their view. They hated the Scabies because they knew that the Scabies hated them. These kids wouldn't have survived what Drew had been through. Yet they felt themselves in every way superior.

After that, Drew walked around in an invisible bubble. Kids gave him a wide berth, fearing infection. Drew sleep-walked through the school day, focusing on things far away. He went over the names of all the small things tucked into the bins of his stepfather's hardware store. He walked the Maine woods in his mind. He revisited all the places Alison had shown him on the Ayn.

After school, he walked to the New White House. His father didn't like him coming here, but he did it almost every day. His fascination with the place hadn't waned. They had fenced off the lawn where people were once allowed to picnic because demonstrations had become too chaotic. By the time the school day was over, the demonstrators had usually gone home. He felt himself at the quiet, orderly center of things. Drew circumnavigated the base of the hill as the sun set so he could watch the play of color in the mirrored surface of the residence. He thought of something Alison had said: "I love colors so much I want to sing them into oblivion." He stayed until the sun sank below the horizon and the building began to glow with a spectral blue light. It was a palace of dreams. It had majesty, which was a quality he had never come upon before.

At home, Drew answered his father's questions with cheerful vagueness. He would never hurt Bostock by telling him about the humiliations of the day. He had someone else to confide in. After dinner, he retired to his room, allegedly to do his homework. He unbuttoned and rolled up his sleeve and unwrapped the gel computer from his arm. Gels were the new technology for people who rejected the idea of implanting cranial computers in their brains. These were soft, wearable, unbreakable computers that could wrap around your arm or neck when not in use. People often wore them under clothing to guard against theft. They had no keyboard. A sensor stuck to the cheek allowed the user to input data by mouthing words. Drew flattened the computer and propped it against his knees as he sat in bed. He had no intention of doing homework; instead, he watched the clock until Alison's image appeared at precisely the appointed hour.

"Hey, you," she said. Drew could see books behind her head in a dimly lit space.

"Hey you, too. Are you in the library?"

"Yep. I always have it to myself this time of day. Uncle Lee will probably come looking for me soon, though. He worries if I disappear from sight for too long although I don't know how I could conceivably get into anything remotely resembling trouble on the Ayn with everyone and I mean *every single freaking human* on this ship watching out for my safety and welfare. But enough of that. I have a surprise, the most unlikely and wonderful surprise."

"Well?" Drew said.

Alison leaned away for a moment and returned with her arm around a dog, who promptly began to lick her face with enthusiasm. Drew didn't know which of them had the bigger grin, the girl or the animal.

"Where the hell did you get him?" Drew asked.

"Her," Alison said. "We fished her out of the ocean. You know that storm that hit the Canadian coast? Whole houses ended up in the sea. She was floating on the roof of something, barking her head off and half starved, poor thing. Luther and I have been feeding her. He thinks she's at least part Australian shepherd. Look at her eyes: one blue, one brown. Don't you love her freckled face?" Alison gave the dog a big kiss on the white blaze on her nose. "We named her Epicurious—Epi, for short—because of how much she enjoys her food. I'm not kidding, Drew, she is just the best thing that's ever happened to me."

"She's beautiful," Drew said with real appreciation.

"Yes. I am no longer the cutest little thing on the Ayn, and that is a good thing. Some of the pressure is off me. Now people pat *her* head instead of mine. She loves it. I love it." Alison buried her head in Epi's fur.

"I'm glad you have her," Drew said.

Alison must have caught something wistful in his voice, because she looked up and peered closely into the screen. "Enough about me. How asinine was school today?"

"Pretty asinine."

"How is your neck?"

"Still red as a beet. Honestly, I think if people would quit talking about it, the rash would just go away."

"Probably," Alison agreed, "but it would also work if you quit *hearing* them. Listening is a choice, you know. Let the words just fall like rain on the roof while you curl up inside, cozy and warm, with an imaginary cup of cocoa. You can learn how to do that. I did, when I lived with Sophie. She was always grousing at us. I learned how to shut her out and taught the other kids, too. You can do it. Remember, rain on the roof."

There was almost nothing Drew couldn't tell Alison. She was a font of sympathy and sound advice. She knew what it was like to be considered a surplus human one day and the center of an almost fanatical love the next. Sometimes he thought she was the only person on Earth who knew.

CHAPTER TWENTY-ONE

Project Lemuel

Hamish's timeline was too optimistic. It took more than five years for OAP to winnow down the lines of research to three options, all involving revisions to the human species. Project Blade Runner involved the downloading of human intelligence into Cyborgs. Project Roto Rooter worked toward the creation of medical nano robots, which would be injected into the human body to clean up the effects of pollution and enhance its ability to cool itself. Project Lemuel had a goal of shrinking human beings to the size of mites. Bostock thought all of this sounded more like science fiction than anything doable within their limited timeframe, but then Hamish sent him to MIT to take a look.

It was February of 2058, and oatmeal-colored snow covered the Great Dome and Killian Court. Bostock hurried past on his way to the modern building that housed the labs doing Bextrand's work. Cody Milton, the head of Lemuel research, welcomed Bostock into an office that was more spacious than Hamish's, but just as cluttered. Milton seemed far too young and raw for the position he held. Hamish had referred to him as a scientific prodigy but added, "His scientific intellect took a giant developmental leap and left his social skills in the dust. He's a real little shite."

Milton started out with a friendly "Just call me Cody" but broke away from Bostock in mid-handshake. "Just a sec, got an idea, gotta make a note. Sit, sit, sit." Cody plopped into his chair and scribbled something on a pad. All the while he continued his choppy and rapid-fire speech. "Hamish says you're no scientist. I'll try to explain things in idiot speak."

"I'm not an idiot," Bostock said.

"Whatever. Maybe I won't try to explain. It would take too long. I'll just show you the results. See this box?" He pointed to a white box, about six inches square, on top of his desk. "How much do you think it costs? Just the box, not the contents."

"From the way you say that, I assume that it is far more costly than it looks," Bostock said.

"Play along. Give me a figure."

Bostock could see he had no choice. "A thousand dollars," he said.

Cody cackled. "Wrong. Higher."

"This could take all day. I have limited time here," Bostock said.

"Okay, have it your way. Counting development, each box costs in the five figures. Price will go down when we start mass manufacture, of course."

"You mean if your option is chosen?" Bostock said. He couldn't help but try to damp the callous high spirits.

"No way I fail. Lemuel is genius." Cody handed Bostock a small metal cylinder. "Viewing scope. Fits in your pocket, but this baby is powerful. Tap here to turn it on and twist this ring to focus. Don't drop it. You want to know what it costs? No, you don't want to know. Let's just say it costs more than the box."

Milton carefully removed the lid of the box. The lid, as well as the sides, were thick such that the interior measured only about four by four inches. The material was some sort of high-tech styrofoam-like substance. "We have air-circulating devices embedded in the sides of this box—better than punching holes. See this?" Milton used a laser pointer to highlight a thin square stuck to one interior wall of the box. "What does it look like?"

"A cracker," Bostock said. "Probably a very expensive cracker."

"Dirt cheap, actually. We call it a Complex Nutritional Grazing Wafer, or CNGW. It will provide one hundred percent of the nutritional needs of our subjects. It's made from algae and yeast. And this," Cody pointed to what looked like a piece of tape running along the bottom of the box, "is a moisture strip that will provide adequate fluids. They just have to touch it and the water bubbles up. They can support the subjects for up to two years. We anticipate that they'll be able to forage and eat just about anything once they're set loose. That's the advantage of Lemuel over the other projects. No continuing costs for cyborgs and nano robots."

"When will you have test subjects?" Bostock asked.

Milton grinned. "See that spot in the corner? Turn on the scope and take a look."

Bostock flipped the switch, and the microscope whirred. He bent and looked into the corner of the box, adjusting the focus until a flesh-colored blur resolved into a huddle of arms, legs, knees, hunched shoulders, and heads that strained to bury themselves in the mass. It reminded him of a mating ball of garter snakes he had once seen. Only the motivation here was fear, not sex.

"They don't like my laser pointer," Milton said. He ran it over them a couple of times anyway.

"Stop that," Bostock said. His heart was thumping in his throat, and something cold clotted in his stomach. "Who were they?"

"You mean, 'Who are they?'" Milton said.

"I'm not sure if the present tense applies here. Do they have language? Memory?"

"We don't know. Our strongest microphones can't pick up anything, but maybe they just aren't strong enough. Here, you need a better look." Milton tilted the box.

"What are you doing?"

"Making them scramble a bit so you can see better."

Bostock watched the naked creatures fight for purchase on the slanting surface and then crawl back into another corner. All the while he hated himself for his curiosity.

"They look ... a little off," he said.

Cody shrugged. "The miniaturization process changes physical proportions, skin texture, that kind of stuff."

"But they aren't acting right either," Bostock said.

Cody's voice grew defensive. "Well, of course. They have to get used to their new form."

"Can they still be called human?" Bostock asked.

"We call them KRILL for Kinetically Recombined Irradiated Liminal Lifeforms."

"None of that says 'human' to me." Bostock handed the magnifier back to Cody. "Who were they?" he asked again.

"Death row prisoners. They volunteered for this."

"Did they know what they were getting into?"

"Something better than lethal injection." Cody's voice was testy. "The experimentation phase isn't over. We'll get closer to human. The great thing about them is that they are incredibly resistant to heat."

"How did you discover that?" Bostock asked.

"You mean did we deliberately broil them?" Cody said. "No, don't look so horrified. It was a lucky accident. A technician was moving boxes between labs. He overlooked a box and left it in a car over a hot weekend in August. The temp in that car was over one hundred fifty degrees Fahrenheit when he opened it up. He expected to find the subjects dead, but damned if they weren't still scurrying around. Not a one died. We continued with heat experiments. Incredibly hearty little guys. Like cockroaches. They can survive an apocalypse and keep on chugging."

"You're turning people into cockroaches," Bostock said.

"I didn't mean that literally." Cody's face took on a peevish scowl as he put the lid back on the box of KRILL. "This is just a beginning. Improvements will come faster when we have more subjects to study. In the meantime, miniaturization of certain populations will head off conflicts and save lives."

"If your project is chosen," Bostock said.

"It will be. The other projects don't go far enough. Their costs are ongoing. We plan to broaden our experimentation and start working in the thousands, rather than a handful. Then we can really move forward."

"How many death row inmates are there who would agree to this?" Bostock asked.

Cody didn't answer. "Do you want to see the Lemuel Units?" he said.

"What are Lemuel Units?" Bostock asked.

"Lemuel Units are the machines that make the magic. The first one was huge, but now they're the size of shipping containers. In fact, we've created them to look exactly like shipping containers. They can be loaded onto boats—"

"Ships," Bostock said.

"Loaded onto ships, taken to target areas, and no one will be the wiser."

"What do you mean by target areas?" Bostock asked.

"Do I have to spell out everything for you?" Cody asked.

⊞

Alone in his hotel room that night, Bostock had his nightly conversation with Drew. It was a short one. Drew had friends over, three fellows from his Secret Service training program. Drew turned the camera toward them, and they gave him a toast with their drinks. They seemed like good young men, and Bostock was glad that Drew finally had a social life after his isolated school years, but he wished on this particular evening he could have had more time with his son. He wanted to be reminded of the stakes, of why he started on this path in the first place.

Bostock didn't want to be alone with his thoughts. He asked himself what he had been expecting when he signed on to work with Bextrand. A miracle. Nothing short of a miracle that would give his son time to have something of a life, if not to grow old. His amorphous idea of a miracle in no way resembled Lemuel. The KRILL were horrifying. They offended his sensibilities. He didn't sleep that night for fear of the nightmares.

The next day, Bostock met with the heads of the other two programs. They were older and more circumspect than Cody Milton. He met with them separately, but each lectured him on the phenomenon of "technological regression."

Lorne Putnam, head of Blade Runner, said, "The entire infrastructure that supports technological progress, from schools, to government, to the mining of rare and precious metals is starting to totter. So improvements in other fields that we were counting on to augment our own research are not coming as fast as anticipated."

Julian Jordan, head of Roto Rooter, said, "Even the motivation isn't there anymore. A young person can't go out now and make a few million with a brilliant idea."

"But isn't survival a compelling motivation?" Bostock asked.

"But what you really need is money," Jordan said with an edge of impatience.

It all sounded like a string of excuses to Bostock. Neither Putnam nor Jordan offered to show him into their labs to see the results of their experimentation. He got the distinct impression that their "products" were not ready for display and perhaps would never be ready.

■

Bostock carried all the information on the three options back to the Ayn in a micro-drive capsule designed to dissolve when swallowed. The capsule, which was the size of a grain of rice, resided in a flesh-colored pouch glued behind his right ear. He knew it would be pointless to protest the elaborate precautions. Bextrand's paranoia knew no bounds. So when he stood before the philosopher, Bostock reached a finger behind his ear and nudged the capsule out of its hiding place. He opened it and plugged the end into a tiny computer port.

Bostock assumed he would be dismissed from the bubble while Bextrand reviewed the information. Instead, he was left to watch this odd philosopher hunch over the screen and read slowly through the material. The hood, beard, and sunglasses obscured his face, so there were no reactions to watch, no way to read the situation. A human vacuum. Bostock had gotten no closer to figuring this man out, judging his motives or his ultimate aims.

"What did you think of the KRILL?" Bextrand asked. The question woke Bostock from his revery.

"I found them appalling," he said.

"Do you think they found themselves appalling?" Bextrand said.

"I have no possible way of knowing that."

Bostock had come here today intending to tell Bextrand that he was finished, that he could no longer participate in this unethical experimentation. Three times he inhaled deeply with every intention of spilling out his resignation on the exhale. But he didn't. He still heard the siren whistle of a hail Mary cutting the air, and he couldn't give up on his son.

Bextrand finished reading and commenced to circle the room with his unnervingly regular steps. *The cuckoo in the Doomsday Clock*, Bostock thought, *a perfect second hand, but one that wipes out all sense of time.* The heat of the bubble and the monotony of the footfalls made him unbearably sleepy. He had not had much rest since his meeting with Cody Milton. He tried to focus on one of the Ayn's accompanying destroyers floating in the distance, but his head started to fall forward twice, and once he had to suck back a line of drool.

Then Bextrand abruptly stopped his pacing and said, "Move forward with Lemuel. Cancel the other two and move all of their resources to Lemuel."

"Are you sure?" Bostock said.

"Of course," Bextrand replied. "The alternative is genocide. Come back this afternoon and I will have your instructions loaded on the micro drive. You may go now."

◘

That night, Campbell snuggled up to Bostock and fingered the bump behind his ear. "Seriously, Sam, what is this thing?"

Bostock pulled away. "Don't pick at that. It's nothing."

Campbell looped an arm around Bostock's neck and pulled him backwards onto the mattress. "It's not nothing. Let me look at it under a light. It could be cancerous."

"It's not cancerous."

"How do you know? I feel something hard in there. It's not normal."

Bostock twisted away and tried to get out of bed, but his legs caught in a tangle of sheets. He pitched forward. His head hit the floor and he came to rest in a heap.

Campbell flicked on the light, jumped down on him, pushed him flat on his back, and sat on his chest. "I need to have a look at this."

Bostock clamped a hand over his ear and struggled to get out from under her, but she had him firmly locked between her knees. "Don't touch it!" he pleaded. "It's not part of me; it's part of my job!"

"What?" With a quick move, Campbell pried Bostock's hand away, slipped a fingernail under the pouch, and peeled it off.

"Ouch!"

Campbell let out a yelp of laughter. "It's stupid spy shit!"

"Give that back!"

Campbell let him take it without a struggle. She was laughing too hard to fight. "You know, it should be a turn-on to find myself sleeping with an international spy extraordinaire, but, strangely enough, it's having the opposite effect. All I can do is laugh. I don't know if I'll ever be sexually attracted to you again."

Bostock rubbed the spot behind his ear. "I think you took some skin with it. You're not supposed to remove it without the remover fluid. Now I'm going to have to glue it back on again."

"Oh, grumble, grumble, grumble. Spies lead a dangerous life. Suck it up."

Bostock placed the pouch carefully to the side. "You didn't mean it about me no longer being sexually attractive, did you?"

"Oh, hell no."

▣

Bostock returned to New Hope and delivered Bextrand's choice to Hamish, who was not surprised.

"What do you think he meant by 'the alternative is genocide?'" Bostock asked.

"Are you not paying attention to the election?" Hamish asked. "Do you not see who's headed for the White House?"

"The election is still months away," Bostock said.

"Yes, but Emile LaFarge and his ignorant brand of Neo-Eugenics are catching fire on the right. He'll win the White House in November."

"So," Bostock said. "The pendulum is swinging again. In four years it will swing back. We don't have two-term presidents anymore. Hell, some of them don't even make it through one term. I can't bear to watch the circus."

"Well, there will be a lot you can't bear to watch soon. It's the fear and the refugees that bring them out of the cracks like cockroaches. And every time they crawl out, they're meaner. Have you not listened to the rhetoric? For a long time we've had the freelancers killing people who try to cross the borders, but let me tell you what is about to happen. First, they will halt any effort to control the private militias. Then they will look for bigger, more efficient solutions. They'll focus on biological or genetic weapons, disease bombs they can plant in streams of refugees. It's already been done."

"It has?" Bostock said in surprise. "I've never heard—"

"Do you think they would make a big announcement? It was during the Hudson Administration. The cholera outbreak in Guatemala was introduced. It got out of hand and spread farther than planned. That was a crude effort—no more sophisticated than settlers giving blankets infected with smallpox to native Americans. This time they will try something that wipes out people faster, before they can move any farther north. They want something that completely hides the hand of the United States. It is likely they'll enlist this office in their efforts. The Neo-Eugenicists in the government have already put out feelers."

"What will you do then?"

"We have two choices. First, we can appeal, through you, to Bextrand. Convince him to take on our salaries and expenses and move us lock, stock, and barrel into the private sector. The disadvantage is that we won't be in any position to affect the genocide. The other choice is to disguise Lemuel as genocide."

॒

Hamish was correct in his predictions. LaFarge won by a wide margin. After the election, Bostock flew to the Ayn to get Bextrand's choice of the two options: privatize OAP or disguise Lemuel as genocide. Bostock planned a quick trip without Drew, who could not get off work. He deliberately left little time for visiting Campbell. It wasn't that he didn't want to spend time with her; it was ... Bostock didn't want to admit it, but it was because he was afraid to look her in the face.

A thick overcast dimmed the sun, but Bextrand hadn't turned on any lights in his bubble. The bare space had a sepia cast that damped Bostock's mood as he waited for the philosopher's answer. He could only speculate on why Bextrand had exiled himself to this stark crow's nest above a dead sea. Thus far this speculation had produced only disturbing shadows that coalesced into a series of nightmares that cast Bextrand variously as the Wizard of Oz, Dracula, and Dr. Strangelove, among others.

Bostock didn't have to wait long this time for a decision. The footfalls slowed, and the philosopher came to a stop. He didn't turn to face Bostock, or even tilt his head in that direction. "We disguise it as genocide," he said. "I'll give you a message to deliver to someone at the Pentagon who will help you. I have allies there who have been considering the contingencies for months already. Come back tomorrow at this time, and I will have the message ready with instructions for its delivery."

॒

Back in New Hope, Bostock dutifully followed the Byzantine and rather dated contact instructions. He left a dead drop, chalked a mark on the fence around the White House, and retrieved a fake dog poop with additional instructions from a sidewalk. Unfortunately, he picked up a real dog poop first and had to find a men's room to clean his hands. He imagined how Campbell would laugh at this story; then he remembered that she would laugh at this part of the story only if she didn't know the rest of it. At precisely three o'clock on a Wednesday, he stepped out of a bank, walked to the curb, and got into a blue car driven by a woman in a yellow hat. Twenty minutes later, he arrived at a safe house in the wealthiest section of New Hope. He walked to the back of the house and opened the door to find a woman he had served with fifteen years earlier seated on an overstuffed chair. She had gone gray and leathery, but it only made her look tougher and more imposing.

Admiral Deanna Falco was clearly surprised to see him. She stood and extended her hand. "Bostock, I wouldn't have expected a straight arrow like you to be involved in this convoluted mess. It's something of a relief. I know you're a good man, so you wouldn't be involved if this effort wasn't"—she struggled for a word—"worthy."

"I thought the same thing when I saw you," Bostock said.

"Well, we're both struggling in the dark. But I hear that you've actually met him."

"Unfortunately, I can't share anything about him."

"Fair enough."

"May I ask how you became involved in this?" Bostock said.

Falco shook her head. "No. Let's just say that we have a small group in the Pentagon who didn't sign on to kill civilians. We knew the Administration would enlist OAP to do their dirty work, so we got to Hamish first. He told us about Lemuel. I can't say I'm happy with it, but I can't see another choice except to retire and walk away, but that doesn't seem right either."

The admiral picked up a remote from the table and clicked it toward a screen on the wall. A map of the Western Hemisphere appeared. Colored lines of various thicknesses traversed the map in a pattern that Bostock instantly recognized. It was one of Campbell's maps of migration flows. Arrows of various colors represented movements of different ethnic, paramilitary, and military groups. Red Xs marked likely areas of conflict among groups. Hashmarks designated coastal areas soon to be flooded.

"Some groups have a path to survival and some don't. We pick the ones that don't. We'll start with small groups near the coast. You'll be in an amphibious assault ship equipped with Lemuel Units. You'll take them off the beaches, miniaturize them, and send them to our base in Greenland, where OAP has set up an area where they are likely to thrive. The Administration will be told that we are 'vaporizing' them, thus fulfilling the mandate they gave OAP, to figure out how to destroy people without leaving evidence. The public will be told nothing."

"A tangled web," Bostock said.

"Fake genocide as an alternative to real genocide," Admiral Falco said. "The fact that it is our best choice suggests that we've all lived too long."

CHAPTER TWENTY-TWO

Intelligence Gaps

Bostock had told her this would be his last visit for some time. It was an unseasonably warm day in early spring of 2059, and the Ayn was off the coast of Maine and preparing to move north for the summer. Bostock and Campbell sat on lounge chairs watching Drew and Alison participate in an elaborate game called "Fucked." It was played with two six-person teams, an inflatable globe, a jet blast deflector as a sort of backboard, a kiddie pool as the goal, and Epi, the dog, as the goalie for both teams. Drew made a running start and took three giant strides up the 45 degree slant of the JBD. He pivoted, and Alison threw him the globe. He caught it and lobbed it toward the kiddie pool. At the last second, Epi deflected it with her body, landing in the pool in the process. She shook off the water with a happy dog smile. The winning team cheered. The losers threw up their hands and shouted "Bitch!" with more affection than dismay.

Campbell and Bostock made appropriate noises from the sidelines, but they had spoken little to each other that morning. The secrecy surrounding Bostock's job had strained their relationship. He was involved in elaborate preparations for something he would tell her nothing about. She stretched out her legs and studied the toe peeping through the hole of her shoe. "So you might be gone for months this time?" she said. Her tone was casual on the surface.

"Yes, I—" Bostock began.

"Or more," she cut in.

"Yes."

"How long have you been working for Bextrand?" The question was rhetorical. She answered it herself. "Years, and I still haven't a clue as to what you're doing or where you go when you leave the Ayn."

"Nothing has changed with the terms of my contract," Bostock said. "You know that. You know I can't say anything."

Campbell saw that he had turned his face away. "Can you say whether you are happy about what you're doing?"

"Happy isn't the word."

Campbell lapsed into silence and watched Bostock's gaze follow Drew as he leapt into the air. She saw the smile of pride as his son caught the globe and threw it to Alison, who fielded it with grace. Drew was no longer a delicate teen. He was a young man now, strong, healthy, and handsome. He had taken up his position with the Secret Service, but he was here with Alison whenever he could get the leave.

"But I still believe in it," Bostock said, and then he repeated with more conviction, "Yes, I believe in it." He stood up. "I'm going to go do some prep for my meeting with Bextrand. I'll see you later." Bostock bent to kiss her and then left.

Campbell had never had a reason to mistrust Bostock, but she sensed that he wasn't trusting himself. She leaned back into her chair. She saw Mason standing nearby, glaring at the game.

When he saw that Bostock had left, Mason came to sit down next to Campbell. He sat on the edge of the chair, elbows on knees, face folded into a look of anguish. "What am I going to do about this?" He gestured toward Alison and Drew. "How do I keep them from having sex? She's a teenager and he's in his twenties. He'll take her away one of these days, but if I ban Drew from the Ayn, she'll turn the whole damn carrier upside down."

"Oh my," Campbell said. She was amazed at Mason's blindness. "You would think a Navy man would realize when a ship has sailed." She almost laughed at the look of surprise that came over Mason's face, but she spoke with sympathy. "Leland, how can you ask Alison to wait for anything in this century? She found her soul mate despite living at sea isolated from the rest of her generation. Be happy for her. She and Drew have the sort of bond that few people ever find. If there is a trace of anything bad in Drew, I haven't seen it. He is utterly devoted to her. Besides, Alison is one of the most grown-up people on this ship. Always has been. Do you deny that?"

Mason rubbed the knots in his brow in silence. Finally, he said with anguish, "I wanted to give her the childhood she never had, but she refused to take it."

"Old story, and she is grown up now." Campbell leaned over and squeezed Mason's arm. "You can't make your kids want the things you want for them. Ask Sam how he felt about not sending Drew to college."

"But suppose she gets pregnant?"

"It's taken care of," Campbell said. "They're using contraceptives."

"So she came to you?" Mason said, "and you said nothing to me?"

"I've always been Alison's go-to for things she can't discuss with you. She started pinky-swearing me to secrecy before I was on the Ayn for a month. I won't apologize for that. She needed someone."

Mason's shoulders slumped. He cast a gloomy stare at the game.

"Look at how happy she is, Leland," Campbell said. "Half the planet is burning and the other half is drowning, but your little girl is happy in this moment, thanks to you and Drew. You've done the most you can possibly do for her."

Mason heaved a sigh. "And yet it will soon fall so short. I guess it's hard to accept my utter powerlessness over her future. I'm obsessing over little things and trying not to look at the big picture."

"You and the rest of the human race."

With each passing day of Bostock's absence, Campbell's mood darkened. It wasn't depression this time, but a sense of something out there that she didn't know about yet: an intelligence gap, a black hole, an unknown unknown. Something with consequences that hovered at the edge of her consciousness, phantasmagorical and elusive. It made her irritable and restless and put her off her food. One evening early in May she pushed her plate away five minutes after she had sat down and left the table without excusing herself. She went up on the deck and stared up at the cuckoo in the Doomsday Clock. "Who the fuck are you," she yelled, "and what have you done to Sam?"

Campbell went below to her quarters, reached under her bunk, and pulled out a plastic bag containing three long gray-blond hairs. She held it up to the light. She had her suspicions about Bextrand's real identity, but she had never been able to confirm them. Within a year of boarding the Ayn, she had collected this sample of his DNA. She got it with the help of Alison, who could be counted on for any sneaky and subversive thing that needed to be done. She never asked how Alison had managed to obtain those strands of hair, but she assumed it was through her contacts in the cleaning staff.

Of course, Campbell's sample meant nothing unless she had a matching sample with a name attached. She had begun the task of discovering that name on her first night on the Ayn when she stood staring up at the elongated, slow-moving shadow that circled inside the green glow of the bubble. The cuckoo in the Doomsday Clock. She kept the puzzle of his identity in the back of her mind to work on subconsciously when she didn't have the leisure to work consciously.

She kept a running mental list of everything she knew about Bextrand. First and most obvious, he was extremely wealthy. Because of that wealth, the company of the Ayn lived better than most people working for the United States Government. They got priority supplies delivered by DeepWater helicopters. The carriers that housed other parts of the government got by on lesser fare. Campbell knew that from her communications with counterparts at the Department of State and Commerce.

Second, he was powerful and the source of that power was money, not government position. He, not the president, was the primary consumer of their intelligence.

Third, he hid his face from everyone. When Bostock told her that even he had never gotten a good look at the man, it confirmed her suspicions that the face must be infamous, or badly scarred, or both.

212 | SUSAN HASLER

Fourth, he was paranoid and security conscious to a ridiculous degree. All of their communications were censored by a small monitoring unit that worked in a restricted area of the Ayn's island. Campbell suspected that this close-knit and reclusive unit worked for DeepWater, but she couldn't confirm it. All the news that came aboard the Ayn—and it was all electronic, not paper—went through this unit. This was not something that was officially recognized, but everyone knew it now, although it had taken them a while to become aware of it. It was a big point of resentment on the Ayn, where intelligence officers felt strongly that they had a right to every piece of information out there.

But it was the censoring itself that finally gave Campbell the answer to her question. She had been in intelligence long enough to know to look hard at the gaps. It helped that she already had her suspicions.

What was missing from the incoming stream of information? Any mention of Alexander Mongold, one of the most notorious men in the world. A dead man, according to reporting, but, still, a man whose influence was ever-present in the sepia tinge of the sky. The press would still be writing about him and about Panacea.

Campbell couldn't type the name "Mongold" into a search engine because it would put her on the radar of the monitoring unit. So she scanned the sources that were most likely to carry articles about him or about Panacea. She was particularly thorough on and around key dates: date of birth, of death, and of the deployment of Panacea. She didn't find a single mention of his name.

Campbell had never believed that Mongold was dead. She was still living in New Hope when she had first heard the news that his body had been found on the charred banks of the Cumberland River. She had instant doubts. The details didn't add up. For one, reports said that his body was found along with several other badly burned bodies. Those bodies were never identified. The news said that he had been identified with dental records. Why would they even think to look at Mongold's dental records, particularly if they didn't know the identity of his companions? He was known as a lover of luxury, not the sort of man to go camping in the dry woods.

Then there was the matter of timing. DeepWater had started refurbishing the Ayn shortly after Mongold's supposed body was found. She suspected that the billionaire had come up with the whole idea of government at sea as a way to create a safe space for himself while keeping tabs on everything in the world with his own damn intelligence service at his feet.

Campbell wanted to do unmonitored research. For that, she had to leave the Ayn. She was entitled to leave, of course. Everyone was entitled to three weeks of shore leave a year. She had never taken her leave before, for much the same reason she quit visiting Franconia Notch Park. She didn't want to see what had become of her old haunts. Nothing good. She didn't have to see them to know that.

Bostock had tried to get her to spend some time back in New Hope with him, but she had always declined. Now that he was off on an extended tour doing something he wouldn't tell her about, she could take the trip without any questions. He would find out, of course, when he got back. She couldn't reasonably pinky-swear the entire carrier to silence about her trip. But by that time, she should have what she needed to know.

⌑

Campbell woke earlier than necessary on the day she was scheduled to leave. She had slept little. It was the prospect of the helo trip as much as concern about what she would find in New Hope that kept her awake. She fucking hated helicopters and didn't trust the damn things to stay in the air. She fought against an urge to delay the trip. The unknowns were festering in the back of her mind. She tucked the sample of hair into a borrowed duffle along with clothes. She wrapped a gel computer around her arm and buttoned her sleeve over it. She felt some of the same excitement she used to feel as a child on the morning of a vacation trip, but it was mixed with dread. She had been living in the bowels of this machine for years without a break, her life divided between its cramped metal guts and the horizontal expanse of sky and sea on deck. This life without the middle distances was probably unhealthy, but what was the healthy alternative when the middle distances didn't bear looking at?

Light was still weak on deck. A haze of smoke dimmed the sunrise, and a breeze ruffled Campbell's hair. She had time to walk a lap on the track before the helicopter was scheduled to leave. She had almost completed her circuit when Alison appeared by the helipad with her own duffle. She dropped it next to Campbell's and waved both arms. "Hey! I'm coming with you!" she yelled.

Campbell had in mind a solitary journey uninterrupted by commentary, but she was careful not to let a frown pass over her face.

"I got an okay growl from Uncle Lee," Alison said, as Campbell joined her. "I promise I won't be in your way. In fact"—and here she lowered her voice—"I'll be staying with Drew. With Bostock away, we'll have the apartment to ourselves. First-time-ever solid, blissful chunk of privacy. Please be okay with this." Alison pleaded with eyes, voice, and the posture of a supplicant.

"Okay," Campbell said. She had a feeling that Mason knew exactly what Alison was up to but had decided to let her have her trip anyway. Good man. They would all keep up the fiction that Mason was in the dark, of course. That would only make it more fun for Alison.

Alison let out a whoop, but cut it short at the sight of Mason arriving to see them off.

"Oh crap," Campbell said. "Now I'm going to have to make a string of promises that I'll end up breaking."

"Yes, you will," Alison said.

▣

Aboard the helo, Alison kept up a steady stream of happy observations as Campbell tried to calm her stomach. She watched the Ayn grow smaller and disappear into the haze. She felt heavy, so much heavier than air. She couldn't shake the feeling that she was about to drop into the sea and sink to the bottom.

"Are you listening to me?" Alison finally said.

"I missed that last bit. Could you repeat it?" Campbell would rather her companion prattle on in this vein than have the conversation turn to her own reasons for traveling to New Hope. Any mention of Alexander Mongold would bring on a Jekyll to Hyde transformation. Alison never forgot her early brush with the huckster genius. It was her first clear memory of childhood: his personal broken promise to her and his role in hastening the death of her mother. She hated him with a virulence that shocked Campbell whenever she witnessed it.

Campbell, too, hated Mongold, but she had loved the city he built, the serene and deliberate beauty of the architecture overlaid with the random color and energy of its refugee population. The juxtapositions had delighted her. Knowing where it was headed and watching it decay had been hard. Now, coming back to it and seeing it utterly crushed between the century's currents was devastating. They arrived in the evening. The city's light was failing badly. The sidewalks and streets that had once glowed at night were now dim. Pollution, including those sulfur particles still being spewed by Panacea, made solar panels less effective. The power grid was overwhelmed by population growth.

Campbell had expected this. What surprised her was the light blazing from the razor-wired, hilltop enclaves of the rich. The government had been bribed into abandoning all attempts to enforce restrictions on burning fossil fuels. The wealthy ran industrial-sized generators using the Arctic oil freed up by the melting ice. Campbell had heard about this, but she was still unprepared for the sight of it. She remembered when the New White House was the only light during brownouts. Now the hilltop glare threw the rest of the city into a profound darkness. Who would dare to walk the blind streets?

The New Library of Congress had been one of Campbell's favorite haunts. Located near the center of New Hope, it had long been spared the decay that had overtaken the rest of the city. Campbell was dismayed to find the walls of this once-beautiful building now pocked with scars. Fences and guards were not enough to protect it from flying bullets and Molotov cocktails. Trash drifted across the brown lawn. Boards covered broken windows. The famous ten-tiered fountain in front was dry. A homeless man huddled in the bottom tier, shielded from the elements with a broken piece of foam insulation.

Campbell had to use her government ID to get in. The place was no longer open to the general public. Inside, the lights were dim and flickering. An umbrella holder by the door held a bouquet of sturdy sticks. A hand-written note stuck to the front said, "For the rats." A guard saw her staring and said, "You'll want to take one of those. The damn things are thick in the stacks and aggressive, too. We finally hired a full-time rat catcher, but he hasn't made a dent yet."

Full-time rat catcher? So that was a career now just like it was back in the Middle Ages? Christ. Campbell grabbed a stick.

Inside, she found that the electronic readers no longer worked, which meant that millions of digitized pages were lost to her. Patrons of the library took their paper reading materials and crowded into an atrium lit with skylights.

A colleague who had recently visited New Hope had advised taking a flashlight from the carrier. "You'll need it, and it's hard to find one in the city. Hold on to it. The pickpockets are everywhere." Campbell was grateful for that advice. Research in this place now felt more like spelunking. After the computer systems had failed, dedicated librarians had started the mammoth task of reconstructing card catalogues, but they didn't get far before layoffs cut their numbers to the bone. Unshelved books and periodicals piled up on every surface. Time and time again, the volumes Campbell wanted were not in their places. She began digging through random piles of magazines, some chewed into nesting material by the rats and interlarded with turds. The smell of rodents was pervasive.

Hours passed before Campbell hit upon a bound volume of *New Hope Weeklies* from the year 2055. That was ten years after the deployment of Panacea. Holding her flashlight in one hand, Campbell flipped through it to August and found a well-chewed special edition of the weekly dedicated to the anniversary. It included an article entitled "The Mysterious Disappearance of Alexander Mongold."

Campbell took out her notebook, but she didn't need it. "This is a gutted fish," she said out loud. Some editor had done a hatchet job, leaving little but vague speculation. The rats had helped by consuming the last few paragraphs. Nevertheless, Campbell read over the piece twice. She sensed that the author, one Ana Delgado, had done extensive research, only to have the bulk of it stripped away. Campbell was starting on a third read of the article when she felt something warm at her ankle.

"Fuck you, rat bastard!" Campbell leapt to her feet and brandished the stick at the retreating rodent. She didn't sit down again. She scooped up volume 14 of the *New Hope Weekly* and took it to the checkout counter, only to find out that checking a book out was no longer an option. "We never get them back," the lady at the desk told her.

Campbell went back to her hotel to wash off the taint of rodent in a short ration of cold shower water. Then she looked up Ana Delgado's phone number and made the call. The voice on the other end of the line was weak and indifferent. It took some persuading to get her to agree to a meeting at her apartment that night.

The building was in *La Ciudad*, the Latino section of New Hope. Like every other section of the city, this one had changed, but whereas most had grown drearier and more subdued, La Ciudad had worked itself into a fever pitch of bright, shallow energy. Packs of children, who called themselves *Calaveras* or skulls, roamed about in gaudy Day of the Dead paint. They left a sweep of graffiti in their wake. They had their own distinct style that relied on bold pattern. They didn't paint over each other's work, but extended and enhanced. One artist took up a motif, copying and then slowly altering the pattern. The childish scribble churned across walls for blocks. "Don't worry about the Calaveras," Ana Delgado had said over the phone. "Most of them are younger than fifteen. They're not violent. Bring coins to give them. You do need to worry about everyone else."

Those words didn't prepare Campbell for the eerie sight and sound of the Calaveras. "*Somos los muertos,*" they chanted in voices that mewled and howled. We are the dead. "*Danos ofrendas.*" Give us offerings. She passed out coins with shaking hands, and they continued on without incident.

Campbell found the apartment building and climbed five flights of stairs rather than risk the elevator. Ana Delgado peered out the peephole before opening the door and quickly ushering her into a room that smelled of smoke, sour body, and garbage. Only one weak lamp cut the gloom.

Campbell judged that Delgado was of her own age cohort, but she looked older. Pollution, poor nutrition, and fear had cut deep lines on her face. Life on land was rougher than life on the sea. Campbell had come to take the safety of the Ayn for granted. She had forgotten what it was like to hurry past alleyways and triple lock apartment doors. She could see that Delgado didn't trust her, probably didn't trust anyone on first meeting.

"Did you have any trouble on the way?" Delgado asked.

"No, the Calaveras were just sweet and sad. Their graffiti is beautiful—unusual—all patterns and no words."

Delgado looked at Campbell as if she were some naive fool. "That's because they're illiterate like most children these days. How can you not know that?"

"I've been at sea." Sensing that she was off to a bad start, Campbell repeated the line that had persuaded the reporter to meet with her. "I think I know where he's been since September fifth of 2049." This was the date of the Boone fire. Then Campbell added the name she had been afraid to mention over the phone. "Mongold."

"Sit down." Delgado motioned toward a stained overstuffed chair. She perched on the arm of a sagging couch covered with bedding in disarray. This was where she slept. There was no other bed in the apartment. The dim lamp sat between them. The reporter crossed her arms over her chest. Her face was wary.

"I read your article from the *New Hope Weekly*," Campbell said, "and I got the feeling that all the meat had been edited out."

"True," Delgado said in a flat tone.

Campbell realized that she would have to spill her own findings before she could expect anything from this woman. "I live and work aboard one of the civilian government aircraft carriers, the Ayn. I'm in the Intelligence Analysis Agency. We went to sea in 2051. We have a mystery man aboard, someone rich and powerful who is the first consumer of our intelligence even before the president. He's called Bextrand, but that's obviously a fake name. I believe that his real name is Alexander Mongold, and I'm looking for proof. I was hoping you could help me, Ms. Delgado."

The suspicion fell from the reporter's face. "Shit. After all these years. You can call me Ana, by the way. Can I get you a brownish, alcoholic beverage that can't be called beer?"

"I'll take it."

Ana stepped over to the refrigerator. This was an efficiency apartment, smaller than the one Campbell had occupied and far more cluttered. Boxes of empty bottles, mismatched dishes, clothing, and other items were stacked along the walls, leaving little open floor. "I see you eyeing my mess," Ana said.

"I didn't mean to—"

"It's all right. We all live like this now. The economy is sinking to the level of barter." Ana handed Campbell a bottle, pushed the bedding on the couch to one side and sat down. "So tell me everything about this Bextrand."

"I can't tell you as much as I would like. I've never actually seen him." Campbell launched into an explanation of the bubble, as well as Bostock's mysterious association with Bextrand.

All the while Ana sank back into the couch, sipping her beer. "Bizarre, but completely in line with what I know about Mongold. Even in hiding he finds a way to be ever-present, to crawl into your subconscious and stick there like a tick, sucking up blood. 'The cuckoo in the Doomsday Clock'—that's perfect."

"So, can you tell me where Mongold was between his disappearance in 2047, after the assassination attempts, and the day they supposedly found his body?" Campbell asked.

"Have you ever heard of the Holy Wallbangers?" Ana asked.

"Weren't they one of the wackier right-wing groups that hid out in the Appalachians?"

"Yes. Wacky and deadly." Ana coughed several times; then held her hand over her mouth for a minute as if to hold back further coughing. She continued. "Actually, it wasn't Mongold who led me to the Wallbangers. I had no particular interest in him when I started my research. I went down to the Appalachians to look into the bone caves. After the fire, the Army swept through the burnt area to hunt down any remaining rebels. They found caves full of bodies, all migrants from the south who had taken *la Pista Áspera* and been hunted down and killed." Ana fell silent, and Campbell could see the shadow of horrid memories pass over her face.

"You went to the caves?" Campbell asked.

"Yes. You know every generation has their 'where were you when?' moments. 'Where were you when the Statue of Liberty was bombed? 'Where were you when Pope John Francis was shot?' For us, it's 'Where were you when all hope vanished?' For me, it was when I reached the first cave.

"I had hiked up from the road, several miles through burned forest. It was still smoldering in places. I looked down and watched my legs grow black from soot as I walked. I felt like I was rotting from the ground up. I was wearing a mask, but it couldn't block out the smell of burning." Here Ana started to cough again as if the memory of the smoke had set her off. When the fit had subsided, she continued. "As I got closer to the excavation site, the smell of human decay broke through, and at first I thought it was coming from my own legs. They were bringing the bodies out, bagging them, tagging them, laying them out like fish at the market. It wasn't a cave like you would see on TV, not something you could walk into. I don't know where the natural cave opening was or how they even knew there was a cave under there, but the Wallbangers had dug holes that reached down a few feet to an underground passage. They threw bodies in until they filled that section. Then they filled in the hole and dug another one a few feet away and started all over again. They must have been doing it for years because there were bodies in all stages of decay. Bodies that will never be identified because their loved ones are dead and scattered. Bodies that could have been my cousins who left Veracruz on a trafficker's boat bound for the Gulf Coast of Mississippi and were never heard from again. Here were people killed by people who had been in turn consumed by fire. Dug up by people already condemned to death. It was an utter triumph of human annihilation. For a few seconds, I couldn't breathe. I tried to suck in air, and all I could do was suck in more death. I passed out, and they had to revive me. I never felt like they brought me all the way back to life."

Campbell observed Ana's face in the dim light of the lamp and saw a detachment that she understood. "Did you write that story?"she asked.

"No," Ana said. "Every time I tried, my hands were too heavy to lift. Other people wrote it. I wasn't the only reporter wandering around the Boone National Forest. I was relieved that others did it for me. I found another story while I was down there." Ana drained her bottle and tossed it into a box.

Campbell jumped at the clattering noise. Her muscles had been tensing as Ana described the caves.

"There isn't enough water to properly wash bottles or bodies anymore. That's why this place stinks," Ana says. "Anyway. To get back to the story I wrote. It came from an interview I did with one of the few survivors.

"His name was Galen. He was young, maybe not even twenty. It was hard to tell because he was so badly burned. Other survivors refused to talk. He couldn't stop, even though his voice was raspy and it must have hurt him to speak. I sat and listened to him for hours. I didn't even ask that many questions. Everything spilled out without prompting, every nasty thing. He could only see out of one eye, but he got a good look at my face. He said, 'You a wetback like what I shot.'" Ana managed a fair imitation of the mountain accent. "It was very matter of fact. I asked him if he hated me. He said, no, so I asked him why he shot us. He said, 'I don't hate deer and I shot more of 'em than I can count. I had to shoot deer to live and I had to shoot wetbacks to live.' He compared us to animals, but there wasn't even any malice in his voice. It was so strange. Then he started telling me one story after another about shooting refugees. He called them all Mexicans, no matter where they were from. He killed men, women, children, whole families together. There was no emotion in his voice. I stopped asking him questions. I wanted to get up and leave, but all of the strength went out of my legs. Finally, I said, 'Talk about something else, please.' That's when he started telling me about the Sinners. Sinners with a capital S."

Ana sat up abruptly. "Do you mind if I smoke?" She fished a cigarette out of a drawer without waiting for an answer.

"Go ahead," Campbell said.

Ana was already lighting up. "I smoke a lot more since they diagnosed lung cancer. I'm like, get it over with, already. The doctors prescribed chemo, like any reporter could afford that. Like there would even be a point to such a thing. I said, 'to hell with it.' I found these. They're laced with THC. Want one?"

"No, thanks."

"So where was I?"

"The Sinners," Campbell said.

"Yes, the Sinners. I had no idea what he was talking about at first. It took me a while to figure it out. The Holy Wallbangers were particularly well-equipped and funded because they had a profitable side hustle—the Sinners. They were rich men who needed to go underground, figuratively and literally. The Wallbangers hid them in their survival shelters. They moved them around a lot, not so much to protect them, but because they didn't want men they viewed as evil to corrupt their own people. Galen told me that some of them were supposedly famous, but they never knew their real names.

"Then he started telling me about this one particular Sinner he had struck up a friendship with. 'Face like he'd been skint,' he said, but he liked him even though he called him ignorant because he 'didn't know nothing' about how to live in the woods. He said the Sinner wore the dumbest shoes he had ever seen. No laces, so they fell off when he walked over rough ground. They were two-tone—cream and oxblood. Solid gold horsebit hardware. Elevator heels. Galen said he couldn't believe anyone would wear such stupid shoes into the woods. I couldn't believe it either because I had seen those very shoes on Alexander Mongold when I interviewed him once. They were custom-made with initials engraved on the horsebit. He wore them all the time. I can't figure out why a man on the run from his identity would wear his custom shoes. Maybe he wasn't thinking straight when he left home. From all accounts, he was half crazy by then."

"MDR," Campbell said.

"What?"

"MDR. Those were my father's initials. He wore engraved gold cufflinks. He was a serial killer. That's how they caught him. Found one of his cufflinks in a well with the bodies."

"Holy shit," Ana said. She reached into the same drawer with the cigarettes and pulled out a piece of metal. "AGM. Alexander

Grant Mongold. See? The initials are tiny, but here they are."
She held it under the light and pointed to the faint engravings
on the cheek of the snaffle ring.

Campbell took the hardware and bent close to examine it. It
was still in good condition.

"How did you get it?"

"Galen gave Mongold a pair of his own shoes and got Mongold's loafers in return. Galen threw them out but kept one of
these in his pocket as a good luck charm."

"He gave it to you?" Campbell asked.

"No, he died that night. I sat with him until the end and then
I took it."

"Big men and their monograms." Campbell shook her head.
She turned the horsebit over and over in her hand.

Ana continued with her story. "I hated Mongold for what he
did to the sky and the Earth and the whole damn human race.
When I heard they had found his body miles downstream, I
went straight to the coroner in that county. That was one body
I *wanted* to see. To tell you the truth, I was hoping it would be
gruesome as fuck. By the time I got there, both coroner and
body were gone. They said the body had been claimed by a representative of the Mongold estate, while the coroner had taken
a job out of state right after he signed the death certificate. No
forwarding address, of course. What a perfect solution for
Mongold. Fake death. It infuriated me. So I wrote my article and
set out to find him. My editor was afraid of shadows, so he
hacked the article into pap."

Ana took a long drag from her cigarette and closed her eyes.
When she spoke again, her voice was so quiet Campbell had to
lean forward to catch the words. "I gave up on my search for
Mongold after a couple of years, when the grim struggle to sur-

vive started taking up all of my extra time and energy." She seemed to sink deeper into the couch.

Campbell listened to the quiet labor in Ana's breathing. Then she reached into a pouch she wore under her shirt. She brought out the plastic bag containing the three long gray-blond hairs. "I need to prove Bextrand's identity beyond a doubt. I have a sample of his DNA. Can you give me any idea of how I might get my hands on a sample of Mongold's DNA?"

Ana's eyes popped open, and she sat up and took the bag from Campbell. She held it under the lamp with hands that shook ever so slightly. "Damn. You bust your ass searching for something and it falls in your lap just when it doesn't seem to matter anymore." She turned the bag over and over under the light. "How many strands are in here?"

"Three."

Ana handed the bag back and lowered herself to her knees next to the couch. She reached under it, slid out a lock box, and punched in a combination.

At first Campbell thought the box was empty, but then she saw that it contained a bag much like her own.

Ana handed the bag to Campbell. "Three strands. What are the odds? It seems like it should have some deeper meaning, but there are no deeper meanings anymore. You need time for depth, and we're fresh out of that."

Campbell examined the bag. The hairs were golden and not so long as the ones she had collected. "How did you get this? I mean how in holy hell did you get this?"

"I got it from Mongold's first failed assassin, a Thai woman named Pakpao Boonmee. Do you remember the story?"

"Of course," Campbell said, "she melted his face and then disappeared supposedly never to be seen again. How did you find her?"

"That's a long story with a lot of sensitive sources. But to give you the gist of it, the Earth's Avengers recruited her to carry out the attack. Afterward, she stayed in the organization, changed her name, and switched from mixing up hair color formulas to making poisons and bombs. She turned out to be quite a genius at it and rose high in the ranks of environmental terrorists. I haven't kept up with her, but I assume she's still blowing things up."

"You spoke with her in person?"

"Yes, several times. She had her own interest in finding out whether Mongold was still alive and kicking. She even got the Avengers to give me some money to fund my investigation. She gave me the hairs. They came from Mongold's own brush."

Before Campbell left the apartment that night, Ana pressed something into her hand. Campbell looked down to see the monogrammed horsebit. "Give this to your friend who meets with Mongold," Ana said. "Tell him to put it down in front of Mongold so he can see that the past has caught up to him."

◘

On the helo trip back to the Ayn, neither Alison nor Campbell said a word. Alison's head and heart were back in New Hope with Drew. Campbell was weighing the impact of the sheet of paper folded into the pouch she wore under her shirt.

The DNA test left no doubt that Bextrand was Mongold. Not that Campbell had had any doubts. She had no intention of making that information known to anyone aboard the Ayn. The morale of a ship's company was a fragile thing, not to be tampered with lightly. Alison's reaction alone could gin up a tidal wave. She would tell Bostock, however, because he should damn well know the real name of his boss.

▣

Back on the Ayn, Campbell started to look for other intelligence gaps. She found one within a week. Her voice came over the tops of the cubicles louder than protocol allowed in the echoing space of the Block. "Something isn't right. The fuck? Something isn't right."

Her words stopped work in the Migration Unit. Analysts sat back and waited.

"Conference room 15, everybody," Campbell said. Now."

They clomped down the metal stairway and met Maeve coming up. She had been in New Hope to attend the funeral of an old partner, the one before Bella. Her hair was freshly buzzed, her nails clipped and filed, and her eyes still red.

"Did you just get in?" Campbell said.

"Fresh off he helo," Maeve said. "I need to talk to you."

"We're about to have a meeting. Can it wait until after that?" Campbell asked.

Maeve nodded. The Migration Unit continued down to one of the tiny rooms that surrounded the old hangar space. Campbell shut the door, cut the lights, and sat down at the head of the small conference table.

"The numbers aren't adding up. The imagery isn't adding up." Campbell unrolled her gel computer. A satellite image of the east coast of Mexico appeared on the screen behind her. She zoomed in on a road crowded with people and vehicles. "Remember this? It was a few months ago. A Mestizo group from Belize moving north. We estimated their numbers at about 1,500 to two thousand. They were unarmed and half starved." Campbell pulled up the same map Admiral Falco had shown Bostock. "Here's the map we put together last fall. The Mestizos are the blue line. The red line is a mix of Guatemalan military and paramilitary groups." Campbell put the map back up. "The Guatemalan group would have caught up to the Belize group before they reached Tampico. Given their past actions, we expected them to kill the Mestizos and take all of their belongings. We estimated that that would happen here. It should have occurred about two weeks ago." Campbell pointed to a small area south of Tampico. "Bella, I had you put in a requirement for imagery of that area. Remember what happened?"

"They said there were technical problems with the satellite transmission."

"Right. We didn't get any more imagery of the area until now. It just came in. This is it." Campbell put up an image of crowds camped out near a beach. "Here are the Guatemalans. The group from Belize is missing," she said. "Here are their vehicles, abandoned near the beach. No bodies. No sign of a struggle. I've checked imagery of the surrounding area. Nothing."

"Maybe they went onto traffickers' boats?" Brian said.

"There aren't enough traffickers in the whole area to take away that many people, even if these people had the resources to pay traffickers, which I doubt. So I'm asking all of you to find out where these people are. Put out requirements to anyone we have near there on the ground. Find out what ships were in the area. This is top priority."

When the meeting ended, they let the others file out. Maeve moved to the chair next to Campbell and placed one hand on the table in front of her and studied it for a moment before she began. "I heard rumors when I was in New Hope." A pause. "Concerning Bostock."

Campbell's mind flashed back to the police woman who had sat down in the dining room in McLean. She had laid her hand on the table in much the same way. An anchor. A focal point. "I don't want to hear this, do I?" Campbell said.

"No, you don't. And I don't want to say it."

"But I have to, and you have to."

"Yes," Maeve said.

"Continue."

"It involves a secret program called 'Lemuel.' Have you ever heard Bostock say that name?"

"I've never ..." Campbell's voice trailed off. She had heard that word, Lemuel, that odd name. It was stuck in a dark place in her mind. She grasped for it. She had heard it from Bostock's lips. "Yes," she said with hesitation. "It was early, dark. He was getting dressed the morning he left the Ayn. He was sitting on the edge of the bed putting on his shoes. I had my eyes closed. I don't think he knew I was awake. I was only half awake. He was muttering, upset about something. I did hear him say it. Lemuel. I remember now thinking Gulliver. Lemuel Gulliver?" Campbell looked down at Maeve's spotted and knotted hand. Not an anchor. Not a focal point. It was a vanishing point. "What does Lemuel mean?" she asked.

"Genocide, according to some reports. Something stranger, according to others."

"Bostock would not be involved in genocide." Campbell could say that with absolute certainty.

"Would he be involved in some highly questionable human experimentation on refugees?" Maeve asked.

Campbell wanted to deny this just as firmly as she had denied the other, but she found she couldn't. "Something has been bothering him, for a long time, but particularly right before he left. I fell in love with him for his open face." But she hadn't seen that open face in a long time. It had closed and turned away, and somehow she had kept that fact submerged in her mind. Campbell felt something buckle at her center. "How did I let this happen to me again?" she asked.

"I don't understand," Maeve said.

"Just tell me everything, every last nasty, incriminating, unsavory thing."

So Maeve began to tell the story she had heard in the basement of the Pentagon, told under the cover of clattering silverware, scraping chairs, and ambient conversation. The story hadn't gone beyond military and intelligence circles yet. But it would. It was a spark of pure fire that would soon take hold in the dry tinder of the capital, a city of refugees. For now it smoldered at the working level of the government, where people mixed largely with their own kind. They knew the consequences of letting it see the light of day, but such a thing couldn't be contained indefinitely. It wasn't surprising that people would confide in Maeve, because she was just the sort of person people turn to when they've heard something deeply disturbing. She was old, wise, and discreet. They took the burden of what they had discovered and dumped it on her. Now she in turn must dump it on the someone who might break under the weight. Her voice faltered now and again, but she gave a full and complete accounting of what she had heard.

"So, Bostock was in charge of this operation?"

"Yes."

"And the people, the refugees, are now what? Not dead but something other than human?"

Maeve reached for Campbell's hand and pressed it. "I don't know more than what I've told you. I don't think it will be long before it all becomes common knowledge. I don't know why people think such things can be kept secret. They always come out, sooner or later. Brace yourself."

Campbell did brace herself, but several months passed with no public revelations concerning the Lemuel Program. Meanwhile, her unit tracked Bostock's work by logging satellite blackouts up and down the coast of Central America.

CHAPTER TWENTY-THREE

The Right Story

What was Alexander Mongold doing now? That question got Ana moving in the morning through the summer of 2059, even if moving just meant making her way to the bathroom, eating a little something, and going straight back to the couch and her computer to work her contacts and smoke THC-laced cigarettes.

That analyst, Campbell, had given her clues. Her friend, Bostock was his name, served as some sort of liaison between Mongold and the Office of Advanced Plans. Ana had heard of OAP in connection to rumored accidents a few years earlier in a lab at MIT.

Ana was too weak to leave her apartment much now, but she could still call in contacts from every corner of New Hope. They came to her looking over their shoulders and speaking in whispers. They came to pay their respects, because she had been a force at one time, and she wouldn't be around much longer. She had partied with them, done them favors, edited their early work, dispensed advice, and shared information and precious hooch. Now they offered her awkward bits of story that they could not fit together themselves.

Ana hated when they pretended her apartment didn't smell bad, when they thanked her and tried to tell her what she meant to them, when they gave her the looks that said, "I know I might be seeing you for the last time and I want to remember." Most especially, she hated it when they said, "I'm praying for you."

He was saying it now, the young man with the bad skin who sat in the same chair Campbell had occupied. His name was Jorge, and he was a distant relative of hers, if memory served.

"Fuck that," Delgado said. She rummaged in her drawer for another cigarette. "How long has God been dead now? A century, at least. Didn't you get the memo? Does this denouement look to you like the end product of intelligent design? Don't you think a few billion people are still praying for something better? It's not happening. How slow do you have to be to still believe? Never mind. What have you got for me?"

"I, well, I've been hearing things from a friend in the Pentagon." Here Jorge repeated the rumors of a secret project run out of the OAP. Ana could tell that his contacts were at the hazy end of a long game of gossip. He described a program to vaporize migrants using laser-spitting drones launched from ships. She had heard other versions of this story. She was drifting off into her own thoughts, when she caught a name that made her sit upright. The effort made her cough. When she could get her lungs to cooperate, she said, "Repeat that."

The sudden attention made Jorge lose his place in his story. "I, um, what was I saying?"

"You said the name 'Bostock.' What about him?"

"Um, Bostock. He's in charge of implementing it, and he's off the coast of Central America now, vaporizing people."

"Vaporizing people" didn't sound at all like a Mongold sort of project. When she had interviewed him, back before the failure of Panacea, Ana had been struck by the image he had of himself as a global über-humanitarian. That was the very term he had used, "über-humanitarian," pronounced with a hush of self-reverence. It was such transparent self-delusion. She had wondered at how genius and fallacy could so blithely coexist in the same body.

"Vaporizing people" did sound like the sort of project the LaFarge administration would take on, however. President Emile LaFarge was a tech billionaire completely lacking the charm and good intentions—misguided though they were—of Mongold. He had a naked, lightbulb-shaped head, hooded eyes, and a protruding lower lip. His forehead was so broad and high he could have used it to display party slogans or paid advertisements. He had founded a new faction of nationalists called the Neo-Eugenicists. Unlike the religious right, they didn't blame the plight of humanity on God's vengeance for human sins. They blamed it on the "breeders." That's what they called the masses of displaced people moving around the planet looking for refuge. They argued that technical solutions could save the planet if not for the wanton population growth among "less-advanced" segments of humanity. Look at New Hope itself, they argued. The city with a "merit population" could have worked, but it was destroyed by the influx of migrants.

Support for President LaFarge was strong in the hilltop enclaves that had been dubbed "Upper New Hope." The rich who lived there were ever more terrified of the rivers of angry and desperate humanity that flowed around them. They kept upgrading their perimeters: stringing more razor wire and electrified fencing, adding security cameras and other forms of monitoring, and hiring more guards. They also resorted to low-tech, but effective, "bottle moats" in front of fences. These were deep ditches lined with rough concrete. Bottles were inserted into the concrete while it was wet. Once it had set, a worker walked along the edge of the ditch with a long iron bar and broke the bottles, leaving the jagged remains sticking up and the shards of glass in place. Anyone who fell into one of these nasty things would be sliced to ribbons. These moats kept the tomato red "Elect LaFarge" signs hung on fences behind them from being torn down.

A child had recently fallen into a bottle moat and bled to death before he was found. Since then, the mood was even uglier in Lower New Hope and more paranoid in Upper New Hope, where Paradise Windows could not put happy faces on the crowds below. Even shut up in her apartment, Ana could feel the tension and hear the sirens, chants of crowds, and occasional shrieks of pain.

Yes, LaFarge would happily vaporize any number of migrants, but Mongold wouldn't be a part of that. From what Campbell had said, Bostock wouldn't be a part of that either. Ana hit up her contacts again, told them to shake every tree that still stood.

The truth about the situation had hid successfully among the wild rumors because it was also wild. Thus far, no one had the discernment, authority, or courage to point it out and say, "That, that one is the truth." It came to Ana midway through the searing summer of 2059. It came on the lips of an old colleague with sources in the Technical Intelligence Agency. It came wrapped up in an apology.

"This one is so crazy I don't even know if I should bother you with it." The aging journalist mopped his brow as he sat forward on the apartment's one comfortable chair. It was too hot to sink back into the cushions.

"Crazy is not a disqualifier," Ana said.

"Okay." He proceeded to relate the story of Lemuel, a program that was not genocide, but something stranger and more unlikely. And, yes, a man named Bostock was in charge of it.

Strange, unlikely, and yet consistent with what Ana already knew about Mongold, Bostock, and the OAP. This was just the sort of idea Mongold would hatch.

"That's it," Ana said.

Once Ana had the right story, she knew where to go to find corroborating information to shore it up. The story grew flesh, while she wasted away. As she incubated it, she could feel it taking on weight, growing bones and feathers. It was a thing that would fly and shriek and rumble the Earth when she finally let it go. An awful thing that would snap the tendons that held everything together.

CHAPTER TWENTY-FOUR

The Box

It was September 1, 2059. The helo trip from Nuuk to the deck of the Ayn hardly gave Bostock enough time to steel himself. Things would have gone downhill in the months since his last visit. His secret work had taken longer than anticipated and taken more out of him than he could ever have imagined. And it wasn't a secret anymore. The aircraft carrier's company had found out about it weeks earlier. Since then, communications had been spotty or maybe people were too angry to return his messages. He lowered his eyes briefly to the white box he cradled on his lap. It was smaller than a bread box yet big enough to rock the Ayn. When he looked up again, he caught sight of the carrier, an island of faded lime green floating in putty-colored waters under a flat beige sky. His hands began to tremble. He pressed them to the box to make them stop.

DeepWater had been sliding on maintenance. The Ayn had begun to resemble something that had sat on the bottom of the ocean for decades. In this autumn season and still relatively temperate northern latitude, she had become a perpetual steel beach picnic. Her decks were covered with accretions: garden

241

plots, clotheslines, grills, and courts for basketball, tennis, volleyball, and badminton. She smelled like mold, salt, and desperation. Everything was repaired and jerry-built. The fencing surrounding the tennis court was bent and rusted, and the net had been mended with old bra straps—nobody actually wore bras anymore, because the world had enough misery. The umbrellas and chairs were torn, wonky, and water-stained. Some had been fished out of the sea.

The downdraft of the helo fluttered the umbrellas and sent trash skittering across the flight deck. Bostock scanned the sorry remnants of government bureaucracy. A hot wave of apprehension almost brought up the contents of his stomach. He squinted. Something was awry, but he couldn't put his finger on it. Then he caught sight of Campbell chasing a wind-borne ultralight gel computer across the deck. She tackled the sheet of silicone, rolled over on her back, and gave the helo the finger.

Bostock broke into tears and laughter. He shook. Last night in a dream he had seen her body hanging from a noose from one of the radar arrays of the Ayn. The vividness of the image had destroyed his equilibrium. Relief took the starch from his knees. When the helo landed, he stumbled and almost fell as he disembarked, but he managed to keep the box level.

Campbell didn't come to meet him at the helipad, but Mason was there. He grabbed Bostock's arm to steady him. They moved away from the copter as the blades slowed. "I'll have someone take that below for you." He pointed to the box and motioned to a junior officer.

"Keep it level. Don't jostle it," Bostock said to the man.

Mason frowned. "Good god, is that—"

"I'll talk about it later."

"Walk with me," Mason said. He tucked his head and started off toward the track, and Bostock followed behind. When they reached it, the other walkers adjusted their pace to give them privacy. Mason didn't exercise much in the way of discipline anymore, but he held the respect of everyone on board. The respect the ship's company had once had for Bostock, however, seemed to have evaporated. He saw looks of hostility. People tried to catch his eye so they could shake their heads at him.

"What's happening here? The Ayn looks like hell."

"Communications are crumbling. We are running short on supplies, and I can't get anyone to send a supply helo. The mini that brought you is the only thing that has landed in months."

"How did people react to the news of Lemuel?" Bostock asked. "Do they all hate me?"

"Not all of them." Mason took Bostock's arm and walked him over to a yellow chalk line that ran lengthwise down the ship. "Just the ones on this side of the line."

Bostock's eyes followed the line down the length of the flight deck. It didn't run quite down the center. About three quarters of the space and people were on the opposition side, including Campbell and all the members of her unit. Now he realized what had felt wrong from the bird's eye view: the two sides were taking pains not to look at each other.

"The ones on that side agree with the idea that any measure, no matter how morally abhorrent, is justified in order that some of us might survive," Mason said. "Most of the assholes are on that side."

"Did it ever occur to you that the subjects of the Lemuel Program might be the lucky ones? They might outlive us all," Bostock said. "The only other choice is death. You need to get ready to take on Lemuel Units. I've already put them on the other ships in the group." Bostock gestured toward the two destroyers that accompanied the Ayn.

"We saw. It pissed off the port side so badly I thought I was going to have a mutiny on my hands. The Ayn will not be a part of it. I secured Bextrand's agreement on that. Lemuel is not compatible with the intelligence function of this carrier."

"You don't even know if anyone is still reading all of those intelligence reports."

Mason lowered his voice to a whisper. "Well, Bextrand is, but beyond that, you're right; I don't know. Do you want me to tell that to the people aboard this ship? Do you want me to say, 'You can stop doing your jobs now?' What would they do then? Sit on their hands and think about their future?"

Bostock didn't have an answer to that. "I need to talk to Bextrand," he said.

"Visit Campbell first. She'll give you an earful of what you're up against with Lemuel. Bextrand hasn't a clue. He has no assets in the human race."

⌗

Campbell's unit was now down to Brian, Maeve, and Bella. Alison served as a research assistant. They worked on the deck today. When Campbell returned to her seat after retrieving her gel computer, Maeve said, "What are you going to say to him?"

"I have no words," Campbell said. "None at all. So when he comes over here and wants to talk to me alone, you are not to leave. None of you. I don't give many orders, but that's an order. Plaster your asses to your seats."

Campbell kept her eyes on her screen, but everyone else on deck watched as Bostock and Mason moved slowly around the walking track. One side watched with approval; the other, with anger.

It had been a difficult few weeks since an analyst had returned from Pentagon briefings in New Hope with the "real story" on Lemuel. It was the same story Ana Delgado had discovered but had yet to release to the general public. Under the best of circumstances, intelligence analysts are argumentative and territorial. These were the worst of circumstances. They had been together on this craft for too long with little in the way of turnover. They could have used some fresh blood to give them perspective, but the government had quit hiring. They had too much shared history, and they had had too many ill-considered affairs. Over-familiarity had taken a toll. Mason had long kept a lid on things by strictly enforcing his own version of the Golden Rule: If you're not good to one other, if you act like a shit, I will put your ass in a sling. He held regular training sessions for managers, mediated conflicts, and counseled troublemakers. This time, however, it had gotten away from him.

The Lemuel Project caused the most incendiary questions to be asked out loud and uncovered rifts that could not be counseled away. What are we willing to do to others so that we might survive? The question had always been there, unspoken in the background even as people did terrible things to each other in order to survive or allowed terrible things to be done on their behalf while they looked in the other direction. Now it was out in the open, and no one could look away or fail to choose a side. The line down the deck of the Ayn had been chalked in the middle of the night by some anonymous party, who had gone so far as to label the sides. Starboard side was "Only Inhumanity Can Save Humanity" and port was "Only Inhumanity Can Destroy Humanity." Perhaps it had been meant as a joke, but people quickly sorted themselves according to their convictions. Mason left the line there because things were calmer when the two sides didn't mix. Then someone scribbled another note on the deck: "Who gives a shit? We're all fucked anyway."

☐

Bostock approached Campbell cautiously. Was she angry, depressed, or both? He threaded his way through tables, umbrellas, and beach towels. She stretched out on a recliner, legs in the sun, pointedly ignoring his approach. Her head bent over the gel computer, which had been brushed off and flattened in her lap. Her subordinates sat in the chairs surrounding her. They were visibly tense.

Bostock jerked his thumb, indicating that they should clear out.

After an awkward moment under Bostock's glare, Brian stammered, "She told us to stay."

"I need to talk to her privately."

Campbell looked up with narrowed eyes and crinkled nose. He had seen that expression before, but never directed at him.

"I can't talk to you," she said. "It's impossible. You belong on that side of the ship with the pro-hubris, let's-play-God party." She pointed across the yellow line. "And I belong here, and there is no middle ground. No. Fucking. Middle. Ground."

"Is this the 'death with honor' party?" Bostock asked.

"Yeah," Campbell said, "it is, in fact."

Bostock lowered his gaze from her eyes and saw that her bare legs were sunburned and peeling. He squatted down and gently touched her ankle. She flinched.

"You need to wear your sunblock, Masha," he said softly.

Campbell leaned back her head and hooted. "Sunblock? Fucking sunblock? Are we still shooting for longevity here?"

His eyes fixed on what looked to be a small lesion on her calf. "Melanoma is a foul way to die."

Campbell motioned for the others to leave and they fled quickly. "I trusted you. Do you know what those words mean? How could you be part of this thing? How could you be in charge of implementing it for fuck sake?"

"Because I want to give people a chance. I want *you* to live."

"Not your decision. I will go on my own terms." Campbell glanced toward the Pri-Fly. "The cuckoo is waiting for you. You'd better go genuflect."

Bostock retrieved the box and took the elevator to the Pri-Fly. He closed his eyes and concentrated on relaxing those muscles about the upper lip and nose that tried to curl in distaste whenever he was around Bextrand. He found the Pri-Fly sparsely manned. Even helo flights were rare these days. He winced at the disorder. Not for the first time, Bostock wished he could don his old uniform just long enough to chew somebody's head off.

Duff was as hostile as usual. He went over Bostock's identification, as he did every time even though it should hardly be necessary anymore. All the while, he kept glancing at the box, licking his lips. Bostock could see how hungry he was to have a look, but he would have been instructed not to touch it. Bostock felt sorry for this man who had spent his life guarding secrets he wasn't privy to. Duff stood back.

Bostock stepped inside the tube and shifted the box so that it was clasped between one arm and his body. He climbed the ladder. At the top, he paused to roll his eyes heavenward. *Keep a neutral face,* he told himself.

"Put it on the table," Bextrand said as Bostock climbed into the room.

Bostock set the box on the table and removed the lid. He reached into his pocket and took out the magnifying device. He pressed a button to turn it on and handed it to Bextrand.

The philosopher turned away from Bostock, took off his sunglasses, and bent over the box. He put the magnifier to his eye. The robe hid his face, but Bostock could hear his breathing quicken. "They're frightened."

"Of course they are," Bostock said. "I have no way to tell them that it's okay."

Bextrand watched in silence long enough for Bostock to grow restless. Finally, he put his sunglasses back on and handed the magnifier to Bostock. "Are they ever happy?"

"I don't know, sir. They eat. They hold each other. I imagine it will take a while for the shock of it all to wear off."

"Physically, they appear to be thriving?" Bextrand said.

"Yes, sir."

"Any sign of them using language with each other?"

"No, sir, but one of them is pregnant."

"Which one?"

Bostock took the magnifier. When he spotted her, he handed it back to Bextrand. "In the far left corner, surrounded by a half dozen others."

Bextrand looked for a while and then straightened. "Put the lid on. Clear the table. We have to talk about your next assignment."

When Bostock had the box in his hands again, Bextrand raised the table and flipped up a computer screen. He began to type in commands.

Bexrand's hands were pale as if they had never been touched by the sun. A burn scar half covered the left one and the right was missing a pinky. The fingernails were deeply ridged and unkempt.

Bextrand finished typing and rotated the table to give Bostock a better view of the image on the screen. It was another map of Central America with colored lines indicating the northward flow of people. Bextrand pointed to a spot where two lines were about to converge. "There," he said. "That's where you go next. Tell me how many Lemuel Units are operational and how you will proceed."

◫

Campbell almost felt sorry for Bostock landing in the middle of this grim controversy that he had helped to create. Almost. Then he came over and demanded a hearing, touched her leg gently, showed love and concern, and left her full of sharp, contradictory feelings that threatened to upend any remaining sense of balance. She could feel herself teetering on the of edge something deep, dark, and familiar.

"I can't climb out again. I don't have the energy," she said to no one in particular. She grew still. She was only vaguely aware of the dull sun on her legs, the yellowed sky above, and the nervous subordinates who returned to cluster around her. Bostock never lied to her. She had come to assume that it wasn't in his nature. She supposed he still hadn't technically lied to her. He had concealed the truth. She had always thought Bostock was the best man she had ever known. Not only thought it, but depended on it and held onto it like a safety line.

No, it wasn't a lie, but a betrayal, not just of her but of what she had assumed were his principles. He wasn't the man she thought he was, and that was a thing she couldn't forgive. She had no desire to argue with him over whether Lemuel was evil or not. She had no doubt that it was sick and unnatural and doomed to an eventual, spectacular failure.

Bostock would be back as soon as he finished with Bextrand. He probably planned to stay a few nights before returning to New Hope. Nausea broke over her. She could not bear to look at his face again.

Campbell turned to Alison. "I need to use your bunk for a few days. You can sleep in mine." She addressed the rest of her unit. "Listen up, people. I'm going to Alison's bunk now to mope. If any one of you tells Bostock where I am or even gives him the slightest hint of it, I will make your life a living hell. I will put dog shit under your pillow. I will spit on your food." She started to leave, but turned back and said, "You know I don't make idle threats."

Campbell's people waited until she was out of earshot and then broke into furious analysis of all they had overheard. Only Alison said nothing. She sat on her lounge chair, hugged her skinny knees, and squeezed her eyes shut against the eerie diffuse light of the beige sky.

"This is bad," said Brian. He was gaunt and balding now, even more overwhelmed by his bushy brows and thick glasses. "She'll be in a pisser of a mood for the next decade if she doesn't get laid before Bostock flies out."

"Don't be an asshat," Maeve said.

"Was that offensive?" Brian asked. "I'm sorry, but you know it's true."

"Yes, but not all opinions should be voiced out loud. We've discussed this before." Maeve directed a scowl toward the Pri-Fly. "What I want to know is what Bostock's presence says about Lemuel. Will it continue?"

A low murmur of obscenities greeted the question.

"Do we have to sell our souls to the Devil before we all die?" Bella said. "Not that I believe in the Devil, but you get my point."

"I think we sold our souls decades ago," said Maeve. "We have survived, which means we aren't innocent."

The conversation continued in tones low enough so that no words would cross the chalk line to the other side of the Ayn. Then Alison broke in. "I don't want to sleep in Campbell's bunk, not with Meg there. How long is this going to last? She can't avoid him indefinitely. How do I even get my stuff from my old bunk while she's there?" Alison's normally soft voice had grown uncharacteristically shrill.

"Relax," Brian said. "Bostock will leave, and you'll be back in your own bunk in no time. Of all the things to get upset over, this is—"

Alison jumped up and fled toward the jet blast deflector, where another game of Fucked was in progress. At her approach, Epi abandoned her goalie duties and came over for some love. The game broke up, and the players drifted toward the lounge chairs. Alison settled into a nearby chaise and pulled Epi's front half into her lap. She buried her face in the dog's fur.

Campbell would find the pregnancy test. Nobody ever bothered anybody else's stuff, so Alison had made no great effort to hide it, just tucked it into the book she had been reading and left it on her bunk. Campbell would have to move the book to lie down. She would find the thick plastic stick registering its plus sign. She would be agonizingly kind to Alison and wouldn't press her over that one failure to use birth control. She would insist on going with her to have the abortion, because of course there would have to be an abortion.

How could a woman give birth to a child who would have no future? She couldn't have this baby, but that didn't stop Alison from wanting it more than she had ever wanted anything. Like most children of her generation, she had trained herself not to wish and want and hope. She was already older than she thought she would ever be. She had never considered future generations. Now she ached with wanting this baby and every moment of this process of pregnancy. Hormones, she told herself. Hormones were making her irrational and tricking her into feeling a warm glow in her center where she shouldn't be feeling anything yet. She couldn't stop imagining pacing the deck with a baby in her arms. A baby that would have a few thousand parents because everyone on the Ayn would love it.

Alison made a wry face. "Love it like a pet, just like they love you and just like they loved me when I was little." She addressed the dog. "I have more in common with you than I do with anyone else on the Ayn."

The sun would set soon. The sky was already beginning to yellow like old parchment. "The sunsets will be glorious," Alexander G. Mongold had said. God, but she hated that man. Alison went below so she wouldn't have to look at the raw red glare.

After dinner, Alison found her way to the berth Campbell shared with Meg. She never visited her friend there because she couldn't stand Meg. The woman spoke too loud, was overly fond of her own opinions, and oblivious to the sensitivities of other human beings. She was just the sort of social aggressor who can make a shy person curl up into a shell in seconds flat.

Alison took a deep breath before knocking on the door.

"Who is it?"

"Alison Leverett." Why did she include her last name? She was the only Alison on the ship and everyone knew her.

Meg opened the door. "Alison Leveret, did you say? The Alison Leverett?"

"Don't make fun of me."

"If you're looking for Campbell," Meg said, "she's not here."

"I know. Campbell asked me to switch bunks with her tonight." Alison hoped that no further explanation would be required.

"Why would she do that?" Meg demanded.

"She wanted to avoid someone," Alison said.

"So she's not speaking to Bostock?"

Alison did not want to gossip about Campbell. "I don't know. She didn't tell me. I just do what she asks."

"Oh, come on, you must know. We all saw him get off that helo today. Still cute after all these years, but his hair is thinning."

"Which one is Campbell's bunk?" Alison asked.

"I'll tell you if you tell me what went down between those two," Meg said.

Alison's eyes fell on the neater of the two bunks, the one with no personal items taped to the wall. She saw a copy of *The Origin of Species* lying on the shelf above it. This would be Campbell's spot, but suddenly Alison couldn't bear to stay for the interrogation she was likely to be subjected to. "I'm going up top to walk. If Bostock comes by, you can't tell him where Campbell is." She fled.

"You'd better have some gossip for us when you get back," Meg called after her.

▣

The sun had set and it was cool on the flight deck. A number of people had brought up blankets and were sleeping on recliners. *I'll do that*, Alison thought. *That would be nice.* First, though, she had to walk to settle her mind. She set a rapid pace in a vain effort to burn off the unpleasant buzz of tension under her skin—tension or hormones, something alien that set her on edge, softened her bones, and made her feel that she barely controlled her own body. She wanted to talk to Drew, but communications were down. She couldn't tell him about the pregnancy because it would only make him sad, and there was nothing he could do to make any of it better. But she wanted to hear his voice and see his face. She couldn't stop imagining what a beautiful baby they would have together.

Alison wished she could scream without attracting attention. She wondered if Campbell had found her pregnancy test yet. She wasn't ready to be forced into a decision, even if it was the only possible decision. No choice. All the generations before her had had choices and had made them so badly, so self-ishly, that there were none left for her to make. If she had a clear mind and energy right now, she would hate them, but no, she couldn't allow something as toxic as hatred to invade her body and harm the small, new life she carried. The life she was going to have to terminate because her predecessors had made all of her choices for her.

The walking wasn't helping. Alison was only growing more agitated. She would never be able to sleep. Maybe it would be better to go to Campbell now and get it over with. She could not have this child. She might as well accept Campbell's support and sympathy. She had no other option. Alison stopped halfway down the runway. She would go back to her own bunk to have it out with Campbell. Yes, that's what she would do, but she would walk a bit more first to get her courage up.

◨

Bostock hesitated at the door of the berth, hoping that Meg wouldn't be there. He knocked and called in. "Bostock here. Is Campbell in there?"

Meg opened the door wearing a towel on her head, an oversized T-shirt, no pants, and a pair of ancient slippers in the form of badgers. "Well, hello, hottie. Come right on in. This is a popular place tonight."

"Is Campbell in?" he repeated. He had no intention of entering the room if she wasn't there.

"No, she's sleeping elsewhere tonight. Evidently trying to avoid someone. Are you two lovers quarreling over your little Nazi doctor project?"

Bostock injected as much menace into his voice as he could muster. "You will cut the crap now and tell me where she is."

Meg stuck out her chin. "I'm not supposed to tell you."

Bostock sized up his opponent. She was vain, insecure, aggressive, superficially intelligent enough to somehow rise as far in the ranks as Campbell had. But she lacked any sense whatsoever, common or otherwise. He changed his tack. "You're just saying that because you don't know."

Meg scoffed. "I know everything that goes down on the Ayn."

"You're out of the loop. You don't even know where Campbell is."

"I know where she is."

"Bullshit. I don't believe it." Bostock filled his voice with contempt. "You like to cultivate a reputation of knowing everything, but it's fake."

"You're full of it," Meg said.

He kept pushing her buttons. "So you don't know or you're too intimidated by your roommate to tell me."

"She's in Alison's bunk," Meg said. "You're boring me. Leave."

Bostock was more than happy to go. Campbell should have known he would find her. Meg was incapable of keeping a secret. Or maybe, he told himself with some hope, Campbell wanted him to find her.

She was alone and utterly still in the dark berth. Bostock flicked on the light. Campbell's eyes were open, but she didn't flinch. He stood a moment. He couldn't detect the movement of her breathing. He didn't see her blink. It had been a long time since she had gone this quiet. The spooked inhabitants of neighboring bunks had taken their blankets and elected to spend the night in lounge chairs on the deck.

Bostock sat down on a lower bunk with great care, as if live explosives were tucked under the blankets. "What are the good choices, Masha?"

Her hands flew up and startled him. She spoke with hands and words and a howl of despair in the back of her voice. "What platitude will you come out with next? That there will always be winners and losers? That there are no win-win options left in the Post-Hope World?"

"I hate that term, Post-Hope World," Bostock said. "What idiot came up with it? We have no right to give up on hope. It's a betrayal of all the generations that have come before us as well as the ones that may or may not come after us. It was the excuse people were waiting for to give up and go down in an orgy of hedonism."

"The hedonism is only for the rich behind their walls in their blast-proof houses with their concierge disaster service teams on call. The rest of humanity is going down in an orgy of starvation and violence."

The tension in Bostock's face seemed about to break it open. "You don't have to tell me that. I'm the one who has witnessed it up close while you've been here. How many years have you been on the Ayn without shore leave? It is worse than anything you can imagine."

"I was in New Hope a few months ago, and it was bad, but I didn't see anything to justify what you're doing. Shrinking the losers down to the size of specks so you don't have to witness their agony anymore? How does that square with your morality?"

"It will give them a chance," Bostock said. "It will give everyone a chance."

"They'll die in droves."

"There was a high survival rate in early implementation."

"Refugees. You shrank refugees."

"Yes," Bostock said. "They had their backs to the sea. They were facing certain death. It would have been a massacre. It has been many times before."

Campbell's voice went deadly quiet. "How did you do it?" She waited for an answer that didn't come. "How did you do it?"

"Okay. I'll tell you everything. Bostock clasped his hands between his knees and stared at them as he spoke. "We took them off the beach in AAVs. It was a slow process."

"What do the machines look like?" Campbell asked. "The shrinking machines?"

"Like large shipping containers with extra-thick walls."

"What are they called?"

"LUs. Lemuel Units."

"What do you call the people you shrink?"

"KRILL."

"Krill? Like little shrimp? How fucking sick."

"It's an acronym, It stands for—"

"I don't give a shit what it stands for. I assume Bextrand came up with it."

"His people at MIT came up with it."

"I have a few words to say about him later. How do you get people to go into these Lemuel Units?"

Bostock didn't want to tell her. If he said it out loud, it might well put a permanent end to their relationship. So be it. Being dishonest with Masha wasn't an option. "We told them they had been exposed to a pathogen. We disguised the LUs as decontamination chambers."

"Like the Auschwitz showers?" Campbell said.

"Not like Auschwitz. We didn't gas people. We had to get them to take off their clothes and jewelry, because those don't miniaturize. The cloth would have suffocated them."

"So what was it like when you opened the doors of those boxes? How many human beings did you squash under your feet?"

"Before the doors open, air currents at floor level sweep them into special containers with food and moistened strips that provide hydration."

"What kind of food?" Campbell asked.

"A sort of cracker that is attached along the walls of the box."

"Sounds delicious. Like a gingerbread house."

"It probably tastes good to starving people. We could never feed them otherwise. We barely have enough food to feed our own personnel. Those people had no chance and we gave them one."

"How many died?"

"Five percent. The ones who were old and weak. I think we can lower the mortality by—"

"Where are the survivors?"

"In Greenland, right across the bay. We've set aside an area of the military base. We're doing everything possible to ensure their survival."

"We can't even ensure our own survival," Campbell said.

"No, we can't."

"How many are over there now? I know that you've conducted at least a half-dozen of these operations."

"Seven thousand or so," Bostock said.

"Shrinking the excess population is the most totalitarian solution I can think of. And it won't work, Sam. It won't work any better than Project Panacea. You can't shrink enough people to lighten the burden on Earth in time. The numbers don't work."

"We have begun large-scale production of the LUs. Soon every U.S. ship will have them. It's an option for survival."

"Are you going to put LUs on the Ayn?"

"Leland is fighting it, but eventually we may need to. Masha, the subjects are the lucky ones. The miniaturization process makes them far more resistant to heat. They may be the only ones to survive. The government was planning genocide, so we disguised this as genocide. It was the lesser evil. I had to make a choice. I know that's not an excuse. It doesn't absolve me from any evil done in the name of Lemuel. I had to make a choice."

"You could have chosen to avoid the evil altogether."

"Which would not have reduced anyone's suffering by one iota."

"So who chooses who becomes a dust mite? Or KRILL, as you say."

"Bextrand chooses based on—." Bostock stopped.

Campbell sat up. "Based on my unit's work."

"Yes."

Campbell covered her face with her hands. "Shit. Crap. Fuck. I knew we weren't doing any good, but I didn't know we were doing harm."

The thought struck Bostock that this could be the thing that pushed Masha into the fatal depression he had been fearing for years. He stood and took her hand. "No, you've never done anything but good. A lot more people are alive than you predicted for that region."

"But are they still human? You said miniaturization makes them more heat tolerant, but what else does it change? Are their memories intact? Are they still themselves or are they something else? Can you communicate with them?"

"You're asking all the questions I asked. We're working on a way to communicate. Their voices are too small. We have powerful microphones, but the sounds are distorted. I know we can find a technical fix for that. We have people working—"

"Or maybe the voices are distorted because they no longer have language," Masha said. "Did that occur to you?"

"Yes. Everything you're saying occurred to me, and I almost resigned a dozen times. If I had seen any hope anywhere else, I would have."

"Would you shrink Drew? Would you turn him into one of your little shrimp?"

Bostock rubbed a hand across his face. "I would give him the choice. Not much of a choice, I know, but more than he's ever had."

Campbell sank back onto her bunk. She began to cry. She let herself go for a few minutes, then wiped her eyes. "Do you know who Bextrand really is?"

"No." The question took Bostock by surprise. "Do you?"

"Yes, I had suspicions for a couple of years. Then Alison helped me get some of his DNA. I went to New Hope to confirm my suspicions. I found someone who had collected a matching DNA sample. Bextrand is Alexander Mongold."

Bostock felt light-headed. He sat down again. "You are fucking kidding me," he said. But he knew it was true as soon as she said it.

"You never swear. You sound like me."

"Mongold drowned in the Cumberland River years ago," Bostock said. "They recovered his body."

"They recovered a body, which was cremated with unusual speed. Not long after that, we got word that we were going aboard the Ayn. Ever wonder why the Intelligence Analysis Agency was the first part of government to be assigned to an aircraft carrier? We're here to be Mongold's own little information service. He can hide behind our security procedures and tap our brains. Like you said, it's a place to hide away from the worst of it.

"You weren't here on the day we boarded. Our security badges were not enough. We went through the most thorough screening I've ever experienced in all my years in the agency. They checked our fingerprints and DNA to ensure we were who we said we were. They scanned our bodies for microchips. A doctor examined us from top to bottom and updated all of our shots. All of our belongings were X-rayed and run through chemical detection machines.

"It was getting dark by the time they finally let us come aboard. That's when we noticed the weird, green glowing thing on top of the Pri-Fly. He had been up there watching us. And he's still watching and giving orders and going over everything we do with a fine-tooth comb."

"The man who killed the Earth," Bostock said.

"Don't be part of this," Campbell said. "Do you really think Alexander Mongold is doing this as a service to humanity? Something is very wrong."

Bostock's brain raced. He should have told Masha everything long ago, despite the oath he took.

Campbell climbed down from the bunk. She sat next to Bostock. "Everyone is talking about the box you brought onboard. What is in that box? KRILL?"

"Yes."

"Show me."

"I stowed the box in the captain's quarters for safekeeping."

"Well go get it and show me." Campbell was using the low, slow voice that could not be denied.

Campbell held the magnifier to her eye and leaned over the box. She adjusted it until the KRILL came into focus. Several dozen men, women, and children. They were naked, huddled together, and staring upward. She could just make out the fear on their faces. She felt like an evil overseer staring down at them, but she could not pull her eyes away. In all of the photos and videos of this group she had seen, the people were on the verge of starvation from the Panacea-caused drought, but these were not. Their bodies had rounded out over the weeks since they had undergone miniaturization. Something about the proportions seemed off to her, though, as if the process had warped the natural human shape. Then she saw that one of the women seemed to be in distress. The others were crowded around her, as if to protect her. Campbell squinted and adjusted the magnifier again.

"Oh my god," she said, "there's a woman giving birth."

Bostock took the magnifier and looked. "We've been waiting for this. She's the first to give birth."

"Let me see!"

Bostock and Campbell looked up to see Alison in the doorway. She had slipped in unnoticed while they were absorbed in the tiny drama in the box.

Alison came over and took the magnifier from a startled Bostock, nudged him aside, and leaned over the box.

Bostock started to protest, but Campbell put a hand on his shoulder. "Let her. She needs to see. She's pregnant."

As she watched, Alison began to tear up. She wiped her eyes with a fist. Campbell handed her a tissue from the box next to the bunk. "The poor woman doesn't need a bath in salt water."

"She's screaming," Alison said.

"Women do that when giving birth," Campbell said.

"Will she be all right?"

"I don't know."

Alison's breathing grew heavy as if in sympathy with the expectant mother. "Won't she and her baby just die like the rest of us when Panacea fails?"

"Probably not," Bostock said. "They can survive much higher levels of heat than we can. There will be things they can eat."

"We don't know how much they have retained in terms of their humanity," Campbell said. "We don't know if they retain language—"

"But they have a future," Alison said. "They have time to get back what they've lost. When I heard about Lemuel, I thought it sounded like pure evil, but this baby will have a future."

"We don't know yet whether it will be born healthy," Campbell said.

"Oh, I think it's coming. It's hard to see."

Bostock started to say something, but Alison held up her hand. "Shh."

They were all quiet for a few moments as Alison focused on what was happening in the box. "Yes! They're all smiling and hugging. The mom is smiling. She has her baby in her arms."

Alison put down the magnifying glass and looked directly at Bostock. "I'm going to have Drew's baby. You will miniaturize me. I'm not asking. I'm telling you."

The old leather sofas in Captain Mason's quarters were in terrible shape. Mason had let Alison jump on them as much as she wanted when she was a child. He even let her draw on them with a marker. As Bostock waited, he read "Alison was here" written in a childish hand on the arm in blue marker and punctuated with a daisy. Her bed used to be in the corner, but when she hit her teens, she had insisted on bunking with the others and trying to live down her reputation as "the captain's little girl."

Bostock knew that he was not waiting for the loving and lenient man who had done his best to spoil his beloved niece. He was waiting for a fearsome combination of mama bear, papa bear, and wounded bear. Mason had lost his wife and daughter to a car accident back when he and Bostock were doing their first tour on a destroyer. Bostock heard the news from their superior and searched over half the ship before he found Mason in the head vomiting up his grief. Such a toxic, profound, gale-force grief that it possessed Mason and almost pushed him over the edge. For years, Mason lived half a life, focused on his work. Then Alison came and restored all the missing parts. Bostock was mortified to be part of anything that threatened her. His face burned, his stomach knotted, and his mouth went dry.

The door opened with a bang, and Mason stormed in and shouted, "What the hell did you do to my little girl?"

Bostock felt like he had been transported back to his recruit days. He thought it best to let Mason storm for a while before he offered an explanation.

"Out of the blue. Out of the blue, Alison comes to me and says—" here Mason's voice broke, and Bostock thought for a second his old friend might break into tears. Panic shot through his system. He didn't think he could bear that sight. But Mason recovered himself and transformed the unborn tears into pure fury. "She said 'good-bye.' She said she was going to leave with you and let you turn her into a dust mite. Then she tells me she's pregnant. Congratulations, Grandad, your son knocked up my Alison. It's lucky he's not here right now, or I would pulp his fucking ass and toss it into the sea along with the sewage. But I can't. So I'll have to settle for murdering you, and believe me, I will kill you before I let you make my Alison part of your unholy mad scientist experiments."

Mason was out of breath from shouting. He plopped down on the opposite sofa. It was time for Bostock to respond now. "Leland," he said, "I told her no."

"Well, Alison didn't hear 'no' when you said it, and she won't listen to me when I say it. You don't understand these quiet, shy little girls. They have a will made of iron. Not iron. Titanium. If they've made up their minds on something, they can stand up to armies. Why the fuck did you show her that box? You wouldn't even let me look at it."

"I didn't mean to. Campbell insisted on seeing it. It's a long story. Trust me that I didn't mean for Alison to see it."

Now the tears began to course down Mason's face. If Bostock could have willed himself to die where he sat, he would have.

Alison was an expert at entering rooms without being noticed. She had been standing just inside the door through half of Mason's tirade. Now she came up behind him, leaned down, and put her arms around him and lay her head on his shoulder. He started. "Why do you do that?" he said. "You're going to give an old man a heart attack."

"I love you more than I loved Mama," she said. "I've tried not to even admit that to myself because it seemed like I was betraying her, but I do. She was too sick to give me what I needed, and my memories of her are fading. You have been everything to me." Alison straightened and came around the couch to sit next to Mason. She took his hand in both of hers. "Not everybody is cut out for being a dad, but you were born to it. When God created you, He said, 'I will give this one intelligence and many skills, but the most important thing I give him will be an absolute *genius* for loving children." Alison freed one of her hands and wiped the tears from Mason's cheek. Then she used the same hand to wipe the tears on her own cheek. "He gave that to me, too. I knew it as soon as I found out I was pregnant. It took me by surprise because I had never even considered the possibility of children. But it was strong. Stronger than anything I have ever felt. But I knew I would have to have an abortion or condemn my child to witness hell. Then I saw this miracle. This woman giving birth. She has a chance to survive. The baby has a chance to survive."

"That baby has a highly uncertain future," Mason said.

"No baby born on Earth has ever had a certain future," Alison said.

"Then just have your baby here," Mason said, "without going through this ghastly program."

"This world won't support a human baby."

Bostock spoke up. "We could have another few years before Panacea goes into final failure."

"It will happen sooner than you think," Alison said. "Everything happens sooner than we think it will. And yet everyone's instinct is to hesitate. My whole lifetime has been watching people hesitate until it's too late." Alison said.

"Please," Bostock said, "let's see how this baby does. I'm starting to have my own doubts about the Lemuel Program, about the motives behind the program."

"Why now?" Mason asked. "You didn't seem to have any doubts the other day. Has something happened?"

"I found out who's behind Lemuel," Bostock said.

"Bextrand. We all knew that," said Mason. "That's why I've had my doubts all along. I'm not even sure that Bextrand is sane."

"I've always harbored doubts about Bextrand, but I had faith in the people in the Office of Advanced Plans," Bostock said, "but last night I found out who Bextrand really is."

"And?" Mason said.

"He is Alexander G. Mongold."

"No!" Alison shouted. "No, I don't believe this. I will not." Her voice had become shrill and so unlike any sound they had ever heard from her that Bostock and Mason both stared. Alison was up and out of the room before they could say anything.

◫

Bostock leaned against the leeward side of the island and went over in his mind all the things he planned to say to Bextrand. He needed an accounting before he could go on with Lemuel. He needed to see the man's face and hear the truth for once. He held the box with both hands. The wind had shifted and grown stronger during the night. It was coming out of the north and had a chill to it. The kitchen staff was harvesting squash and tomatoes into big stainless steel bowls. Others were securing loose furniture and taking down awnings. The tank tops of the day before had been exchanged for windbreakers. People shot quick glances at the sky as they worked. Whereas yesterday glances had been directed across the chalk line, now the line was forgotten and smudged by feet going back and forth.

Bostock squinted at the sky. The clouds to the north reminded him of bruised flesh, purple edging into yellow. Something was about to break.

When Bostock arrived at the Pri-Fly, Duff gave him a narrow-eyed glare of disapproval. Bostock was not supposed to make requests of Bextrand. It should always work the other way around.

Bostock shifted the box under his arm—he had his reasons for bringing it again—and climbed up the ladder.

As always, Bextrand continued to pace without acknowledging his visitor.

Bostock reached into his pocket and brought out the object that Campbell had given him. As the philosopher came around, Bostock slapped it down on the table. The noise attracted Bextrand's eye. He continued for two steps until the shape of the thing slipped into a corresponding hole in his memory, and he stopped.

He didn't look at Bostock. After a pause of a few seconds, he came forward and picked up the horsebit, turned it in his hands, and examined the letters in the engraving, AGM.

Bostock focused on Bextrand's mirrored sunglasses. What was he thinking?

"What do you have to say, Mr. Mongold?" Bostock said.

The philosopher put down the bit and resumed his pacing. He came full circle before he said, "Do you know who renamed this carrier when she was decommissioned?" He asked as if he hadn't heard the name he had been running away from for years. His eyes fixed on his own feet as each made its regular appearance from beneath his robes, thrusting out, ball of the foot landing before the toe.

As soon as he asked the question, Bostock knew the answer. "You did," he said.

"Correct. I named it after Ayn Rand. Are you familiar with her philosophy?"

"I know the outlines. I tried to read one of her books once."

"But you could not finish it."

"Right," Bostock said.

"She was a dreadful writer, but she captured minds with her vision. Do you know why?"

"No," Bostock said, although he had an idea. This wasn't the subject he came to talk about, but he would let the man go on because he had to make a judgment about Bextrand's character and sanity, a judgment that would have critical consequences. Everything the philosopher chose to talk about and everything he said must be weighed as evidence. Still, Bostock found Bextrand's slow speech and meandering approach to a point maddening. He bit back an urge to stick out a toe and trip him, just to see him sprawl on the floor.

"Rand captured men," Bextrand said, "because she identified a burden and gave them a way to throw it off without seeming to do so."

"The burden of caring for their fellows?" Bostock asked. He remembered now the distaste that he had felt toward Rand's message.

Bextrand took off his sunglasses, slipped the hood back off his head, and turned to look directly at Bostock.

It was not so much the ruined face that startled Bostock, but the eerie fixedness of the gaze. *The man is insane*, he thought.

How did I not realize that the man is insane? The eyes held raw pain. The face was misshapen, haggard, and lacked eyebrows. The most heavily damaged area was under the cheekbones, where Pakpao had massaged the mask most deeply into the skin. Here, flesh had the appearance of melted plastic.

Bostock forced himself not to look away. He tried to connect this face to the image of Alexander G. Mongold that had once been ubiquitous on magazine covers and television and social media. Perhaps the eyes were the same? Or the same eyes with a different person behind them? The manner, the movements, everything else was different. Bostock had a sudden moment of doubt. "You are Mongold, aren't you?"

"I was." Bextrand replaced the glasses and hood and resumed pacing. "I was the Atlas who dropped the planet. And I was very sorry. Am very sorry. Do you know why I live in a bubble?"

"So a grateful world doesn't kill you?" Bostock said.

"I've never heard sarcasm from you before. But never mind. Yes, of course that's one reason. In one sense, I'm still hiding. In another, however, I've stopped hiding." Bextrand made a gesture that encompassed the 360-degree view. "See the sky I created? The dingy, dreary, dismal, eerie, awful sky? Not so long ago, a few days of a sky like that would have been enough to make a man howl with depression. Now we've had years of it, and the world has never seen such suicide rates. I went underground, literally under the ground, to hide from that sky—as well as from all the people who wanted to kill me, of course. Justifiably wanted to kill me. Now I force myself to stay up here with nothing else to look at. No Paradise Windows for me. I don't deserve them."

Bostock considered this. The view from this bubble could easily drive a man crazy.

272 | SUSAN HASLER

"Yes, I am very sorry for what I did," Bextrand said, "but I have never thought of myself as evil. We Titans never do. What will you do with us? Sure, you can bring us down. You can chop off the head of a dictator or overthrow a system, but that's a time-consuming, resource-intensive, violent, and chaotic process. Needless to say, there is enough chaos in the world now, and more would mean an even earlier end. You get nowhere going after Titans these days. Besides, as unjust as it may be, we are the ones who have the resources. The Earth has no time to bring us down. We have had enough of violence. Avoiding it was one of the prime reasons behind Lemuel in the first place. That's one reason you signed on so eagerly, isn't it?"

"I signed on to give my son a chance," Bostock said quietly.

"He never really had one," Bextrand said. He returned to his earlier subject. "Rand rebranded what was once considered a deadly sin—greed—and turned it into a virtue. A brilliant marketing move. She relieved the burden of guilt, largely guilt based in religion, but other sources figure in as well. Never underestimate guilt. Never undercalculate the lengths a man will take to avoid blame—in his own eyes, first of all, and only then in the eyes of other men. He will build labyrinths on Earth and in his imagination and try to lose himself in them. He will run with bare, bloody feet through a burning forest. He will try to tear down the old guilty self and rebuild on a slate that can never be clean. Guilt is heavier than osmium and its weight only increases with age." Here the philosopher heaved a sigh so profound that it interrupted the regularity of his stride.

"Objectivism offered to free man from the guilt of the selfishness that came with industrialization and the rise of the market economy. It made self-interest a virtue and shifted blame off the backs of the wealthy. It sanctified the individual. It made certain people feel superior. Freedom from guilt and the drug of elitism are what kept people reading to the end of those mind-numbing tomes."

Bostock found nothing original in Bextrand's musing. "You're an objectivist?" he asked.

"No, of course not." Bextrand abruptly stopped his pacing and went to the table. He flipped up the screen and rapidly keyed in a few commands. An image appeared. It was Atlas straining under the weight of the globe. Bextrand hit a couple of keys and the image flipped 180 degrees.

"Rand's mistake was that she had it upside down," Bextrand said. "Atlas was resting on the world, the natural world and the backs of the poor. The poor suffered and bore up or perished as they always have, but the natural world broke.

"Most 'isms' start out well enough," Bextrand continued, "but it's dangerous to follow one to its ultimate consequence. It turns out that the ultimate consequence of individualism is the annihilation of all humanity." Bextrand snapped the computer shut and resumed his pacing.

But does he really care about humanity now? Bostock wondered.

"Objectivism, neoliberalism, neoconservatism, laissez-faire economics, Chicago School, were all part of the same religion. Their gods were self-interest and profit motive, which were declared as infallible as the Pope. I used to be one of them, and then I lost my religion." Bextrand made a slow half circle before he spoke again. "I lost my faith. It takes courage to lose one's faith, but sometimes you have to do it to regain your full humanity."

Bostock said, "I don't understand. That runs counter to—"

"Everything you've been taught." Mongold finished the sentence for him. "It's dangerous to have total faith in anything because so few things in this world are worthy of it."

"God?" Bostock said. "For those who still believe?

"Do you believe in God?"

"Not a specific god or religion anymore. I just believe that there's something out there too large for me to understand."

"Good," Bextrand said. "Nonspecific is good. The devil is in the details. Most people don't actually have faith in a God because the concept is too large for them to understand. They have faith in man-made interpretations of God, little chunks of wisdom or dross, depending on whatever the priest, pastor, reverend, what have you, is selling. These "men of God" promise certainty in an uncertain world. Their message is that you shouldn't think for yourselves, let God think for you. Let me think for you. Here are the rules. Do these things, or don't do these things, and you'll get a big reward. The last thing sheep want to believe is that you have to figure the rules out for yourselves, that you have to do this over and over throughout your lifetime, and that at the end of your life you may still be wrong. You may discover that what you had faith in—whether it be a set of rules, a theory, or even yourself—is not only unworthy, but deadly.

"So, you may ask, what do I believe in now? What is my 'ism'? Because if you're a philosopher, you have to have an 'ism,' right?" Bextrand waited for an answer from Bostock but got none.

"You can call my philosophy 'anti-ismism.' It sounds like a joke, doesn't it? It's not. All 'isms' are created by man and are therefore fallible. They all start out with good intent, but follow any one of them to their ends and they will lead you to darkness and destruction. A disciple will follow his 'ism' right off a cliff because he has forgotten how to use his own eyes and ears and chosen to hand over responsibility to someone or something else."

Bextrand stopped pacing when he reached Bostock, removed his glasses, and once again stared directly into his face. "It's like the dilemma you face now. You came here today to find out whether I'm evil or crazy or otherwise untrustworthy. You came to find out whether you can justify faith in me. Am I right?"

"Frighteningly so," Bostock said.

Bextrand replaced his glasses and resumed pacing. "And you will leave here today not knowing." He gave an odd, bitter-sad laugh. "I would tell you if I knew myself, but I don't. I think I'm sane on most days, but I require a prodigious amount of compulsive activity to get through a day. It's the guilt, I think. I named this craft the Ayn as a reminder of the power and uses of guilt and the promise of release from guilt. Also, I couldn't resist the irony." A convulsive twinge crossed the lower half of his face. It might have been a smile. "Do you know how I came up with the idea for Lemuel?"

Bostock didn't answer. He had no desire to spin like a music box ballerina so that he could follow Bextrand's progress around the room. The man was behind him now, the thin voice niggling at the back of his neck.

"It was that phrase 'reduce man's carbon footprint.' Everyone was calling for it but somehow no one could do it. After the big ice sheets vanished, it wouldn't have been enough even if we had tried hard. Man was still too big, too heavy, too full of himself, too dishonest, and too clumsy to avoid fatal damage to the Earth. No, the only solution was to reduce man's actual footprint, to make him too small to cause harm. To humble him."

Bostock said, "It sounds strange to hear the word 'humble' come from your mouth."

"Yes," Bextrand said. "I admit it. I am the patron saint of hubris. If I had ever had anything like humility, the world would be a more livable place. But too late. It's hubris or nothing now. People told me that the idea of shrinking people was science fiction, but science fiction is just next year's news. You just have to set the goal and put the right pieces into place. I assembled just the right mix of talent: molecular physicists, microbiologists, and a number of other 'ists' that no one else would have thought of putting in the same room. I used my resources and persuaded the government to direct its resources. It was like the first moon landing; focus the will and you will find the way."

"Like you did with Panacea?" Bostock asked.

"Yes," Bextrand said. "I failed with Panacea. I gave up trying for a while. Then I had to try." He took a deep breath. "Because you have to try. What other choice is there?"

Bostock did not like hearing his own words coming out of Bextrand's mouth. It caused a faint wave of vertigo.

Bextrand stopped his pacing. "Why did you bring that box back?"

"I wanted you to see something. A baby was born last night."

Bextrand was at Bostock's side in seconds. It was the first impulsive and non-deliberate movement he had ever seen the philosopher make.

"Let me see," Bextrand said.

Bostock took the lid off the box, set it on the table, and handed over the magnifier.

Bextrand laughed as he stared down into the box. It was a natural laugh this time, a pleasant laugh, the sort of sound that Bostock could never have imagined coming from this man. "They're not so frightened as they were yesterday. They must have been terrified with a woman about to go into labor. Just now, they looked up at me, then went right back to watching the baby. The mother is nursing. It must be a normal baby because they're all behaving as if everything is good, normal." He watched for almost half an hour, only making the occasional comment in a voice filled with awe, for all the world like a new father at the glass window of the maternity ward. When he finally handed the box back to Bostock, he said, "They're human enough. I'm sure of it now."

And you're human, Bostock thought. *Teetering on the fuzzy edge of sanity, but still human.*

Alison walked the track for an hour after leaving Mason and Bostock, keeping up a furious pace until she made her decision. Then she stopped and went through a full set of stretches slowly. Now she stood in the captain's galley watching Luther slicing onions newly harvested from the deck gardens.

"Hey, sweetie, are you hungry?" Luther asked.

"I'm just checking to make sure those onions aren't making you cry," she said.

"Oh, no. I'm too tough to cry. Besides, I know the secret. Chop fast and use a sharp knife. I always sharpen my knife before I start."

"Now that you mention it," Alison said, "I am hungry, but not for onions."

Luther wiped his hands on his apron and gave her a big smile. "I figured out how to make something that tastes almost like one of those good old peanut butter cookies. Would you like one?"

"Oh, yes."

"I'll get them out of the pantry. I'll be right back."

A minute later, Alison was munching her cookie and heading for the door, while Luther was trying to remember where he had laid down his knife.

Once out of the galley, Alison ran down a couple of corridors and then slipped into a side nook and readjusted the position of the knife she had tucked into the waistband of her shorts. It had nicked her skin and drawn blood, but she ignored that. The knife had a six-inch blade. Would that be long enough?

Alison had never outwardly shown any tendency toward violence, but she had always told herself she would kill Alexander G. Mongold if she ever had the chance. It was the first thing she had said after her mother died. When she heard he had drowned in the Cumberland River, she had been disappointed at the thought that she would never have the opportunity to say, "My name is Alison Leverett. You promised me air that my mother could breathe. You killed us all. Prepare to die." She would never have the chance to swear at him, spit in his face, and then pull a small knife out of her pocket and sink it into his heart. It had to be a knife, because a knife was slower and more personal.

Alexander G. Mongold was alive, and she knew exactly where he was. He had been hovering over her for a decade, waiting all this time to deliver one more blow, to make one more promise he wouldn't keep. For one night she thought she might get what she wanted more than anything else in the world, something Mongold had taken away from her. Then she found out that it was all another big lie. Lemuel would go just as wrong as Panacea. That baby and the other KRILL could all die after a few months or turn into something monstrous.

She could kill him, she was sure of it, because that year she had been lost had deposited a hard little nut at her center, and everything she needed to kill was inside its shell. It was her duty to kill Mongold and keep him from pulling another cruel joke on the world. As far as she knew, she was one of only three people who knew who Bextrand really was, and the other two weren't going to do it. She owed it to her mother and every other human being on the planet. Alison believed in justice, not that she had seen much of it in her lifetime, but she still believed in it.

She went back to her bunk to arrange a better way to conceal the knife, which was once again biting into her skin. She would wear a windbreaker. She had one with a pocket inside. All she had to do was cut a hole at the bottom of the pocket and slip the blade through. The handle would hold it in place. If she stood straight, the point wouldn't nick her. All she had to do was zip the hoodie halfway up, and the knife would be accessible, but not visible.

Now she just had to get an audience with Bextrand.

CHAPTER TWENTY-FIVE

The Spark

The main newspaper of New Hope had folded, and many of the people Ana needed to reach didn't own computers. She chose an older method to get her story out–broadsheets disseminated by a coalition of anti-government groups. The story was what they had been waiting for, a spark. They translated it into a half dozen languages and on the morning of September 2, the broadsheets landed in distribution points all over New Hope and other major U.S. cities. Stacks of the papers appeared in stores, on street corners, and in the lobbies of apartment buildings. From there, the story spread like fire.

The Secret Service army that had protected the New White House had already begun to shrink. Men and women who had taken a solemn oath disappeared. It was not because they weren't getting paid—their salaries would be the last thing to be cut—but because they sensed a change in the atmosphere. It was eerie guarding that strange, mirrored house, that lonely circle of emptiness in the seething city. The Secret Service guards could feel the hatred directed toward LaFarge like a current that passed from the people, through their own bodies, to the president.

Drew was beginning to wonder if there was anything to protect inside that glittering mansion. LaFarge had made no public appearances in months. The motorcades that periodically emerged from the executive adit likely were decoys. Drew had no love for this president but was not one to abandon his duties or his oath. He was too much his father's son for that.

On the morning of the second, Drew was getting off the night shift when his supervisor begged him to stay for the daylight hours. "We are dangerously short-handed. I don't care if you sleep on your feet. We just need more of a show of force. I'll try to get some reinforcements from the Capital Police. We won't have trouble today. There are no planned demonstrations and it's going to be too damned hot for people to hit the streets."

Neither the supervisor nor Drew knew about the broadsheets yet. No one connected with any sort of authority was included on the distribution.

Even without knowing about Ana's story, Drew felt something off in the city. He disagreed with the idea that heat would keep people home. Most of the city's population didn't have cool homes to crawl into. The power grid had been down for a month due to a combination of sabotage and poor maintenance. The smog was so bad that solar panels were useless. The masses would be hot and angry. Bostock had taught Drew to read the signs of bad weather brewing. Certain prerequisites had to be present for a storm: moisture from the Gulf of Mexico, atmospheric instability, a trigger like a collision of air masses. Drew had taught himself to read the signs of coming unrest in the same way. He felt the tension in the Capital rising under the press of heat from above, and he watched for the trigger.

The sun burned through a yellow haze and rose into the dingy sky. The mirrored White House was to Drew's back. If he turned to look at it, he would see his own face staring out of a blinding sulphur glare. The lawn had been closed to public picnics for years. Water was scarce, so maintenance staff no longer used sprinklers to keep the grass green. The blank brown hillside stretched in front of him, dropping seventy feet to an iron fence built atop a two-foot stone wall. Beyond that was the Executive Ring, the huge roundabout that circled the lawn. Six avenues formed the "spoke streets" that radiated out from the ring before meandering through the city's hills and along the river. New Penn Ave. was directly in front of Drew.

Drew watched workmen preparing to install a new section of fence that had been knocked down by a suicide bomber in a panel truck full of explosives the day before. Miraculously, the truck had not exploded. Once upon a time, that truck would have been big news in the Capital whether it exploded or not. But two other bombs had gone off yesterday, one in a post office and one at the gate of the Vice-Presidential Mansion.

Drew saw the workers remove the damaged section of fence, unpack the new one and set it into place. Then they leaned it against the old fence and sat down under the shade of a tree. One Secret Service agent, a relatively inexperienced man named Harper, guarded the gap in the fence. Drew radioed in to his boss. "What's going on with the fence? They've stopped working." A minute later, the boss called back with the explanation. "The bolts are the wrong size. They're waiting for new ones."

"We need more than one guard on that gap. Do you want me to go?"

"I've already sent Wilson. He's closer."

Drew watched Wilson move from his post along the south fence to the gap. Gone were the days when Secret Service agents wore suits and guns hidden in harnesses under jackets. They were as heavily armed as combat troops now. Still, two guards seemed thin protection. He scanned the traffic on the Executive Ring for any sign of drivers behaving erratically and then his eyes followed New Penn Ave. due east past Capital Police Headquarters, through the Financial District, then out into the squatters' shacks that rippled in the waves of heat. Hidden beneath the road was a tunnel that provided a direct link to police headquarters.

The forecast high for the day was 106 degrees. People were dying out there in the shacks. One could almost imagine the souls rising in the rippled air. They were dying in parks. Dying in basements. The current heat wave had already taken nearly three hundred people in New Hope alone.

Grief. Anger. Heat. Humidity.

Drew monitored his body's reactions. Lack of sleep rendered him more vulnerable to the heat. When his heart rate quickened and his head began to swim, he called for a temporary to take his post, went into one of the cooling huts, and gulped down electrolytes. Then it was back out into the oven. Those breaks were all that stood between him and heat stroke. Millions in the city had no relief.

The new bolts arrived at ten thirty. The workmen moved the new section of fence back into place. They were preparing to secure it when Drew caught a flash of dancing color along the fence to the south. It was about three dozen Calaveras, children who dressed in gaudy Day of the Dead skeleton make-up. They moved in packs committing minor vandalism in the Capital and other cities. They were rowdy but relatively harmless. Given the world they had inherited, Drew considered their rebellion remarkably restrained. He radioed down to Wilson. "Calaveras coming from Ohio Ave. Tell Harper to stay cool. They're just kids."

The Calaveras spotted the work on the fence and started toward it at a run, emitting the eerie whoops and shrieks they were known for. The workmen panicked and started running up the hill.

"Kids," Drew repeated. "Unarmed kids. Don't fire." He started down the hill at a fast trot.

The Calaveras reached the fence. "*Danos ofrendas*," they yelled and grabbed the iron bars. The new section, held only by a couple of partly screwed in bolts, rattled.

"Come on, kids," Wilson shouted. "You need to disperse now."

"But we don't feel like dispersing," one of the Calaveras yelled back.

"Get back or I'll shoot," Harper screamed.

This prompted taunts and obscenities in both English and Spanish. The Calaveras shook the fence and it gave way. They whooped in triumph and pushed into the breach. Wilson fired into the air, but it had no impact on the frenzied pack. Harper panicked. A hideous glow-green skull advanced on him. He raised his weapon and fired directly into it.

Drew arrived in time to see the figure collapse and hear the mannered whooping turn into the screams of frightened children. He radioed for an ambulance and backup. Meanwhile, Calaveras were screaming for their own backup from the surrounding streets.

Harper seemed frozen in place with gun still raised. Drew came up behind him. "Get out of here," he ordered.

A drawn-out, tortured word rose in the screams: Alma. A small figure pushed in from the back of the crowd and threw herself down beside the corpse. "Alma!" she cried, trying to shake the body to life despite the gaping exit wound in the back of the head. She looked up at Harper and said, "She was my sister."

Sirens sounded, and more Secret Service agents came running down the hill. Drivers stuck in traffic in the Executive Ring abandoned their cars.

Harper was still frozen.

"Get out of here!" Drew yelled into his ear.

Another shot fired. At first Drew thought that Harper had killed another protester, but the bang wasn't loud enough. Somebody had a small-caliber weapon. Harper doubled over and collapsed, alive but bleeding profusely from a wound in the stomach.

Drew fired at feet to back the crowd up, while Wilson brought down the shooter with two rounds. The Calaveras retreated into the Executive Ring, hiding behind empty cars. Drew radioed to his supervisor. "We need to park a big truck in front of this gap until we can get it closed. The biggest vehicle you've got."

"The SWAT truck is in the tunnel. It will be there in less than two minutes."

"I don't want SWAT. They lost one of their own last week. They'll be out for blood. They'll blow the situation out of control."

"It's already out of control. And the SWAT truck just left the service adit." Drew looked toward the north and saw it bumping over the lawn at the base of the hill.

"How's Harper?" his boss asked.

"Wounded but alive. Losing blood fast."

"The ambulance is leaving the service adit now. You and Wilson load him in and come back with him. If you try to run back up the hill, you'll be easy targets. Who knows how many guns are out there."

After exiting the ambulance in the service area, Drew and Wilson rode the elevator to the top of the hill. They were unaware that it was the only elevator that went all the way to the top. The Secret Service operations center was located just under the skin of the hill, to the side of the residence. It had its own adit, disguised by an arbor covered by a Lady Banks rose. Unlike the grass, the rose was kept watered. It was coming to the end of a profuse blooming season. When they brushed against it, it rained yellow petals onto their bloody uniforms. Drew had no time to consider how odd he looked. He saw something coming down New Penn Ave.

"Wilson, look." Drew pointed.

"Jesus," Wilson said. "The whole city is emptying into the streets. Ohio Ave., too."

Voices soon came across the radio to say that crowds were converging from every one of the spoke streets.

"What idiot decided to put the New White House at the center of a bullseye?" Wilson said. "Listen to it. Doesn't that make your blood run cold?"

The crowds were mimicking the weird, rhythmic calls of the Calaveras. The sound seemed to pulse in the heat waves, growing louder as the crowd neared. The first people were pouring into the Executive Ring now. Someone torched an abandoned government car to wild approval.

The SWAT team had taken up positions behind the low stone wall at the base of the fence.

Don't start shooting, Drew thought. *If you start shooting, this city will explode.*

A Molotov cocktail hit the sidewalk near the SWAT truck and exploded with a crack and a sheet of flame. That was the signal for a hundred more projectiles to arc through the air. Not Molotov cocktails this time, but grenades. The area around the fence erupted in billowing gray clouds of dust.

"Shit, this was planned," Drew said.

The sound of the explosions and the screams of the wounded were lost in the roar of the crowd. A survivor opened fire and was answered by fire from the buildings surrounding the Executive Ring.

They heard a low boom, and a section of New Penn Ave. buckled and collapsed into the ground. Someone had blown the tunnel to Capital Police Headquarters.

Drew and Wilson dropped to the ground and began to fire as the crowd rushed the hill. Bullets hit the wall behind them, spraying them with shards of mirrored glass.

"Let's get inside. We run through the broken window on three," Wilson said.

"Wait," Drew said. He was looking over his shoulder. "There is no inside."

Behind them, where bullets should have opened a path into the NWH, was a blank concrete wall covered with an intricate web of wires.

Drew turned back to see a grenade rolling toward his face like some child's stray ball. *What am I dying for? Alison, will you*

...

CHAPTER TWENTY-SIX

Before the Broil

Thanks to the total chaos, the news from New Hope didn't reach the Ayn right away. Bostock had one more night of believing he still had a son. He spent that night with Campbell, who had given up on shutting him out. They were about to turn the light out when she rolled over to look Bostock full in the face.

"With Doomsday coming, I'm starting to wish I believed in God," she said.

Bostock knew better than to take this declaration at face value.

"Do you know why I hope there's a God?" she asked. A sudden spark of wild energy in her face announced that this was likely to be a naked riff.

"Um?" he said.

"Because I want to be there when he or she or it conducts the 'lessons learned' session to end all lessons learned sessions. I want to see God stand before the big whiteboard in the sky and yell, 'Listen up, people. Settle in, because this is going to take a long time.'"

Campbell jumped up and launched into performance art. "See the columns I've drawn on this board? On one side we have successes and on the other, failures." She pretended to write on a board. "First, I'll talk about the successes. There are none. Once you homo sapiens developed your big fat brains, you fucked up every last good thing you ever did. Now, the failures.

"Who here is from the UK? Can I see a show of hands? Where is that clever Scot, James Watt?'" Campbell pretended to locate an invisible man in an invisible audience. She pointed. "There he is, folks, inventor of the first efficient coal-powered steam engine. Got the Brits hooked on fossil fuels, and then they conquered a lot of people who were minding their own business and got them all to take the carbon out of the ground, where I put it, and put it up in the air, where it's not supposed to go, which is why we are having this post-Apocalypse wrap up somewhat earlier than planned.

"Americans, raise your hands. You believed in the pursuit of money over all other things, thus ending life and liberty. Where are the Koch brothers? Aha, I see you over there trying to avoid me. Just leave now. Out. I'll speak to you privately later.

"Russians, you created Socialist Realist art to tout your big industrial leap forward. The industries produced crap, the art sucked, and you fucked up a freaking enormous expanse of mother Earth.

"Farmers, your cows farted methane.

"Now, you hunter gatherers, don't think I'm going to let you off the hook just because you didn't have the carbon habit. Before you came along, I put some amazing animals on Earth. Wooly mammoths? They were elephants with shag haircuts.

How cool is that? Did you have to kill every blasted one of them? How many wooly mammoths can one tribe eat? They weren't fucking potato chips. And you killed my giant lemurs, sloths, and kangaroos. Kangaroos the size of cars. If you had just tamed them, instead of killing them, mankind wouldn't have had to build amusement parks for the kiddies. Just put 'em in a pouch and let 'em ride until they puked."

Campbell abruptly stopped. Her shoulders slumped and her face grew slack. The frenetic riff was over. She lay down next to Bostock and pressed her face into his shoulder. He put his arm around her.

"Surely the human race has accomplished great things," Bostock said.

"No," Campbell said. "I used to think that, but now I see it as human propaganda. The human race made a fucking religion of itself and in the process, degraded and destroyed—how does that old song go?—all things bright and beautiful all creatures great and small." After a few moments of silence, she said, "The whiteboard was too much, wasn't it? Do you think I've been a bureaucrat too long?"

"Quite possibly," he said.

Bostock and Campbell were still naked the next morning when someone knocked on the door. "I'll be with you in a minute," Bostock called. He grabbed his pants.

"Bextrand wants to see you now." The voice was Duff's. He yelled through the door. "It's urgent."

"I'm coming," Bostock replied. "Give me two minutes. You can go. I'll be up there shortly."

When he opened the door, Duff had gone back to his post, and Alison stood in his place. "I heard that you're going to meet with Bextrand. I'm coming with you," she said.

"No," Bostock said. He pushed past her and headed down the hallway at a fast clip, but Alison was right behind him. "Duff will never let you in."

"Yes he will. Nobody says no to me on the Ayn."

"Surely you haven't charmed that cold slab of meat?"

"I have a superpower," Alison said. "Generally, I am too proud to use it, but it's there."

"Fine, we'll see how far you get."

⊞

Duff broke into a grin when he spotted Alison. She returned the smile with an animation and sparkle in her eye that Bostock had rarely seen. "Hello, Uncle Charlie."

Before this, Bostock wasn't even sure that Duff could blink. Now the man squirmed like a happy puppy.

"I'm going along with Bostock to see Bextrand," Alison said. "You don't mind, do you?"

Duff frowned and said gently, "Now, Sweetie, you know I can't let you do that if you're not on my list."

"Please, Uncle Charlie. Just ask. Tell him I want to volunteer for Project Lemuel."

"Why would you want to do that?" Duff said.

"Just ask, please."

"Okay, I have to step in here to talk to him. It's a rule." Duff squeezed himself into the tube, and the door shut.

"I thought you weren't going to be involved with anything connected to Bextrand," Bostock said.

"I have to talk to him," Alison said.

"What are you up to? Who are you? I thought you were this shy little—"

"Shy people can fake it," she said.

Duff came out looking sheepish. "I'm sorry, but he says no."

"Oh, thank you so much!" Alison gave Duff a peck on the cheek and was in the tube and up the ladder in a flash.

Duff was stunned into inaction.

"I'll handle it," Bostock said, and followed her up the ladder.

"Bostock here," Alison said in a fair imitation of his voice, or at least enough to pass for it over a speaker. Then she climbed up into the room with Bostock right behind.

Bextrand stopped pacing and backed into the glass wall. He held out his hands to ward her off. "Women aren't allowed to come in here. Especially tiny, angry women. I won't have it. Go!"

For a moment, Alison seemed disoriented to be trapped in this spare, strange bubble in an angry sky with clouds racing all around. She swayed on her feet. Then she steadied herself and advanced on Bextrand. "Do you recognize me?" she said. "It's been a long time. It was Great Hope Pavilion, 2043, and I was sitting in the front row with my mother. You took my drawing of the clouds and sky and held it up to the cameras and promised us air my mother could breathe."

Bextrand's legs failed. He slid down the glass until he was sitting on the floor. He took off his glasses, and Alison let out a gasp at the sight of the scarred face. "I remember," Bextrand said. "I'm sorry. I know that an apology is hopelessly inadequate. But it's sincere."

"How can you be the same person?" Alison asked.

"I am and I'm not. We've both had a hard time since then. I'm trying to put it right."

Alison advanced another step on Bextrand. "You're trying to fool us all again. Make a big promise and then pull the rug out from under us. I was ready to walk into one of your damn machines."

"You should. You must," Bextrand said. "Soon. Today."

"How can you possibly think that I could ever trust you?"

The sound of a helo interrupted the conversation. Bostock turned to see a heavy-lift helicopter approaching from the south and struggling in the wind. A Lemuel Unit swung below. "What the hell does he think he's doing? He's going to tear up the LU and the deck. I thought you and Mason had decided that no LUs would come aboard the Ayn. "

"The situation has suddenly changed," Bextrand said. He pulled himself up to a standing position. "I got a communication through my emergency network. With a nervous glance at Alison, he moved to where he had a better view of the helo.

The wind had picked up and big drops of rain began to pelt the bubble. Only those involved in the drop were up on deck.

"Why is he putting it down in this weather?" Bostock asked.

"Because there's no time to wait," Bextrand said. "That's why I called you up here. The news just came in over my emergency channel. Two hours ago terrorists blew up Panacea. Everything is gone, the people, the equipment. The India system has been down for a month. I had them move an LU from one of the destroyers to give the people on the Ayn a choice."

Bostock felt something leaden fall through his body. "How long have we got?"

"I don't know," Bextrand said. "Days? Hours? We can still save anybody near an LU. I put out the order for them to run the units day and night for as long as they can. We can save the people on the Ayn if that pilot can put the machine down safely."

"I assume you'll be saving yourself, as well," Bostock said.

"No, you both will be happy to know that I am electing to remove myself from the stage before the next act. I have a contingency system in place for the end. If I wasn't such a coward, I would stick around for the Broil. It would be an appropriate punishment for me, wouldn't it? But I am a coward." A sad, distorted smile crossed Bextrand's ruined face. "Sometimes, during storms, I piss myself."

The motion of the helo banking away from the Ayn drew their eyes outside. The pilot came around again to make another attempt to bring clumsy moving objects together gently. "He's damn good," Bostock said, "but I don't know." Then another movement caught his eye. His reflexes were fast. He lunged and grabbed Alison's arm, and the knife clattered to the floor.

"I think I just wet myself again," Bextrand said. He looked at Alison, struggling in Bostock's grasp. "It's all right," he said. "I understand. You would have been doing me a favor, really." His voice was kind with no trace of the stiff self-consciousness that had always annoyed Bostock.

Alison quit struggling, and Bostock felt the tension drain from her body. He let her go, and leaned over to retrieve the knife. She took a step toward Bextrand, and Bostock grabbed her arm again.

"It's all right,"Alison said. "I'm not going to try to kill him; I just have a few questions. I need honest answers. Can you give me honest answers?" she asked Bextrand. "Are you capable of that?"

"Yes," he said. "Alexander G. Mongold was not, but I am."

"I'm pregnant," Alison said. "If I go into one of those machines, does my baby have a chance? Is there something you're not telling us? Some nasty surprise like Panacea?"

"Did you see the baby?" Bextrand's face softened into something less frightening. "We had a beautiful, miraculous baby. You could, too. I can't guarantee you anything, because we haven't had years for testing, but I can say that I don't know of any nasty surprises. With Panacea, I was so full of myself that I ignored warnings. This time, I acknowledge that there is a lot of uncertainty. I can't give you any guarantees. The only thing I am certain of is that we don't have much time. I want you to live, Alison. I want your baby to live. Please believe I am sincere in that."

A loud scraping sound drew them to the windows again. The LU had come down roughly on the deck. The cargo hook was released, and the helo swung away from the Ayn.

"I'd better go down and see what condition it's in," Bostock said.

"Wait," Bextrand said. "There's something else." An awkward look came over his face. "I don't really know how to say this. I don't know how to deal with ..." He stopped and stared down at his hands, turning them this way and that. "You might say I'm out of practice at being human. I have to give you bad news. It came in along with the other news. The captain is probably seeing it now, so I should tell you before you go down. I don't want to be the one to tell you, but there we have it. There's been a coup in New Hope. A mob stormed the White House. I know you have a son who works there."

Bostock's knees almost gave way. Alison made a soft, choking noise.

"I'm sorry." Bextrand's face registered panic at the raw emotion he saw before him. "I, um, none of the Secret Service survived. You have my deepest sympathy, condolences, thoughts, prayers if you believe in that sort of thing, all of that." Bextrand's voice trailed off.

⊞

Bostock and Alison felt their way down from the bubble on legs that struggled with the reality of the ladder. The captain's assistant waited in the spot where Duff usually stood. He spoke to them in a voice that was devastatingly kind. "The captain needs to see you both right away."

Bostock saw Alison sway and put his arm around her. Thus they made their way to the captain's quarters with blood rushing in their ears, and their surroundings floating and indistinct.

Mason stood stiff and formal in the center of the room, dressed in his best uniform. Campbell was off to the side, her face pale and opaque.

Mason saw their faces and said, "You already know?"

"Is it certain?" Bostock said.

"Drew died at his post," Mason said. "He was a hero." He stepped forward and threw his arms around Bostock and Alison. Campbell joined them. She pressed her face into Bostock's neck and stroked Alison's hair.

Bostock wanted to scream at the word "hero." He didn't want his son to be a hero; he wanted him alive. What did it mean to be a hero when there would be no one to remember the sacrifice? He wanted to yell and curse, but he felt a vibration that stopped him. A vibration and a keening emerging from the slight figure in the middle of their huddle.

The inhuman sound that came from Alison set up a tremor that seemed to shake the whole ship. Certainly it would at the very least tear apart her body.

"Alison," Campbell said, "your baby. Don't do this to your baby."

The sound abruptly stopped, and Alison said, quite calmly, "You're right." She pulled away from the group. "I'm going into the Lemuel Unit. There won't be any more discussion of that. I want to be alone now." She left the room.

"Is there still a U.S. Government?" Campbell asked.

Mason shook his head. "I don't know. LaFarge is dead. He was trying to escape through the tunnel under New Penn Ave. when they bombed it. They think it was someone inside the Capital Police who planted the bomb. I got the news from a friend holed up in the Pentagon. It's the only building in New Hope still under control of the government. The rest of the city is burning. Even they weren't entirely sure of what was happening elsewhere. The transmission broke off and I couldn't get them back on the line."

"So we're cut off."

"Yes. But that's not all. Moscow is taking advantage. Two of the other government carriers have been captured by Russian destroyers. They're headed for us."

<hr />

Wind and chatter thrummed in the old steel of the Ayn. The weather had deteriorated so quickly that they barely had time to lower the LU into the hangar deck before the winds began to shear off the temporary structures from the flight deck.

News of the fall of New Hope and the arrival of the LU raced through the carrier. There was no getting ahead of it now, but Captain Mason called the top managers into his office to let them know what was up so they could inform their people in whatever way they saw fit. They filled the leather couches, squatted on the floor, and stood around the edge of the room. Meanwhile, everyone on board knew that a meeting was taking place.

Mason held up his hand to forestall questions as he entered. He didn't take a seat. "I'm not going to sugarcoat this. We've all known what was coming for years. Panacea has been blown up. We don't know how quickly things will heat up. It doesn't matter. New Hope is in chaos. The U.S. Government isn't functioning. Russian destroyers are on their way here. They've captured two other carriers and they're coming for us.

"So what are your options? First, you can do nothing. The 'do nothing' option is as fatal now as it has always been. You can expect interrogation and probably execution by the Russians. Even if they for some reason don't come, the deck of the Ayn will heat up like a griddle and be unlivable sooner rather than later. Second, you can choose to take one of the red pills. The infirmary will have them ready. I've ordered the deck-edge safety nets removed if you would like to bury yourselves at sea.

"Third, you can walk into the Lemuel Unit. This option is only open to those with no medical implants of any type. Nonorganic material does not miniaturize. Undergoing the process with an implant would lead to your death and probably that of other people around you. Obviously, there are no guarantees for those who go into the unit. The survival rate goes down after the age of sixty. And none of you will survive unless we can successfully get you moved to shore in Greenland. When the weather lifts, we have a volunteer to fly the boxes to the military base at Nuuk.

"I leave it to every man and woman aboard to make his or her own decision. I already see you starting to argue and grumble. Stop it. No one will survive if we can't pull together right now. The one thing I want you to make clear when you brief your people is that I'm not going to tolerate any squabbling. I'm ordering Security to toss anybody who breaks this rule overboard. This is not a joke. None of this is a goddamn joke."

Campbell didn't like silly drama, so she had long ago culled from her unit any analysts who showed tendencies toward panic, temper tantrums, and displays of pique. She also got rid of those with whiny voices. Those still with Campbell had no family off ship. They had been together for a long time and had nothing to hide from each other or prove to each other. The discussion regarding options for the end of humanity was calm and lacking in hand wringing or self-pity.

They pulled their chairs into the space between cubicles. For the occasion, Campbell made a rare pot of coffee. The bean had grown far too expensive for regular consumption, but now there was no reason not to enjoy what was left of their precious stash. All eyes followed the pot as Campbell filled each cup with the solemnity of a teishu at a tea ceremony. The Ayn had begun to yaw in monster waves, but Campbell didn't spill a drop. When all cups were full, she proposed a toast. "To Russian Roulette with all the chambers filled."

No other cups were raised.

"Really," Brian said, "that's your toast?"

"You have something better?" Campbell asked.

He thought a second and then said, "To our tiny little futures."

Everyone took a sip except Alison. She merely touched the cup to her lips and then set it down on her desk. Moans of pleasure went round the circle.

"Oh, God this is good. Now I can die happy," Maeve said.

"Are you opting for suicide?" Brian asked her.

"No, I'm going to walk into the LU. Survival rates are low for old people, but I'll take a shot at it, anyway. I know a few hours ago we were all against it, but now that the apocalypse is written on our calendars in ink and not pencil, things look different. I would like to see what the world looks like from the mite's eye view. That would be completely new, and it has been a long time since I've experienced something completely new."

"I guess I'm going in, too," Brian said. "I don't want to die like a strip of bacon frying on the deck."

"You could stay below and die like a potato baking in the oven," Bella said. "There are options. Alison, what are you planning to do? And why aren't you drinking your coffee?"

"I'm pregnant," Alison said. "My baby and I are going into the LU."

"I assume that Drew knocked you up?"

"Irrelevant," Alison said.

"Highly relevant," Bella said. "Part of him has taken up residence in your nether regions, where it has joined forces with part of you and will grow until it's too big to get out. Then it will come out anyway."

Alison broke in. "Don't you have anything better to do on what may be your last day on Earth than gossip?"

"No, actually," Bella said. "Most human activity is pointless now. I could cry and hug everyone and tell you all how much I love you, but, eww. If you're not going to drink that coffee, Alison, do you mind?"

Alison handed Bella her coffee.

"Double-fisted coffee drinking is just the thing for the end of times," Bella said. She quickly sipped down Alison's full cup to lessen the danger of spillage.

"So you're going into the LU, Bella?" Brian asked.

"Yes, I suppose I will. After decades of being size 16, I might as well try out size negative five hundred."

"Actually, we'll all be totally naked," Maeve said. "You will have the privilege of viewing all of Bella's tats."

"I apologize in advance," Bella said. "My youthful tattoo humor didn't age as well as I thought it would."

"Don't forget to take out all of your piercings," Maeve said. "You'd better start early. It could take hours."

Brian turned toward Campbell. She had gone still and didn't even seem to be following the conversation, but now all eyes were on her.

Campbell looked up and said in a cheerful voice, "Pills and booze. It's something of a family tradition."

"But you have to come with us," Brian said. "We need you."

"You've been my deputy for decades; don't you think it's time to step up?" Campbell asked. "I hereby put you in charge of taking care of all our people going into the LU, especially Alison and her baby. I recommend going to the library and reading up on childbirth. In fact, I want all of you to do that. Consider it my farewell assignment to you. Now, I need some alone time." Campbell got up and headed down the stairs of the Block.

▫

Alison had no second thoughts as she watched technicians preparing the Lemuel Unit. She had looked into Bextrand's eyes and made her decision to trust him despite everything. Once the decision was made, an odd peace came over her. Or, rather, it came from within. A message of comfort from her baby, she thought, a message telling her that she was doing the right thing for both of them. She mentally enclosed herself in a tunnel and focused all of her energy on trying to hear that tiny voice and see that tiny light at the other end. Everything else was death and grief. If she let herself be distracted, if she looked to any side, she risked being swept away. Epi shared this safe space. The dog stayed by her side, leaning her body slightly against Alison's leg.

The first group, fifty people, lined up next to the LU. They wore only the sheets from their bunks. The sound of wind roaring across the deck above made it difficult to be heard.

"This is like dying," Bella whispered; "you have no idea what's on the other side." She stomped her feet and drew her sheet closer about her.

"I thought Campbell would be here to say goodbye," Brian said. He had his eye on the door.

"If you think she would show up for teary farewells, then you don't know her very well after all these years," Maeve said. "She said her goodbyes when she served the coffee. She looked into each of our faces and touched our hands as she handed us the cups. Didn't you notice?"

"That was goodbye?" Brian said in obvious distress.

"That was goodbye," Maeve said.

"I wish someone had told me."

Maeve reached out and gave Brian a hard pinch on the cheek. "In case everything doesn't go well, this is goodbye."

Captain Mason was there to say his farewells. He knew the name of everyone aboard the Ayn and dispensed handshakes to some, hugs to others. He saved Alison for last. He wrapped his arms around her and kissed the top of her head.

"You take care of that baby," Mason whispered into her hair.

"We'll both take care of it," Alison said. "I'll see you soon. You'll be in the last group, right?"

"Whatever happens, I'll be there for you when you need me," he said. "Just close your eyes." Then he stood back and spoke to the whole group. "I'll respect your privacy and go now. Please, everyone who is not going into the unit come with me. To the rest of you, I wish you fair winds and following seas, my dear, dear friends." The captain turned away and quickly herded the other visitors out the door.

The LU techs had come with the unit. They had been inside, lying on the floor, when the helo set it down on the deck. They had worked for hours getting the unit ready to go. One of them held up his hands. "Listen closely. Once again, if you have any sort of implant you must not go into the unit. You should have already had any pre-2025 fillings removed by the dentist. Bio-fillings are safe. I want you to check one more time for jewelry or anything else nonorganic on your person. Now, I want you to form a single line. First, Liam over here will wipe your feet. We have to keep the floor of the unit as clean as possible. Then I will take your sheet right before you go in. It's no time for modesty. No one cares about your cellulite right now. Once you're inside, move to the back. It will be crowded, but not for long."

There was hesitation. No one wanted to be the first to go into the LU. Then Alison stepped forward with Epi. When the tech started to protest, Alison said, "Don't say it. She goes with me. You don't want a scene, do you?"

"How dirty are her feet?" Liam asked.

"Cleaner than yours," Alison said. She bent and lifted each of Epi's feet, and the frowning tech wiped them off. She wiped her own feet, slipped off her sheet, handed it to Liam with an air of unconcern, and went in with Epi on her heels.

Another pause. "What the hell, maybe I should break the tension," Bella said. She stepped forward, handed her sheet to the tech, and bent so that everyone could get a clear look at the tattoo on her behind. It said, "If you can read this, your standards are too low."

Everyone laughed, and now the line moved faster.

When they were all inside the LU, no one said anything. They tried to avoid touching each other's naked bodies. The light went off. First they heard a high whirring, then a metallic banging that made them cover their ears. Then the sound moved their bones such that arms and legs jerked involuntarily. Some people fell to the floor.

Alison felt the cells of her body separate and fly away. She tried to call to her baby, to comfort it, but she couldn't find her voice.

No one had warned them about the pain. Maybe the techs didn't even know about it, because the subjects couldn't scream. The pain was cold and it burned and it sang through every cell of their bodies and negated everything it touched. They lost consciousness for a few seconds.

When she opened her eyes, Alison was lying alone on a surface that bore no resemblance to the clean, smooth floor of the LU. It was uneven and pitted. A furred creature was beside her, whining and shaking.

Alison struggled to stand and was immediately hit by a warm wind that swept her off her feet and into a gauzy sort of tunnel. The others appeared as if coming from a great distance, and they all tumbled together into the tunnel, which fed them into a large room, or, rather, a small KRILL box, just like the one Bostock had carried. She lay dazed, but no longer in pain. Everything was white, nothing but white, both inside and out. Her body felt stiff. If she had remembered anything, she might have compared it to a new pair of shoes, yet to be broken in, but she did not remember shoes.

Captain Mason had borrowed the magnifier from Bostock. He went down to a room where KRILL boxes now covered the floor. He moved slowly among them, searching for one he had marked with a slash of ink. He found it at the back of the room.

Mason gently removed the lid of the box, regretting all the while any disturbance he might be causing and hoping there would be no fear. Alison would have told them about his visit, if she could speak, if she was still Alison.

Mason put the magnifier to his eye. It took a minute to adjust it, and even then the image was hazy to his weak eyes. He felt like a sick old man looking down at his naked shipmates. He had wakened some, but others slept right through the removal of the box lid. They must be exhausted. It was difficult to recognize anyone. Would he even be able to tell which one was Alison?

Then he saw her. Epi was curled next to her. *How well can she see me?* he thought. *Am I a blur?*

"I love you," Mason said softly. He didn't know how her ears would perceive the sound.

Alison awakened and looked up at him, twisting her head as if confused. She didn't seem frightened, but she didn't wave or try to communicate in any way.

Mason looked at her a few moments, then replaced the lid to give them their privacy. He mouthed the word "goodbye."

He had misled Alison. He wouldn't be in the last group to go into the LU. Mason had a pacemaker, which had been implanted when Alison was thirteen or fourteen. He hadn't told anyone on the ship about it then or since. He had explained his time off-ship as a training course.

He hadn't exactly lied to Alison. He had told her that he would be with her and he intended to be. He believed in guardian angels. More than once he had felt the presence of his own mother after she had passed, always in difficult times. He felt sure he could do that for Alison.

Mason settled down in a corner and sat with the box in his lap for the rest of the night.

◻

Bostock and Campbell had worn themselves thin with arguing. She still refused to go into the LU. Already several hundred of the inhabitants of the Ayn had submitted themselves to the miniaturization process, which was continuing through the night.

Campbell lay in Bostock's arms. Apropos of nothing, she said, "If I hadn't forgiven him years ago, I would have self-immolated."

Bostock knew she was talking about her father, something she rarely did.

"Lately, I almost understand him, which is something I thought would never happen. It's frightening. Or rather it was frightening. Now it doesn't matter."

She paused for a long time. Bostock took hold of her hand, but said nothing, afraid if he said the wrong thing, she wouldn't tell him what was on her mind. It was the thing that was keeping her out of the LU. He was sure of it.

"We called it the Leskov problem," Campbell said. "Leskov was my paternal grandmother's maiden name. She came over from the old country and never learned English. She lived for forty years in a little ranch house in Arlington surrounded by mementos from Russia and African violets. The whole place smelled like Tide detergent. She washed everything in it: her clothes, her dishes, even her body. I hated that smell. By the time I came along, she had shrunken into an angry, bitter little apple doll. When we visited, she would harangue us with long diatribes in Russian. Once she started hitting me with her cane because she thought I had stolen a Fabergé egg. I was five and she gave me a blow on the head that required seven stitches." Campbell reached up and pushed back her hair to reveal a pale scar above her ear. "See? My father had to pull her off. After that he didn't make me visit her anymore."

Bostock put his fingers to the scar, barely touching it, as if the wound were still fresh.

"When I was sixteen," Campbell said, "my father told me, 'Leskovs get strange, inert, and angry as they age. Your grandmother was a vibrant woman, a loving woman even, when she was young. Then she succumbed to the family gene. My uncle gave in before he was forty; my grandfather, even earlier. They sat with their heads in their hands and moaned and rotted. I fight it. You'll have to fight, too. That's why I make you do so many things and learn so many things. Those are resources you can draw on.'"

Campbell looked up at Bostock. "That monster loved me and he gave me monster genes. The murders came out of the Leskov gene. He couldn't fight it. Or maybe that was his way of fighting it. For years I hated him for his failure, and now every day I understand it better."

"You are not your father," Bostock said.

"Those times I dumped you? It was never you. You were perfect, almost too perfect. It was always because I didn't want you to spend your old age trapped with a zombie. When I took you back, it was because I thought this world wouldn't last long enough for the gene to get me. Also, when the depressions lift, I have this short period of feeling superhuman, but you probably know that already.

"You were right. I avoided going off the Ayn for fear of what I would see. It was cowardice. This ship doesn't smell like Tide, and there are no African violets, but it's just like my grandmother's little house. It's a hermit crab's shell. Some days I can barely get out of my bunk. I just stare and I know I'm freaking everyone out, but if I move, I'm afraid the anger will take over and it is so much stronger than I am. It's like I've got a tumor growing in my brain. It's been there all my life, but now it's taking over and eating up all the good cells."

"Maybe the tumor won't survive the miniaturization process. It will be like starting life all over again."

"I *do not* want to start life all over again," Campbell said. "It was hard enough the first time. I'm tired. That's the last thing I want. There is nothing you can say or do to make me change my mind on that."

"I won't go into the LU without you," Bostock said.

Campbell laughed. "That bit of leverage might have worked if I didn't know about that motorcycle accident you had when you were twenty-seven. You have two orthopedic implants. You had to fight like hell to stay in the Navy."

"How do you know that?" Bostock asked.

"I did a background check shortly after we got together."

"You told me you looked into my face the first time and trusted me completely."

"There's an old Russian saying, Доверяй, но проверяй, Trust but verify. Campbell leaned over and kissed Bostock. "Don't get too outraged; you just tried to mislead me, you know. Please, respect my decision and don't try to change my mind. I want to die while I'm still me, and by that I don't mean while I'm still five foot nine. I mean while I'm still Campbell and not some gray cloud of fucked-up brain chemistry. Also, I want to die with you. That is the best outcome I could ask for."

▣

Under the pressure of a hot air mass descending from above, the polar vortex parked over the North Pole weakened and began to break up. Its ragged edge encompassed the Ayn and the whole Baffin Bay, bringing high winds, a sharp drop in temperatures, and then swirling snow and whiteout conditions.

The Ayn's meteorologist shrugged when Bostock and Mason came once again to consult with him. "Like I told you, I have no idea when we'll see a break. Radar is down. All communications are down. Anything that can go down is down."

"Can you give us any clue when this storm will dissipate? Will we get enough of a calm to fly a helo to Nuuk?" Bostock asked.

"I don't know," the meteorologist said. "Like I told you before, there's no precedent for—"

"Come on, Kyle; there's no precedent for any goddamn thing that has happened this century," Mason said. "We have a superheated mass of air pressing down on a polar vortex. Make an educated guess."

"We've never had a warm air mass the size of this one, nor have we ever had one coming straight down on a polar vortex. Calm is the last thing I would forecast, at least at first," Kyle said. "Look, with all my equipment down, I'm as blind and ignorant as everyone else. I want to go into the LU tonight. I know I'll probably end up floating in a soggy box on the waves, but it's a shot."

"Fine," Mason said. He turned and left the room with Bostock right behind. They kept their arms out to avoid being thrown into the walls by the movement of the ship.

"We have to go talk to Bextrand," Mason said.

"Is he still up there?" Bostock asked.

"As far as I know. The phone connection went down."

"Well that bubble is the last place I want to go right now, but I see there's no choice."

Duff was sitting rather than standing in his usual spot. He clutched a trashcan full of vomit. Nevertheless, he struggled to his feet at the sight of Bostock and the Captain. "I'm sorry, sir," he stammered. "I tried to stay standing, but—"

"It's fine, Duff. You don't need to be here. No one is going to bother Bextrand. Go into the LU while you have the chance."

"No," Duff said, "I belong here."

"Let us in," Bostock said.

"I have to check with the boss."

"Just let us in," Mason said. "This is an emergency, and we don't have time for crap."

Duff keyed in the code and opened the door. Then he fell to his knees and commenced to vomit again.

"You go first," Mason said to Bostock. "I don't want to fall on you in case my hip gives out."

Bostock was up the ladder quickly. He yelled through the microphone and waited for a response, but it didn't come. He called down to Mason, who stood at the bottom of the tube looking up. "Tell Duff to pop the hatch. Bextrand isn't responding." Bostock couldn't hear the click over the roar of the storm, but when he pushed the hatch, it opened. He stuck his head into the space and saw Bextrand at eye level. The philosopher had strapped himself to his foam bed. His hood had slipped down to the pillow. He was staring up at the sky goggle-eyed and stiff with fear. Bostock wasn't sure he was even alive at first, but then Bextrand turned his head and yelled over the noise.

"Don't try to stand. Crawl."

The disposition of the philosopher's bubble high above the Ayn's center of mass meant that any rotational movement of the carrier was amplified, turning it into an amusement park ride for masochists. Bostock was not too proud to crawl. Indeed, he inched along the floor on his belly, not even trusting to get up on his knees.

With much moaning and groaning, Mason made it up the ladder. "You are a fucking lunatic, Bextrand," he yelled over the wind. "I've always known it, but I never had the opportunity to tell you before. You are a lunatic."

"You are not hurting my feelings," Bextrand said. "I'm aware of it."

Bostock crawled up next to Bextrand and grabbed hold of one of the straps just as the bubble gave a violent lurch that tried to send him backward. "Are you all right, Mason?" he called.

"'All right' is not a term that could be used to describe any human on Earth, but if your question is 'did I fall back down the ladder,' no." When the bubble lurched the other way, Mason took the opportunity to slide on his belly toward Bextrand's bed. He collided with Bostock and grabbed on to the strap.

"This is too intimate," Bextrand cried. "I think you touched me."

"Suck it up," Mason said. "I have to get those KRILL boxes safely off the Ayn. Tell me the best time to do it. Surely you ran models of what would happen if Panacea was turned off. What does it do to this storm? Will the wind die down?"

"I hesitate to make a prediction," Bextrand said. "That's where I went wrong before."

"You put the LU on the Ayn to save people's lives. Now those people are trapped in boxes, and I need to know when I can get them ashore," Mason yelled.

"My guess is that there will be a short period of intense precipitation, lightning, and wind. More intense than anything we've ever seen. Then the heat should burn it off and dissolve the cool air mass. Then there may be a short time before conditions become unlivable."

"Can you be more specific than 'short time'?" Bostock asked. "What did your models say?"

"My models said we would lower Earth's temperature by two degrees. So screw the models."

"Why do you stay up here?" Bostock asked.

"Atonement," Bextrand said. "It's ghastly and it will never be enough. And that is even more ghastly."

▣

Bostock and Mason made their way back down to the captain's office, where they collapsed onto the old leather couches and took a moment to breathe. "All we can do is wait out the storm, hope we don't catch a rogue wave, and send a helo up with the boxes as soon as the wind dies down."

"I've been talking to Harding," Bostock said. "She's the best pilot we've got and she's volunteered for the mission. There's another LU at the facility, so she can go into that."

⊞

The KRILL boxes were loaded onto the helo, which waited on the elevator at the hangar level for the first break in the weather. A minimal crew continued to man the ship, gamely doing their duty.

The sulphur dioxide particles began to dissipate, slowly at first, but rapidly accelerating as the heat stored above the stratosphere broke through.

Thunder was the first indication of the change on the Ayn. It rumbled and cracked in steel that had borne the landing of jets with less noise. The hot air burning through the cold set off waves of sheet lightning, followed by yellow bolts striking thick and fast. Bostock and Mason watched from vulture's row along with the helo pilot who had volunteered to go up with the boxes and her crew. They could taste the electricity and feel it raising the hair on their heads. They would not under any circumstances wait out such a spectacle below. They had to see it and feel the terror and the thrill. They were adrenaline junkies awaiting their greatest and probably last fix. Their eyes glittered as they watched the falling snow melt into rain. Water and slush poured off the flight deck, mixing with giant waves breaking over it.

⊞

Below, Luther was holding a party in the mess hall. After he had been shut out of the LU by an artificial hip, he had raided the freezers in the captain's galley. Now, fighting the movement of the ship, he served out the remaining delicacies. He kept a smile on his face as he set out his biggest stock pot and threw in containers of frozen juice concentrate. The guests poured in all the alcohol they had stashed away—vodka, gin, Scotch, Everclear, whatever they could get hold of. They drank toasts to as many current and former passengers of the Ayn as they could remember. Punch sloshed down shirts, into laps, and over the sticky floor. People sang and hugged. Whenever they began to grow weepy and lugubrious, Luther told a joke. They were bad jokes, but you didn't need good jokes when everyone was drunk.

"It's time to march with the saints!" Luther yelled. "Get them little red pills and let's go out singing, Hallelujah!"

They moved out of the cafeteria, into the corridors, and up the stairs. They fell over each other and picked each other up. When they reached the deck, they linked arms and sang "When the Saints Go Marching In" and walked toward the edge.

▪

Bostock put an arm around Mason as they watched a wave sweep the singers off the deck and into the sea. He felt a shudder go through his friend's body.

"I never wanted to be around for the end," Mason said.

The storm raged for another hour, and then the heat began to burn through. The overcast thinned and dissolved into a searing blue.

"Let's move!" Bostock yelled. The helo came up on the elevator, while pilot, crew, and ground personnel ran to meet it. They loaded the boxes and the helo rose into warming air.

Bostock watched for a few seconds; then something else caught his eye. The space above the Pri-Fly where the philosopher's bubble should have been was now a charred skeleton, evidently fried by the lightning.

Mason came up behind Bostock. "He had men up there last week making modifications. I think he had them rig it to attract the lightning."

＊

Bostock said goodbye to Mason, hugged him, and left him sitting at his desk with an album full of photos of Alison, a glass of water, and a bright red capsule. Now he stood behind Campbell with his arms around her. They were on the Ayn's elevator, thirty feet above Baffin Bay. The Russian destroyer was in sight, plowing through the seas toward them for no good reason.

"Why do they even bother?" Bostock said. "They'll be dead soon, too."

"It's like an elderly billionaire who continues to accumulate money he'll never spend," Campbell said. "They never found a bigger purpose, or maybe it's just something to do to pass the time."

Bostock and Campbell were the last on board. They had their pills in hand.

"Look at that blue sky," Campbell said. She smiled, tilted her sweating face into the sun, leaned her head back against Bostock's, and breathed deeply. The heat was already beginning to push the limits of human tolerance, but the sky was miraculous. "I thought I would never see that color again, and now there it is, in the sky and reflected in the water. I can die happy. How about you?"

Bostock put his arms around her. "Maybe 'happy' isn't the word, but I'm fine with it. Maybe I'll see Drew again. Maybe not. Maybe we all disappear into nothing. Maybe nothing has ever had any meaning."

"Well, crap. Just like billions of human beings before you, you will die without finding the meaning of life, and here I am fresh out of violins." Campbell laughed.

Bostock laughed, too. "Well, if you put it that way." She was ready; he could feel it in the way she stood. He wasn't ready just yet. He needed a few more moments with her. "Can I ask you something? How is it that you have shared a room with that awful Meg for years and you never let me stay with you three days running?"

"Oh, Meg was easy to live with. She was such a shit I never felt the need to apologize to her for anything, and I never gave a crap what she thought of me. I could ignore her completely." Campbell turned around to look directly into Bostock's face. "It's much more arduous to live with someone you love. Full of mistakes, apologies, and remorse. But all that is in the past."

"You have such a lovely smile on your face right now," Bostock said. "You really do seem to be happy."

"I'm about to make the most beautiful dive of my life, a perfect swan dive into the blue sea with you by my side. No one will see it. No one will give me a medal. It will leave no ripples behind. But, fuck it, I'm going to make it beautiful anyway. I'm alive at this moment. I survived for decades without faith or hope, and I did not become a monster. " She repeated the words slowly. "I did not become a monster. That may seem like an unambitious life goal, but think how different our world would be if more people had adopted it. But enough talk. I have made it to the end of my life, and I am filled with love for you. It's perfect." She turned, kissed him, and then broke away. "It's time." They touched the red pills together in a toast and swallowed them. "On three," Campbell said.

"One, two, three."

A half dozen steps forward, and their feet left the steel of the Ayn at the same instant. Campbell's dive was perfect grace; Bostock's, serviceable. Whether or not it mattered was a question no one was left to debate.

EPILOGUE

They were not empty vessels starting completely anew. They had the memories of butterflies who could return to places they've never been, count on the experiences of predecessors they could not name. The KRILL couldn't call forth their human memory by conscious effort, but it was there, large but shadowy and always in the background. If a clear snatch of the past came to one of them, it came cloaked in a holy light like a vision. Those visions would one day become the basis of a religion.

They lived and fed among the lichens in a world of radical shape, color, and texture. The greens could be dusty-soft and bluish, or biting yellow and full of lethal vulpinic acid. The oranges were clear and fiery or rusted almost to brown. The blues could be deep and rich as cobalt or powdery and pale. If the former inhabitants of the Ayn remembered its hard, gray metal chambers at all, then it was as vaguely as a bird might remember the shell from which it hatched. Now the lichens were everything: food, shelter, and hazard. The KRILL were small enough to see that a lichen was not one thing, but an intricate symbiosis of organisms, of fungus and algae. If there was a world beyond lichens, they had no time to contemplate it.

The KRILL learned to speak again, not their old languages, but a new tongue fitted to the differences in their mouths and throats, as well as to differences in their lives and surroundings. Alison had no conscious memory of Drew, but she didn't hesitate over the name of her son when he was born. She chose a new word that sounded something like "dew," but with a strange sort of vowel that sent breath shuddering along the alveolar ridge.

Their naked children rose with the sun and crept out from the overhanging scales. During the night, drops of moisture had collected at the tips of fungal filaments. They squealed at the sight of globes trembling with sun dogs, rainbows, and skewed reflections of the blue sky. They could play endless games with the dew, testing the limits of its surface tension until the drops broke and spattered them with water.

Alison smiled at her beautiful son, who looked back at her quizzically with his forehead screwed into an assymetrical frown that she loved more than anything else in the world. She kept one eye out for predators. They were many and merciless. Life at the bottom of the food chain was savage and gorgeous, lacking in guilt and ambition, focused completely on now. You had to survive this moment to earn the next, and to survive you needed to be aware of every shadow, sound, and scent. She was rarely afraid, however. She sensed the presence of a god, a benign, loving, protective god ready to wrap her in warmth. She had even seen his face once, looming large, and so kind, in the sky above the sterile white plane where her memories began.

Acknowledgments

The production of my fourth novel coincided with ovarian cancer and a pandemic. I needed some help from my friends to get through it. Fortunately, I have wonderful friends and family.

I thank my husband, Stephen White, for taking care of me during a year when no one else could come in to help. He had to postpone his own orthopedic surgery and limp around on two pain-wracked knees fetching me bowls of gruel. He read my novel and, as usual, didn't see any mistakes. This is the role of a spouse.

I owe so much to Martha Woodroof. Martha, while coping with her own stage-four cancer, coached me through my chemo, read multiple versions of KRILL, offered solid suggestions, kept in communication daily, called the ambulance when I was laid out on the kitchen floor, and taught me how to face uncertainty with good humor. She is the wisest woman I know.

Chris Bolgiano, a wonderful nature writer, read and offered comments on this work. Chris felt that my timeline was too slow, that the climate effects I described would come much sooner than they do in the novel. She is probably right. In the end, however, I left things as they were because I didn't have the energy to rewrite the whole thing on a different timeline. So please take this work as an effort to get people to think about the unthinkable and not the predictions of an expert.

I needed a copy editor I could trust. Bill Spencer stepped up. Bill is a long-time friend, a fine humor writer, and a retired professor of English. He did an absolutely spectacular job on a manuscript that needed a lot of touching up. Any errors that remain in this book are undoubtedly the result of me not accurately inserting his edits.

I thank my friend and writing partner Janice Lierz of Bear Page Press for being a constant source of advice and support.

The late Phil and Joyce Richardson were perfect, generous, and enthusiastic writing friends. I miss them mightily.

Thanks to Judi Hill and my Wildacres writing family. I hope I will not have to suffer another year without seeing them.

Finally, I give my love to all of the people who made me feel like I wasn't alone during a time of isolation—Audrey White, Chet White, Eli Estrada-White, Louise and Hank Phelan, Barbara Camph, Milda Carroll, Carolyn Elkins, Michele Serocki Bluhm—who sent me amazing cookies when I really needed cookies—and too many Facebook and Twitter friends to name.

About Susan Hasler

If Susan Hasler had her druthers, she would have preferred to be the person who entertains others, brings joy to others, or heals others. Unfortunately, she lacked talent in areas of entertainment, joy-bringing, and healing. This, combined with poor planning and the need for a job when only the CIA was hiring, led her to become a person who warns others. In other words, the least popular person at any party. As a CIA analyst, Hasler worked the Soviet threat, proliferation, and terrorism. Warning is a grim business that eventually warps the mind. She has always been aware of this and countered it with warped humor. Seventeen years after leaving the CIA, she still can't escape the warning mentality or the warpage. So cautionary tales it is. Go elsewhere for fairytales.

Made in the USA
Middletown, DE
15 January 2022

58757097R00186